To Ethan James Bowers, welcome to the world little man.

SILVER BULLET

MARK L'ESTRANGE

Copyright (C) 2019 Mark L'estrange

Layout design and Copyright (C) 2019 by Next Chapter

Published 2019 by Evenfall – A Next Chapter Imprint

Edited by Emily Fuggetta

Cover art by Cover Mint

This book is a work of fiction. Names, characters, places, and incidents are the product of the author's imagination or are used fictitiously. Any resemblance to actual events, locales, or persons, living or dead, is purely coincidental.

All rights reserved. No part of this book may be reproduced or transmitted in any form or by any means, electronic or mechanical, including photocopying, recording, or by any information storage and retrieval system, without the author's permission.

Prologue

THE MAN FLICKED HIS WHIP BESIDE THE HORSE'S right ear. The sound of the snap made by the leather lash urged the animal to run faster, although it was already exhausted from the journey. The wheels of the wooden cart harnessed to the poor animal bucked and jerked each time they crashed against a jagged rock or discarded branch in their path.

In the distance the man could see the dark red hues of the setting sun seeping into darkness as night began to take hold. He glanced over his shoulder, afraid of what he already knew would soon be there, hanging in the sky like some razor-sharp sphere tolling his fate.

He cursed his bad fortune as he cracked his whip once more, urging his faithful steed to move faster.

As he rode on, his mind reeled with the reminder of the events which had led to his present predicament. He had set off early enough that morning, allowing him ample time to make his various deliveries before reaching home before dark. What he had not anticipated was that old Simeon would forget that today was his wood delivery day, and that he would send his sons out to the next town to help with the building of a new barn for his brother. Old Simeon was too fragile to unload his order himself, and it would take too long to send word to the town to bring his boys back, so the man had no choice but to do it all himself. Old Simeon had been very grateful, it was true, but the extra time it had taken for the delivery had thrown the man's carefully planned schedule completely off.

From then on it had been one disaster after another. His next customer, because he had spent so much time at old Simeon's, had gone out by the time he arrived, so he had no choice but to wait until they returned to make his second delivery. But worst of all was when his horse threw a shoe en route to his next drop. He was almost three miles outside of town, and his horse was obviously in too much discomfort to continue dragging the cart, so the man was left with no option but to unhitch his wagon and walk his horse into town to have the blacksmith there fit a new shoe.

By the time the man was back on the road, he knew that he was desperately behind. Having made his final delivery, he considered taking lodging in the district for the night, for he knew that the journey home would doubtless take him longer than the remaining daylight allowed. But then he thought about his wife, Hanna, and their little girl, Katerina, alone in their cottage for the entire night, and tonight of all nights.

He decided that he would have to make it home, come hell or high water. The cart was now empty and so easier for his horse to pull, and the smithy had checked all its shoes to ensure that the nails were tight. He even considered leaving his wagon behind and just riding his horse so that he could make better time. But then he remembered that he would need his wagon first thing the next morning otherwise he would lose a day's wages. Working for Silas, the town coffin-maker and wood merchant, he knew from experience meant that wages were only paid for actual work completed. There was to be a burial at 11 a.m. the next morning, an elder from one of the wealthiest fami-

Prologue

lies in the district, and he had been contracted to transport the deceased's coffin on the parade through the local villages on to the church.

So, left with no choice, the man had decided to race for home as quickly as his poor horse could carry them.

Now, with barely a mile left to go, he realised that he had been far too ambitious to think that he would reach home before dark.

The sky ahead slipped behind its cloak of night, and at that moment the man heard the first howl emanate from somewhere in the darkness. He could feel his body, drenched with perspiration from a combination of exertion and anxiety, start to shiver. For a moment he wondered if indeed his tremors were as a result of the cold night air, or fear.

More howls mingled in unison in response to the first, and the man held tightly onto the reins as he lashed out once more with his whip to urge his horse to make haste up the last hill before they entered the outskirts of his village. The horse galloped on, eager to fulfil its master's wish, its flanks streaming with sweat as it breathed heavily through its flared nostrils.

As they raced down the other side of the hill, the man could at last see the shadowy hulks of the surrounding dwellings, which signified he was finally back in his village. *Only a little farther to go*, he assured himself. Usually, on a night such as this, there would be lanterns lit on the front porches, or at the very least, firelight from inside the dwellings seeping under the door frames or shafting through the open windows in the summer. But tonight, just as he had expected, all was in darkness. None of his neighbours wished to draw to their presence the attention of anyone, or anything, outside.

As he pulled back on the reins outside his cottage, his horse whinnied and snorted before coming to a complete halt. The man jumped down from his trap just as another loud howl crept through the darkness. Fighting the urge to leave his steed and race for the comfort and relative safety of his home, the man instead unhitched the wagon and led his horse into the small stable block beside his home.

There was straw and water already in situ for the horse to dine on, and the man made a silent promise to venture out later to feed his mount something more substantial and palatable as a reward for the service it had rendered in reaching home so quickly.

Once he had secured the stable door, the man raced up the wooden stairs to his cottage door and hammered on the wood. From inside, he could hear the scrape of furniture against the bare floorboards as his wife shot out of her chair to let him in.

As she fumbled with the locks, the man could hear another awful howl springing forth from the darkness which surrounded him. This one was immediately joined by several more, until he could feel them closing in around him.

"Hanna, quickly, they're coming closer!" He leaned against the door and whispered as loud as he dared in an attempt to urge his wife on. Through the door he could hear his poor wife straining and crying with frustration as she wrestled with the largest bolt. The man cursed himself for not having greased it as he had promised his wife he would before leaving on his journey that morning.

Finally, he heard the bolt shoot free. The man pushed against the door, almost knocking his poor wife over in his haste to gain entry. Once inside, he slammed the door and slotted each of the bolts firmly into their sheaths before turning around and falling back against the wood, breathing heavily.

His young wife ran into his embrace, and the two of them stayed in that position until the man had recovered his composure.

The only light inside the cottage came from the fireplace and a single candle placed in the middle of the table. The man looked around the room to ensure that his wife had secured all the shutters so that no light could escape and be seen from outside. Once he was satisfied, he released one last long sigh before he held his wife's tear-stained face in his hands and wiped her cheeks with his thumbs. They kissed passionately and then hugged each other in a tight embrace.

"I was starting to think you were not going to make it," the woman spoke with her face nestled in her husband's chest.

"It was touch and go for a while, but how could I leave you and Katerina alone on such a night?"

"Silas's wife called round an hour before dark; they were worried that you would not make it back in time and offered us to go and stay with them tonight."

"You should have gone, at least then you and our daughter would have been safe, warm and fed."

Hanna leaned away from her husband and gazed up into his face. "How could I sleep not knowing if you had made it home safely?"

In the glow from the firelight, the man caught sight of a pair of emerald green eyes, framed by a mass of wavy dark-brown hair. "And speaking of the imp," he announced.

His wife looked puzzled for a moment before following his gaze and seeing their six-year-old daughter peering around the door of her bedroom.

"Katerina!" her mother scolded. "You should be asleep by now."

The man crouched down and held out his arms. His daughter, taking the cue, ran to him, and he lifted her up, kissing her all over her little face.

The child squealed with a combination of joy and revulsion in a desperate attempt to wipe away her father's sloppy kisses before he could plant any more. Once the battle was over, the man clasped his daughter close to him, and she reciprocated, placing her head on his broad shoulder, letting her flowing locks cover her face.

Her mother moved forward and gently uncovered her daughter's face. The little girl smiled back at her, compelling the woman to soften the expression of reprimand she was trying to impose. Hanna knew that their daughter could wind her father around her little finger whenever she wanted. There had even been times when Hanna had had to insist that Katerina be punished for pushing things too far, when her husband had still been willing to turn a blind eye.

Hanna ruffled her daughter's hair playfully. "Bed, young lady," she commanded.

"Papa, carry me," the little girl urged cheekily, keeping her face buried in the folds of his jacket.

"Come on then, little one." The man carried his daughter back into her bedroom, while his wife began to serve up their dinner.

He stayed with his daughter for a while, watching her angelic face in the dim light as her eyes grew heavy with sleep. Once he was satisfied that she was drifting off, he bent down and kissed her forehead before leaving the room, securing the door behind him.

The little girl opened her eyes. She had heard something, but she did not know what. She listened intently in the darkness. She had no way of knowing how long she had been asleep, but it seemed like ages. She lay in her bed, holding her breath, waiting for the sound to come again.

Then she heard it!

A howl, somewhere out in the woods that surrounded the village.

She had overheard talk from some of the elders in the village about the werewolves that came when the full moon was bright, but she had no inkling as to what they were discussing. When she had asked her mother, she was told that the werewolves were merely folklore, stories made up by the elders to keep the villagers in line.

But Katerina knew instinctively that there was more to the story. She had seen the concern in the eyes of those who discussed the situation whenever another full moon was on the cusp. Whenever her father had his friends over, they would stay up late into the night after her mother had retired, drinking and discussing what they could do to rid their village of this terrible situation.

The little girl had mastered the art of pretending to be asleep when her mother would come in and check on her before going to bed. Katerina knew that if her father had men over to talk, that talk would invariably turn to the topic of the werewolves, and she was eager to learn more about them than either of her parents was willing to divulge in her presence.

Now, as she strained to listen to the sounds of the night outside her window, she knew immediately that those strange howls were not being made by any old mountain wolves. She had heard their cries on several occasions in the past. The ones she was now listening to were far deeper, more guttural, and distinctly more sinister.

A child's fearless inquisitiveness can often outweigh their dread of reprimand, and such was the case with Katerina. She knew that if she dared to try and venture out to take a look at what all the fuss was about, she would be in serious trouble with her parents.

There was no way that she would be able to undo the bolts on their front door by herself, and even if she could, the racket she would create would be more than enough to stir her parents from their sleep. So that idea was a non-starter.

However, she was aware of the trap door in the floor of her wardrobe which led to the crawl space under the cottage. Her father had shown it to her once when he was measuring it for a new trap door, after the old one had worn through. Having removed the old wood, he had placed a temporary board over the hole, but Katerina knew that he had not had the time to make the replacement as yet.

Inspired by this knowledge, she slid from under her covers and crept stealthily over to her wardrobe. She edged the door open gently, as she knew that the hinge creaked if you yanked it. In the darkness the little girl fumbled to find the edge of the board, shifting all her toys and shoes over to the other side to make it easier for her to move it.

Katerina shifted the board just far enough to create an opening to allow her to pass through. Before venturing through it, she retrieved her boots from the mass of jumble she had created and pulled them on so that she would not cut her feet on the stones and splinters of wood in the crawlspace.

As she lowered herself into the hole, she heard the howling once more. It appeared much closer than before, but she surmised that it was probably because she was now being exposed to the elements.

She crept along the dirt floor on her hands and knees until she reached the end of the porch, beside the steps which led to her front door. She stayed there for a moment and looked out at the surrounding area.

The night sky was filled with stars, the clarity of which she had never seen before. She gazed at them twinkling in unison as if to put on a special show just for her. The moon was bigger and brighter than it had ever been in her experience, which, granted, was somewhat limited as it was only on rare occasions that her parents had allowed her to join them on their porch so late at night, and never when the moon was full.

As she watched the stars perform their mystical dance, Katerina was so mesmerised by the display that she did not realise that she had emerged from under the protection of the crawlspace and was now out in the open, in front of her dwelling. The autumn air was crisp and carried the aroma of wood smoke from the surrounding chimneys.

Prologue

As her eager little eyes grew accustomed to the darkness, Katerina could just make out shadows moving through the woodland surrounding the village. The cold night air did little to hinder her sense of excitement and wonder, as she started to make her way towards the woods and those enticing shadows.

As she passed by the last cottage which marked the boundary for the village, Katerina heard a cacophony of howls from the woods. But to her eager little ears, they sounded like the sweetest music that had ever been composed.

She walked on, determined in her quest to leave the sanctuary of her home far behind and to venture forth to face whatever fate awaited her in the darkness.

The moment she crossed the threshold and entered the copse, the fleeting shadows, which she had gazed at so fondly when she first ventured outside, began to emerge from their cover behind the trees and slink slowly towards her.

Katerina was not afraid. Any grown man in the village in her position would have been far too afraid to venture out on a night when the full moon brought forth these creatures of folklore, whose stories had been passed down from generation to generation as a warning of foreboding and terror. What's more, they would not have been ashamed to admit to their fear. But the little girl sensed from within herself that these beasts were a part of her ancestry, and to try and deny her kin would be tantamount to denying the reason behind her very existence.

As the werewolves drew closer, Katerina held out her little arms towards them in an offer of embrace. Her face beamed as a broad smile spread across it, and her emerald eyes sparkled in the moonlight.

The leader of the pack advanced upon her until its snout was within inches of her face. It sniffed at her for a moment before nuzzling her neck. Katerina closed her arms around its mighty head, which was, in itself, almost as big as her tiny body.

After a moment, the lead werewolf turned back to the rest of the pack and lifted its head before howling a message which only they, and Katerina, could understand.

As the pack advanced to surround the little girl, she reached out to stroke each one in turn, ruffling them behind the ears as if they were no more threat to her than tiny puppies.

She did not even flinch when the leader opened its massive jaws and sank them into her neck!

Chapter One

GERALD CROSS, PHD, PROFESSOR OF ANTHROPOLOGY at West Central university in London, crouched down to utilise the protection afforded him by the overgrown thicket hedges which banked the far end of the field. He carefully removed his camera equipment, including the night-vision scope lens, from its purpose-built case and laid it all out on the picnic blanket to ensure that everything was in situ.

As dusk began to settle, he wanted to make sure that he had all he needed close at hand to ensure he would not have to fumble around in the darkness and waste valuable time trying to locate a particular object.

The digital recording equipment that he had borrowed from one of his colleagues at the university, was already set up in place, with the remote microphones strategically placed around the enclosure. He had tested the receiver and was satisfied that each of the recorders was functioning properly.

Tonight had to be the night!

His passion for studying ancient rituals and customs had taken him throughout central Europe on several fruitless escapades, investigating one theory after another, until finally, he had found himself in his own backyard on what he hoped would be the verge of the greatest scientific discovery in decades.

If his research was correct, he was within hours of witnessing a life-changing phenomenon which would quite literally challenge the hitherto scepticism of many of his colleagues around the world.

Indeed, he had suffered years of derision and mockery at the hands of the scientific world for his research into the ancient myths and rites of cults and religious orders. But such was his conviction, he was more than willing to put his reputation on the line in his quest for the truth. His fellow scientists often boasted of their open-mindedness, but in reality, he had come to believe that the majority were not prepared to go out on a proverbial limb if they believed that in any way it might leave them open to ridicule by their peers.

Gerald, on the other hand, had grown an extremely thick skin over time, and the sniggers and nudges which would pass between those who attended his seminars and private lectures he had given for the Royal Society had long since ceased to annoy him. He possessed an enviable courage of conviction, and that was something he was extremely proud of, and no one could take that away from him.

After tonight, he hoped that he would finally have the recorded proof that would show his alleged peers once and for all that he had been right all along. Where would their scoffing and sanctimonious postulating be then?

With his equipment prepared, he sat back and waited. A chill wind crept through the foliage, sending a shiver through his upper body. It was a warm night, so the sudden blast of cold air took him by surprise. He zipped up his jacket as high as the buckle would go. Even the sound of the teeth interlocking seemed to make too much noise, and he checked himself for allowing his paranoia to seep through.

Chapter 1

He waited in silence. The anticipation he was feeling reminded him of Christmas mornings as a child, waiting patiently in his room for his parents to call up that it was time for him to go downstairs and see what Santa had brought him.

Gerald gazed towards the western sky and noticed that the last of the daylight had disappeared. He turned around and could just make out the first signs of stars dotting the night sky. The moon was beginning its ascent, and already he could tell that it was going to be even bigger than the meteorologists had anticipated.

As time passed, Gerald could feel himself starting to fidget, and so he made a conscious effort to try and remain still. Even when something small and furry scampered across his leg, Gerald did not move for fear of drawing attention to his position.

Although he knew that his quarry would doubtless not be arriving for several hours, he was apprehensive as he suspected that they would send scouts on ahead to ensure that the area was clear. Plus, he was in no doubt that should he be discovered, those same scouts would think nothing of disposing of him, rather than risk the wrath of their leader by suggesting that they call a halt to the night's festivities.

Finally, after what seemed to him an eternity, the scouting party arrived.

Gerald heard the distant rumble of their vehicle a good twenty minutes or so before he could make out the first signs of them walking across the field. He counted five in all, judging by their torchlights.

He reached down and started the digital camera as he did not want to miss a moment of what was about to unfold.

In the shadowy moonlight, Gerald watched as the five converged in the middle of the open expanse of ground, doubtless to receive their orders from their commander.

Sure enough, within a few minutes they split up and started

to search the surrounding area. Gerald could feel himself subconsciously trying to shrink back into his shelter as one of the party inspected the area a few feet in front of him. The beam from their torch inched ever closer to his vantage point, and for a split-second Gerald steeled himself, awaiting discovery.

He held his breath.

Just then, something scuttled out from the bushes to Gerald's left and disappeared into the blackness. The searcher reacted swiftly and spun around as if in anticipation of coming face-to-face with an intruder. Once he realised that there was no real threat, he eventually moved on, allowing Gerald to let out the breath he had been holding in.

The search continued for the best part of an hour. During that time the group covered the entire area before finally converging back in the middle of the open field.

Cautiously, Gerald removed an earpiece from his coat pocket and placed it securely inside his left ear. Reaching down, he switched on the receiver and was delighted when he managed to pick up, albeit faintly, what the men were saying.

"They will be arriving soon, so start gathering the wood for the fire, and I'll wait back at the turning to make sure no one else tries to enter the path."

Gerald could just make out a combination of mumblings of agreement from the others, and he watched as they split up once more to set about their tasks. He continued to watch as the remaining men started piling logs on top of one another in the field. They appeared to be working in silence with only the occasional grunt or mumble slipping past their lips.

Gerald angled his camera into position so that he could start recording the activity. In time, he could hear the rumble of more vehicles converging on the area, and soon after a group of about fifty people entered the scene.

Through his infrared scope, Gerald tried to focus in on the group as they drifted towards the hill of stacked wood, but even with his colleague's state-of-the-art equipment, the light was too poor for him to make out specific features.

All those entering the fray seemed to be dressed in some form of ceremonial robe, which reminded Gerald of a masonic function he once attended when he was considering — the advice of an extremely insistent colleague — joining the order. But as he had expected, the ritual and ceremony were not to his taste, so he had to decline his friend's offer, much to the man's chagrin.

Gerald noticed that some of the group were carrying bags, and once the pyre had been lit, they produced from them several bottles of what appeared from this distance to be wine. As the bottles were passed from person to person, each member of the assembly took a large swallow. The bottles were passed back and forth several times until Gerald presumed the contents had all been drained.

As the flames from the fire lapped up the sides of the wooden structure, one of the party walked up to it and stood barely inches away. When this individual discarded their robe, Gerald could see through his lens that she was a stunning dark-haired woman. Even from this distance, the contours of her figure were easily defined in the firelight. As she allowed her robe to slide down her body and fall behind her, she raised her arms out to the side and, almost in unison, the rest of the gathering also disrobed.

Now Gerald could see that there appeared to be as many women in the field as men. They all stood unashamed in their nakedness, illuminated by the fire's flickering light.

The woman raised her arms out to her sides, and each member of the crowd turned to face her, waiting for their leader to speak.

"Come together and be one!" the woman commanded, and immediately those in attendance began to dance around in a circle and cavort with each other. Initially, each man and woman seemed to move effortlessly from partner to partner, exploring the other's body as they writhed and cavorted, exploring with their hands and tongues.

After some time, they appeared to pair off as if by some mutual agreement, and each couple immediately began to indulge in intercourse like porn stars obeying their director's instruction of 'action.'

The woman herself stood alone at the head of the congregation with her back to the fire, enjoying the spectacle she had instigated.

Gerald continued to capture the scene, firing off multiple shots as he carefully scanned the group. As he zoomed in closer with his lens, he started to notice the bodies of those involved in the mass performance growing darker. At first, he put it down to the night filter he was using combined with the poor lighting. But then he started to concentrate his focus on those closest to the firelight to give him the clearest view.

As he zoomed his lens in on one particular couple before his eyes he noticed what appeared to be thick, dark hair sprouting from both their bodies. Neither of them seemed particularly perturbed by this manifestation, each lost in the throes of their union.

Gerald moved away from his camera for a moment and stared at the ensemble without the aid of his equipment. He rubbed his eyes with his thumb and forefinger as if attempting to clear his vision before returning to his viewfinder. He squinted slightly as he strained to home back in on the couple. To his astonishment, the hair now almost covered both their bodies, and it was hard for Gerald to distinguish one from the other.

Slowly, he began to scan the rest of the group, his mind still unable to fathom exactly what was transpiring before him. But as his lens alighted on each couple in turn, he could see that the same metamorphosis was taking place.

Chapter 1

Gerald could feel the excitement starting to send shivers through his spine.

This was a moment he feared he would never experience, even in his wildest dreams.

He began to imagine the expression on the faces of his esteemed colleagues when he produced his evidence that werewolves actually existed. Until now, he was part of an extremely minute and, some of his peers would argue, insignificant group of scientists who genuinely believed that lycanthropy was not merely a psychological state of mind which only took place in the fevered imagination of the victim, but a physical manifestation which had existed for hundreds if not thousands of years.

Through his own personal research, Gerald had painstakingly pieced together evidence from several cultures throughout the world, which, if properly interpreted, proved the existence of such a phenomenon. Yet with all that, he had nearly lost his seat at the university the last time he presented his findings to the board.

But now, things were going to be very different.

Gerald quickly looked down to ensure that the digital camera was still recording the events in the field. Satisfied that all was as it should be, he returned to his lens.

The assembly now appeared to him to be more werewolf than human. Each body was now completely covered in thick fur, and when he focused in on some of the faces, he noticed they all had long snouts and protruding ears.

As his lens drifted across the writhing canine bodies, the sound of howls began to fill the night sky. Several of the beasts had lifted their heads and howled as if in obedience to their master, the moon.

Then suddenly, one of the beasts turned its attention towards Gerald!

For a moment he felt himself frozen to the spot. It could well have been a trick of the poor light, but Gerald was convinced that the beast was looking directly at him, and what was more, it seemed as if the creature was able to penetrate the darkness and even the thick clump of bushes which concealed its prey.

Gerald slowly started to scan the field once more. This time, however, he noticed to his horror that one by one, each of the beasts had ceased their sexual liaisons, and now their focus was aimed directly at him.

Gerald turned to look at the woman at the head of the bestial army. Unlike the rest of the pack, she was still in human form. But alas, as with the rest of them, her attention was focused on his hiding place.

As if by silent command, the werewolves started to charge towards him.

There was no time to gather up his equipment; Gerald knew that his only chance of flight was to make it back to his vehicle before his attackers reached him. With the camera strap secured around his neck, he tried to negotiate his way down the embankment in the darkness. The hefty lens attached to the front of the equipment caused the camera to swing back and forth, thudding against his chest like a punch from an assailant as he made his decline. With each return, the force of the blow caused Gerald more pain, until he felt sure the next one would send him over backwards.

As he leaned over and squinted in the darkness trying to see his way, the camera swung out in front of him further than before, almost knocking into his face. In anticipation of the return blow, Gerald made a grab for the lens. The movement caused him to miss his footing, and before he could prevent it, Gerald pitched head-first down the grassy slope.

As he tumbled down the rest of the embankment, Gerald felt the wind being sapped from his body. When he finally came to a stop, he was gasping for air, unable to move as the effects of the damage his poor body had sustained set in.

He could hear the howls of the approaching animals growing

louder, and by the time he had recovered his composure, he could see them all jostling for position at the top of the hill.

Gerald watched as a cloud of mist rose from their slavering jaws, dispersing into the moonlight. Their mighty chests rose and fell in anticipation of imminent attack. They viewed their prey through blood-red eyes, each one focused intently on their victim.

Before Gerald had a chance to move, the pack descended on him, ripping him to shreds as they fought over their feast.

His last thought before his heart gave out was the painful irony that he had sacrificed himself in an effort to prove his belief, and no one was ever going to know about it.

Chapter Two

"Oh, baby...baby...baby!" Roger cried out in ecstasy as he finally climaxed. When Jenna felt his ejaculate explode inside her, she heaved a silent sigh of relief. For her, that morning's entertainment had not resulted in any such pleasure. But then, she had not expected it to. Roger's early-morning wham-bam extravaganzas invariably left her feeling completely unfulfilled and somewhat used as a means to an end.

Having drained his load, Roger rolled off her and lay on his back, breathing deeply. Jenna knew that this was the part when she was supposed to sound grateful and express her satisfaction. But in truth, she had long ago given up on bothering to fuel the fire of Roger's ego. Over time, he had managed to complete that task very successfully, unaided.

The familiar sound of Roger lighting up his first cigarette of the morning was all the inspiration Jenna needed to throw back the covers and officially start her day.

"Hey, wait a minute, babe, where're you going?" whined Roger. "I fancied a cuddle for a while."

Jenna ignored her boyfriend's appeal, grabbed her dressing

gown from the chair by her side of the bed, and slid her feet into the pink fluffy slippers he had bought for her last Christmas.

As she reached the bedroom door, Jenna turned back. "If you wanted a cuddle, you should have waited before lighting that." She pointed to the Rothman's protruding between Roger's index and middle finger. "You know I can't stand them!"

Without giving him time to reply, Jenna left the bedroom and made her way to the bathroom for her shower.

"Can you bring me a coffee as you're up?" Roger's cry went unanswered as Jenna closed the bathroom door behind her. Through the wooden barrier she could hear him repeating his question, so she reached into the shower cubicle and turned on the water to drown out his voice.

As luck would have it, when Jenna emerged from the shower Roger was sitting in the kitchen engrossed in a conversation with one of his mates, discussing arranging a boys' night out.

She slipped into the bedroom and quickly dressed, stopping only long enough to apply some light make-up before gathering up her overnight things and preparing to leave for work. She called out to Roger from the front door as she left the flat. Although she knew he would be too engrossed in his conversation to reply, at least it would not give him an excuse to say later that she had left without saying anything.

The morning traffic was surprisingly light, and Jenna made it into the office within half an hour. After dumping her things on her chair, she waved good morning to those of her colleagues scattered around the open-plan office and made her way to the coffee shop within the main complex.

Jenna ordered a double espresso and a breakfast bagel and found an empty table by the window. As she ate, her thoughts turned back to her uncle Gerald. She checked her mobile once more, just in case he had left her a message while she was driving in. But still there was no word.

She considered calling him. But she had already left umpteen messages over the past week without receiving any response. In truth, this was not the first time her uncle had forgotten to call her to assure her that he was alright. Jenna knew how passionate he was about his work and that he often lost track of the time when he was out on one of his many excursions around the globe.

Jenna had insisted on buying him a mobile, even though she knew that she would have a battle on her hands in forcing him to remember to carry it, let alone use it. Her uncle was extremely set in his ways, almost to the point of obsession. He still refused to pay any of his bills by direct debit, never ordered anything online, insisted on using a cheque book rather than paying for things with his debit card, and refused point-blank to allow any of his students to e-mail their work to him, much to the chagrin of the university's head of year, who had to deal with the complaints.

Although her uncle was only in his sixties, he embodied the old-fashioned notion of an absent-minded professor. A true academic, he had never married, nor to her knowledge ever come close to it. Instead he embraced the life of a bachelor, allowing himself the luxury of guiltless self-indulgence. Even though to him, that basically meant being able to read well into the early hours without interruption and to disappear for the purpose of research whenever the mood took him without having to plan ahead or make excuses to anyone.

Their relationship had never been especially close, at least not in the traditional manner. A tragic accident had seen Jenna lose both her parents at the tender age of fourteen. Being an only child, and without any other relatives to speak of, Jenna had been destined to spend her formative years within the walls of some cheerless institution within the social welfare system. However, at the last minute her uncle Gerald had come forward and fought tirelessly for the right to look after his dead sister's only child.

Chapter 2

Jenna had only met him on a couple of occasions previously when he had come over for dinner. But, although she never expressed it at time, she had been immensely relieved when he stepped up to save her from a life in care.

The introduction of a teenage girl into Gerald's quiet academic existence had proven to be a huge upheaval for the quiet, soft-spoken bachelor. However, he'd seemed to appreciate instinctively that his sacrifice was nothing compared to the grief that his niece was suffering, and to that end, he had been willing to make whatever changes necessary to help see Jenna through that horrendous time.

Gerald owned a very modest flat, barely big enough for himself. Nevertheless, he had arranged to have his study converted into a second bedroom for his niece and left Jenna to instruct the decorators to ensure that everything was just how she wanted it.

Jenna had never been the brightest pupil academically, and before her parents' death she had begun to associate with some older children she knew her parents did not approve of. Initially, Jenna had slipped back into her old ways, quickly realising that her uncle had no idea how to discipline a teenage girl.

She found herself pushing the boundaries further and further, almost as if she wanted to test just how far he would allow her to go before trying to rein her in. Gerald allowed Jenna to wear make-up and buy clothes she had only been able to fantasise about before. As her skirts grew shorter and more revealing, and her tops tighter, Jenna found herself in the company of men far older than her tender years. At weekends especially, she would often drift in during the small hours, only to find her uncle Gerald sitting in his armchair reading.

He would always greet her with a smile and ask how she had enjoyed her evening. Never once had he mentioned the lateness of the hour or demanded to know who she had been with.

But everything came to a sudden head one night when a car

she was travelling in with a couple of friends was stopped by the police for speeding. The driver was breathalysed and found to be over the limit, and a subsequent check proved that the car had been reported stolen earlier that evening. Although Jenna had had no idea about any of this, everyone had been carted off to the station, and once her age had been ascertained, her uncle Gerald was called to come and collect her.

The two other girls Jenna had been with in the car were both collected by their parents before her uncle arrived, and each was given a sound berating by their parents, much to the amusement of the officers on duty, as well as those waiting to be processed.

But when her uncle Gerald had arrived, he'd appeared to only be concerned with Jenna's wellbeing and embraced her for the longest moment, while tenderly kissing the top of her head and reassuring her that everything was going to be fine.

From that night, Jenna changed her attitude completely.

She had begun to knuckle down at school, and through her uncle's encouragement, she'd discovered the joy of reading for pleasure as well as for academic advancement.

The pride she'd seen in her uncle's eyes when her grades began to improve was clearly evident, and with his encouragement and infectious enthusiasm, Jenna had made her way to university and graduated with a first-class degree in journalism.

"Still no word then, I take it?" Jenna's reverie was broken by the arrival of her friend and co-worker Trish. Without being conscious of it, Jenna had been staring at the blank screen on her phone, as if praying for it to suddenly burst into life.

Jenna turned to her friend and smiled warmly. "No, I'm afraid not. I've left him countless messages, but still nothing."

Trish slung her shoulder bag onto the chair across from Jenna's. Searching in it, she removed her purse. "Would you like another one of those?" she indicated towards Jenna's coffee with a nod.

Chapter 2

Jenna took a sip and winced. Her espresso had gone cold.

"Yes, please. Here, take the money."

"Don't worry, I've got it."

Jenna watched her friend make her way to the counter. Trish was the assistant editor for the fashion section of the magazine they both worked for, and she spent much of her time out on location, ensuring that designated shoots were proceeding according to plan. Although she had two assistants, Trish was a bit of a perfectionist — or control freak, as her mother called it — and insisted on being close at hand most of the time.

Jenna took another bite of her bagel. That, too, had turned tepid since her last bite, but at least it was still edible.

When Trish retuned with her tray, she placed it on the table and removed the items from it one at a time before discarding it in the rack beside their table. She moved Jenna's unwanted coffee to one side and replaced it with her hot one.

Jenna thanked her friend and blew on the hot drink before taking a sip.

Trish slid into the seat opposite her. "So, have you considered calling the police?" she asked, cutting open the sticky bun she had opted for and thickly spreading it with butter and jam. "I know it may sound a little extreme, but he has been incommunicado for quite a while now."

Jenna shrugged. In truth, she had given the idea a great deal of thought, but knowing her uncle, he was probably just so caught up in his research that he had lost track of the time.

Trish took a sip from her steaming cup of tea, all the while watching Jenna's expression as she mulled over her suggestion. She could tell from Jenna's face that her friend was anxious.

After a few minutes, when Jenna still had not answered her, Trish felt compelled to speak up. "I hope you don't think I'm interfering, but it's obvious from the look on your face that you're worried."

Jenna slipped her hand across the table and gave her friend's a gentle squeeze.

"No, of course you're not interfering," she assured her, "it's just that I'm used to him not calling me because he's forgotten, just, not for this long, that's all."

Trish nodded her understanding.

They had been firm friends virtually from Jenna's first day at the magazine. It had been Trish who had shown her around and let her in on who to avoid if she was easily offended by sexual innuendo.

Trish was ten years older than Jenna, and she often thought that if she had been blessed with an elder sister, she would have wanted her to be just like her friend.

She was also a very good listener and never seemed to judge others by the way they chose to live their lives. Listening to her speak, Jenna often felt humbled in her friend's presence.

The two had spent many a fine weekend at Trish's flat, discussing everything from world politics to which celebrity they would like to get off with. If the weather was particularly poor, the two of them would stay in their pyjamas all day, losing themselves in box-sets and dining on take-aways, all washed down with several bottles of wine.

They would often talk well into the early hours before sleep finally claimed them.

Whenever Jenna was feeling low, Trish was like a breath of fresh air, dispelling her gloomiest thoughts like autumn leaves in the wind, and she was immensely grateful to have her friend with her now.

Trish shovelled the last of her bun into her mouth and licked her sticky fingers before wiping them on a paper napkin.

As she swallowed, another thought struck her. "You know the other thing is, if, heaven forbid, anything had happened to your uncle, then surely the police would have contacted you? Your uncle does have your number in his phone, doesn't he?"

Jenna nodded as she gulped down the last of her espresso.

"He only has my mobile and his home phone number in his contact list. I had to put them in because he could never remember either of them."

"Well, there you are then," Trish replied, lifting her hands in a gesture of confidence. "I'm sure if anything was wrong, they would have called you by now!"

Instinctively, Jenna glanced at her mobile once more. Trish's words made perfect sense, as usual, and they gave her some reassurance, which she desperately needed.

"Thanks, Trish, you always seem to have the knack of cheering me up."

"That's what I'm here for," replied Trish with a cheesy grin. Pleased with her suggestion, she pushed with her feet and leaned back on her chair, lifting the front two legs off the floor like a bored schoolgirl in class. But she mistimed the manoeuvre and had to make a desperate grab for the table to save herself from falling backwards.

The two women instantly burst into a fit of laughter, attracting glances from those seated around them.

One of those who had noticed Trish's antics was Colin Fenn from their accounts department, who had just finished paying for his coffee at the counter. Most, if not all, of the women who worked at the magazine knew to avoid the silver-haired old man, as he was renowned for his lecherous innuendo. Sure enough, as he walked past their table, he could not help but give Trish a sly wink as he licked his lips in his usual provocative manner.

Trish immediately made a face and held her index finger in front of her mouth, as if she were about to gag.

Jenna, who had only just finished laughing at Trish's earlier stunt, was overtaken by another fit of uncontrollable giggles.

"Jesus," said Trish, "I'd rather sleep with a cobra; at least if it died during the night from the excitement, I would get a decent pair of shoes out of the bargain!"

Chapter Three

THE TWO FRIENDS ARRANGED TO MEET FOR LUNCH before both making their way to their respective offices.

Jenna switched on her computer and began dealing with the e-mails that had been sent in over the weekend from some of their international offices. As usual on a Monday morning, there was a stack of expense receipts she needed to upload to the company's account database before forwarding them onto their accounts section.

She kept her mobile in front of her, checking the screen every ten minutes or so, but to no avail.

Even though Trish had managed to ease her concerns over breakfast, now that she was alone again Jenna could feel the anxiety concerning her uncle's whereabouts starting to creep in once more.

During the morning period she made a conscious decision that if she still had not heard anything by the evening, then she would contact the local police force and instigate enquiries.

On her insistence, her uncle had written down all the details of where he was going and left them on the front of the fridge. Unfortunately, he had not been able to confirm exactly where he

Chapter 3

would be staying at the time of leaving, but he had promised to let Jenna know once he was settled. Alas, when he'd phoned, Jenna had missed the call, and the message he left did not specify the name of his hotel.

Naturally, she had tried calling him back, several times in fact, but all her messages so far had remained unanswered.

A diary message pinged on Jenna's screen, reminding her that she was down to minute-take a meeting in thirty minutes. Jenna had already collated all the necessary paperwork the previous Friday, so she checked that the meeting room was vacant and began to set up for the board members. Once the room was ready, Jenna quickly went to the toilet as she knew from past experience how these meetings could drag on. Several of the board members loved the sound of their own voices, and depending on who was acting as chair, they were often allowed to drone on to their heart's content, with no consideration for the poor minute-taker.

Before heading into the meeting, Jenna checked her mobile once more, and her heart leapt when she noticed she had received a message. But much to her disappointment, it was only from Roger, reminding her that he was due to be away for a few nights at a conference.

Roger's mother was one of the senior board members, which was the only reason her son was given the position he now held, along with the inflated salary. As a result, he was often called upon to attend such conferences, which Jenna suspected were in reality nothing more than an excuse for a grand piss-up.

The board meeting — as Jenna expected — took far longer than was necessary, and by the time it was over, Jenna was already late for her lunch date with Trish. Roger's mother, Cecelia, caught up with Jenna by her desk just as she was about to leave.

"Can I have those minutes on my desk by this afternoon please, Jenna?"

Jenna smiled and nodded her confirmation.

Jenna knew that Cecelia did not approve of her dating her son. As far as Cecelia was concerned, Roger was merely sowing his wild oats with Jenna until he was ready to settle down with a nice girl, whom his mother would doubtless choose for him.

Cecelia had never said anything specific to Jenna about her feelings. But by the same token, she had never made her feel welcome when the two of them visited for Sunday lunch.

Jenna took the stairs two at a time rather than wait for the lift.

As she approached the glass revolving doors at the entrance to the building, Colin Fenn was just returning through them from one of his many smoking breaks.

Jenna pretended not to notice him as she entered her portion of the rotating circle. Just then, the doors stopped moving, and as Jenna pushed against the glass pane before her, it refused to budge.

She looked up to see Colin's beaming face pressed against the glass of the section opposite her. Jenna looked straight at Colin through furrowed brows and placed her hands firmly on her hips in an attitude of irritation.

Colin laughed and moved forward, automatically releasing Jenna's side. He mouthed something to her through the glass, but Jenna could not hear what he said and did not hang around to find out what it might be.

The sandwich shop which they had agreed to meet at was only a few minutes from the office, and when Jenna arrived, she saw Trish already sitting at a table with bottle of mineral water in front of her.

"Sorry I'm late," Jenna apologised as she took her seat. "I had to take minutes for one of their stupid meetings, which ran on forever. And then I bumped into your secret admirer at the swing doors playing silly buggers."

Chapter 3

Trish looked shocked. "What secret admirer?" she asked quizzically.

Jenna smiled. "Why, Colin, of course."

"That's not funny, are you trying to put me off my lunch?" Trish leaned over the table and playfully slapped her friend on the arm.

"Better than the Atkins diet," Jenna retorted, picking up her menu.

The waitress came over, and the two girls ordered their food. Jenna felt as if she could really do with a glass of wine but opted for water instead. She knew from past experience that drinking during the lunch break made it almost impossible for her to concentrate when she returned to work.

"Anyway," Trish began, "speaking of love's young dream, how's Roger these days?"

Jenna sighed. "Don't ask!"

"Still the profound pain in the arse, I presume?"

"Yeah, you could say that."

"Let me guess, still smoking in bed in spite of how many times you've told him it makes you feel sick? Still leaving his dirty underwear on the bathroom floor and expecting you to pick it up? Still calling you from whatever public house he's just about to be thrown out of and expecting you to come and get him, even if it means you having to get out of a warm bed just to do so?"

Jenna nodded as she took a drink of water.

"Oh, and let's not forget his gracious consideration for you during your lovemaking, if you can call it that! Is he still favouring you with his five-minute quickies?"

"All the above," agreed Jenna, "and last night he brought up the topic of us moving in together, again."

Trish raised her eyebrows. "Please tell me you're not actually considering it?"

Jenna shook her head. "No way, but you know what he gets like if I refuse to discuss the situation outright."

Trish was the only friend that Jenna had confided in about Roger's behaviour. At first, she had felt that she was being disloyal to her boyfriend by revealing all his juvenile antics, as well as his selfish bedroom performances, but after a while, Jenna needed to unload, and anyway, what were friends for?

Once, when she had actually built up the courage to tell him she was leaving him, Roger had threatened suicide. When she'd told Trish, her friend had told her that she should have called his bluff. She claimed that people who threatened to do it were only doing so for attention and to get their own way. Although at the time Jenna had felt her friend's observation was a little harsh, she knew how Roger could act like a petulant child when he could not get his own way.

Even so, as Jenna had not been a hundred-percent convinced that Roger would not carry out his threat, for the sake of a quiet life, she had reassured him that she would stay. But she had also warned him that he needed to shape up, and through floods of tears he had sworn upon all that was holy that he would.

That had been over a month ago, and Jenna was still waiting for this miraculous transformation.

Each time she spoke with Trish, Jenna realised what a coward she was being by not breaking up with Roger. She just needed to focus her attention on the situation and sum up the fortitude to finally make the break.

Jenna's other concern was that when the time came, Roger might put the knife in and convince his mother to fire Jenna. She certainly would not put such an undertaking past him.

But right now, she had something more important to worry about.

"I take it there's been no word from your uncle since breakfast?" Trish's question shook Jenna from her reverie.

"No," Jenna replied dejectedly. "I've decided that when I get

Chapter 3

home tonight, if there's no message from him on the answering machine, I'm going to contact the local police and ask them to start a search."

"Wouldn't he have called your mobile rather than leave a message on the machine?"

Jenna smiled. "He can't always remember how to access the address book on his phone, but he eventually learned his home number by heart."

"Won't Roger be peeved that you're not going to stay at his tonight? I mean, like you should even care?"

"His mummy has booked him in for a conference, so he's going to be away anyhow."

Trish nodded. "Do you remember where your uncle is staying?"

"It's written at home on the fridge door; it's somewhere near Shropshire if memory serves."

Trish could see the faraway look in Jenna's eyes. She leaned over the table and placed her hand over her friend's. "I'm sure he will be fine," she offered comfortingly.

The rest of the afternoon dragged. Jenna could not help glancing at the time on her computer screen every couple of minutes. She finished typing up the minutes from the morning's meeting and e-mailed them to Miriam.

Once she had dealt with everything urgent that had come in since lunchtime, Jenna decided that the rest could wait until tomorrow. It was still a little early, but her focus was on her uncle, so she shut down her computer and left.

Chapter Four

Kevin Roop stood behind the counter of his D.I.Y store and watched the two young women argue over which type of paint they intended to buy.

As they were his only two customers, Kevin was able to give them his undivided attention. In truth, he was glad that none of his usual clientele was around, bothering him with asinine questions about what size screws they needed and which type of hammer worked best on specific heads of nails.

Indeed, Kevin had a vested interest in these two women. He desperately wanted to shag both of them!

But the sad truth was that neither of them were willing to give him so much as the time of day, and if it were not for the fact that his was the only D.I.Y shop in Huntley, they would probably have shopped elsewhere.

Kevin was seventeen, and although, as a result of many years lugging around gas bottles and sacks of compost and the like, he had shoulders that most bodybuilders would envy, the rest of his appearance did nothing to inspire admiration from the opposite sex.

His long blond hair, which always looked greasy due to a lack of washing, was unkept and constantly in his eyes, forcing him to swing his head back violently to sweep it away, whenever his hands were full.

Like his hair, his complexion still suffered from an overproduction of oil, which left its mark in the form of acne.

But even if the girls were prepared to overlook his general appearance, he did not do himself any favours in the way he often spoke to them. His elder brother Nick had always taught him that women needed to be dominated, otherwise they would not show their men proper respect.

Sage advice which Nick had picked up at their father's knee.

Kevin had always looked up to his brother. Their father had drunk himself into an early grave when Kevin was still in nappies, so his elder brother had become his male role model, and the one he would always go to for advice and guidance.

Their mother Sandra, once her husband was gone, had spent most of Kevin's childhood drinking and prostituting herself around town. Kevin and Nick had had more 'uncle's' when they were young than either of them could remember. So, Nick was generally the only one at home to make sure his younger brother did not set fire to the place.

The Roop clan had always had a bad reputation in Huntley.

Kevin's father, before he became known as the town drunk, had made a tidy living by dealing in stolen property, both that which he himself purloined, as well as anything which happened to come his way via some of his unscrupulous acquaintances.

From there, he moved on to intimidation, and obtaining money with violence by scaring some of the more vulnerable business owners in town to pay him protection money. In fact, the shop Kevin was serving in was the result of his father harassing the previous owner, and elderly proprietor named Jefferson, who had agreed to will Kevin's father his D.I.Y business in return for protection.

A few months after the necessary paperwork had been

formalised, old man Jefferson was killed disturbing a burglar. Nothing could be proved at the time, but everyone suspected that Kevin's father had a hand in it.

Once his father was dead, Kevin's mother tried to run the business herself, but she soon grew bored with the day-to-day handling of the trade, and having to deal with people had never been a forte of hers. But, now that her husband and breadwinner was gone, Sandra knew that she had to find money from somewhere, and working for herself certainly beat having to do it for someone else.

She gave it her best shot, but her love of drinking and partying made it almost impossible for her to keep regular shop hours. The one advantage she had was that there was no other D.I.Y store in town, so despite her lackadaisical attitude towards business she managed to keep her head above water.

When her eldest son Nick was expelled from school at fifteen for fighting, she used the excuse to force him to work with her, giving her more free time for drinking and visiting the beauty salons. Nick was only a couple of months shy of his sixteenth birthday, so the local social services, already knowing the family well, did not try too hard to intervene and encourage Sandra to force her son back into education.

As a youngster, Kevin would go straight to the shop from school and wait there with his big brother until closing time. Nick would fill his young head with all manner of schemes and plans he had for his future.

Unfortunately for the young Kevin, his brother's aspirations appeared to be along the same lines as their father's. Except that Nick wanted to be more involved in major crimes, explaining to his younger brother that their father had merely been small-time.

Kevin idolised Nick and tried to learn all he could from him.

Unfortunately, this also meant him discovering all he knew about the opposite sex from a man who thought nothing of bringing home a different girl each night and using them for his own sexual pleasure before tossing them out into the street.

Nick would often leave his bedroom door slightly ajar, almost encouraging Kevin to spy on him with his latest conquest, which Kevin often did. Sometimes, the poor girl would notice the young Kevin staring at them and object — strongly. But this usually resulted in Nick telling her to shut up and let him concentrate.

Some of those girls would leave straight after, swearing never to return as they slammed the front door. But to Kevin's surprise, they often returned.

Nick told him it was because they enjoyed being part of a spectacle and only made a fuss because they believed it was the proper thing to do.

Once Kevin turned sixteen, his brother promised him that he would arrange for one of his regular conquests to bring a friend over so that he could finally sample the delights of the female flesh. But things did not go exactly according to plan.

The girl herself was not really to Kevin's taste, but as he was more interested in losing his virginity and impressing his brother, he pretended to be interested in her. For a start, she was far older and fatter than her friend who introduced them, and she was wearing so much makeup she looked to Kevin as if she were about to enter a circus. It turned out that she was really the other girl's aunt, and she was temporarily escaping the drudgery of marital bliss, looking for a little excitement and adventure.

The four of them began the evening in the living room, making their way steadily through Sandra's stash of booze.

When it was time for them to split up, Nick winked at his younger brother and led his girl into his bedroom.

The girl's aunt, who up until that point had been sitting across from Kevin, took the initiative without any encouragement and crossed over to where he was perched on the end of the couch.

Kevin's immediate instinct was to shuffle away from the older woman, not just because he did not fancy her, but because he had never been in such a circumstance before. But he had nowhere to go, as the arm of the couch was already jutting into his side.

The woman, noticing his reluctance, held out her glass for the two of them to clink before she drained what was left of Sandra's scotch in one shot.

Kevin followed suit. Throughout the evening he had been sipping slowly from his glass, as he still had only minimal experience with alcohol, and then only with beer.

The woman placed her glass back on the table.

"Well, here we are then," she purred, using her well-manicured index finger to gently brush Kevin's hair behind his ear.

Kevin wanted to retort with something witty and clever, but his wits abandoned him.

The woman leaned in and pursed her lips before blowing gently in Kevin's ear.

The feeling made him squirm. It was not altogether an unpleasant sensation, quite the opposite in fact, but it still made Kevin feel uneasy. He wished that they could just get on with it so that finally he could pop his cherry and no longer have to lie to his mates so much about how much pussy he was already getting.

The woman began to trace a pattern around his earlobe with her finger.

They had not even kissed at this stage, and that was one thing Kevin knew how to do from watching films and his brother in action.

Kevin took in a deep breath and turned his head so he was facing his date.

The woman looked even less appealing to him from this

Chapter 4

distance. Her skin was caked with thick concealer, which close up did nothing to hide the ravages of time etched on her puffy skin.

But he knew that he had no choice. If he caused a fuss or told her to go, Kevin knew that Nick would go ape with him. Especially if the woman's niece took umbrage and left before Nick had enjoyed his fun.

Steeling himself, Kevin leaned in and pressed his mouth against hers.

The woman immediately responded, parting her lips and sliding her eager tongue into Kevin's mouth. The woman's tongue tasted of brandy and nicotine, and mixed with the heady scent of her sweet perfume, Kevin was afraid for a moment that he was going to spew.

Fortunately, the woman removed her mouth from his and, curling her fingers around his neck, pulled him closer as she began to nibble on his earlobe.

Meanwhile, her other hand slid casually down Kevin's torso until it came to rest on his groin area.

Kevin moaned unconsciously as the woman began to knead his genitals through the thick fabric of his jeans.

He closed his eyes and concentrated on the sound of the woman's broad brass bangles jangling together as she continued to rub and massage the shaft of Kevin's rising dick.

Finally, the woman began to unzip his jeans. She shoved her hand inside and manoeuvred his penis out of hiding. Kevin glanced down for a moment and could not believe that it was the bald head of his dick that he could see, bobbing up and down between the woman's fingers.

Without warning, the woman ceased nibbling on his ear, and before he had a chance to respond, she had swallowed his erect penis right down to his throbbing testicles.

Kevin cried out in ecstasy as the woman's eager mouth sucked on his willing shaft.

He rolled his head back and stared at the ceiling before closing his eyes.

Then, without warning, Kevin ejaculated in the woman's mouth!

It all happened so quickly, Kevin did not even have a chance to warn her of what was coming. The woman immediately removed her mouth from his erupting fountain of goo and began to spit out what was already inside her mouth onto the carpet.

Kevin could feel his legs starting to quiver as the last of his seed squirted out onto his leg. By the time he opened his eyes, the woman had already leapt up from the sofa, and she was gagging and coughing as if she were still trying to dislodge something from her throat.

Kevin hoisted himself off the sofa to try and calm her down, but the woman pushed him away so violently that he fell backwards over the arm of the couch and ended up on the floor.

"You fucking little shit!" The woman spat the words out, not bothering to try to hide the loathing and contempt in her voice.

Kevin held a hand out as if to plead with her to keep her voice down while he used his other to push himself off the floor so that he could stand.

Once he was up, he placed a finger over his mouth. "Shush."

"Don't you shush me, shithead." The woman turned away to face the living room door. "Janice, come on, we're leaving!"

Now Kevin could feel the panic rising within him.

He knew that it was too soon for Nick to have had his fun, and if the woman's niece adhered to her aunt's demands, he knew that he would get it in the neck from his big brother.

Kevin moved up behind the woman. He could tell by the rising of her chest that she was just about to shout out again.

In desperation, Kevin slapped his hand over the woman's mouth to prevent her from screaming. The woman began to struggle and fight with him, and although Kevin towered above her, the violence of her writhing and kicking almost caused him to lose his balance once more.

Kevin whispered in the woman's ear at first, begging her to keep quiet, then offering her inducements like more alcohol if she would only calm down. But the more he spoke, the more fervent her attempt to break free grew.

Without warning, the woman clamped her teeth around Kevin's middle finger. Such was the ferocity of her attack that it felt to him as if she was trying to chew down to the bone.

He released his hold slightly, and the woman seized the advantage by bringing her high heel crashing down on his instep. The sudden pain in Kevin's foot caused him to relinquish his hold on the woman altogether, and he staggered back, trying to grab his injured foot whilst maintaining his balance.

The woman turned to face him.

Kevin could feel his face flush, and uncontrollable tears began to stream down his cheeks. Through his blurred vision, he could just about make out the expression of pure malice on the woman's face. Her features were twisted into such a foul grimace that anyone would have thought that Kevin had tried to murder her, not try to keep her calm.

The woman held up her fingers like ragged claws, and she ran at Kevin like a wild animal.

Out of pure instinct, Kevin moved out of her way as she rushed by him and swung his right fist in an arc, catching the woman on the side of her head. The blow sent her reeling off balance, and she crashed to the floor, just catching her forehead on the coffee table as she went down.

"What the fuck is going on in 'ere?" Nick demanded, appearing at the door.

"Auntie!" Nick's date screamed at the top of her lungs as she rushed to her relative's side, almost knocking Kevin off balance in her haste. "What's that little turd done to you?"

Before Kevin had a chance to offer an explanation, Nick

grabbed him by the collar of his shirt and flung him to one side. Such was the force behind his brother's action that Kevin found himself, yet again, dumped on the floor.

Amid much screaming, shouting, threats and finger-pointing, the two women made their way out of the house, despite Nick's assurances that he would sort Kevin out later if they would only stay for another drink and allow the situation to calm down.

But the two women were having none of it!

Once they had gone, slamming the front door behind them, Nick was in no mood to hear explanations. For the next five minutes, Kevin stayed curled up in a ball on the floor while his big brother laid into him with kicks and punches, accompanied by every vile name he could think to call him.

That was the first and last time Nick allowed Kevin to double-date with him. But despite everything, Kevin still idolised his elder brother, and he was willing to do anything he told him, regardless of whether it was legal or not, and take any battering his brother saw fit to hand out if he made a mistake.

Eventually, Nick moved up into the big time, but he did not stay there for long before he was involved in an armed robbery, which resulted in two watchmen being killed.

Nick was now serving eight years at her majesty's pleasure in London.

Now Kevin's days were mostly spent behind the counter of the shop, being helped less and less by his mother. As much as he hated his life, his brother's incarceration had brought him home to the fact that the glory of being in the big time was not worth the risk involved.

It was better for him to keep his head down and get on with his work.

At least the job had some perks.

The two girls he had been watching choosing paint were definitely one of them. They looked to Kevin as if they could be

Chapter 4

models. Both were slim, one with long dark hair and the other blonde with her hair tied in a ponytail.

Over time, Kevin had dismissed most of the girls in Huntley as either being tarts or too stuck-up to bother with, so the arrival of fresh meat was always a welcome change.

Kevin moved to the far end of the counter, pretending that he was dealing with something under a shelf, but in actuality, he was just desperate to obtain a better vantage point so that he could see the girl's legs.

They were both wearing skirts; the blonde had on a particularly short, pleated one with long white socks and white pumps. She reminded Kevin of a schoolgirl, and he immediately felt himself starting to harden. The dark-haired one had on a longer, straight skirt with tights tucked into boots. The tights, although quite thick, could not obscure the perfect shape of her legs.

Becky Graham and Stella Braithwaite had only been in Huntley for a week. They had arrived in town together from Reading having just finished their final year training to be beauticians. They had rented a small house on the outskirts of town with a view to starting up their own business.

They had decided on Huntley as a location, having stopped there briefly the previous year on their way to a rock festival.

Stella was the first to notice the unwanted attention they were receiving from the man behind the counter.

"Hey, don't look now," Stella whispered in her friend's ear, "but I think we're being watched by the bloke behind the counter."

Becky immediately spun around, catching Kevin's eye and forcing him to flush beetroot. He quickly looked away and pretended to shuffle some papers in front of him, but his act was not fooling anyone, especially Becky.

Stella knew from several past experiences that her good friend had always lacked something in the tact department, so she immediately regretted the way she had phrased her initial statement. To Becky, it was like a red rag to a bull.

Becky, oblivious to the fact that she had done anything wrong, turned to her friend and asked, "When you say 'watching,' do you mean he was just looking in our direction, or was he having a quick perv?"

Her voice was not exactly loud, but in the small shop it carried enough so that Stella suspected their watcher had heard every word. She wished now that she had kept her observation to herself, at least until they had left the shop.

Stella, starting to feel her own face flush, pretended to show Becky something written on the can she was holding. "Will you please lower your voice, he must have heard you," she urged.

This time Becky, too, kept her voice low. "I think we should have some fun with him, what d'yer think?"

In spite of herself, Stella felt the corners of her mouth crease up.

She nodded.

The girls grabbed some brushes and assorted accoutrements to go with their choice of paint and made their way to the counter.

Kevin had his head buried in a catalogue as the girls approached. He made an attempt at pretending that he was unaware of their presence, but his act was not at all convincing.

"Will that be everything?" Kevin asked, focussing on the items that the girls had placed on the counter.

Becky gave Stella a sly wink. "Well, actually," she began, leaning in closely towards Kevin as if she were afraid someone might overhear her. "We were wondering if you stocked body paint?"

Kevin looked up. As his gaze met hers, he immediately felt heat radiating through his cheeks once more.

He frowned. "Sorry," he stammered, "body paint?"

Now it was Stella's turn. "Yes, you know, paint that you use

Chapter 4

to cover each other with." With that, she began to trace a line down Becky's arm from her shoulder to her wrist.

Becky shivered as if the thrill of her friend's touch excited her.

Without warning, Becky swung her right leg up onto the counter, causing her pleated skirt to ride up, exposing her bare leg.

Kevin could not help but look. His eyes followed the line of Becky's leg until he could see her powder-blue panties.

Stella moved forward. "You must have seen the adverts online?" she offered, placing her hand on the inside of her friend's thigh and slowly gliding it towards the mound of Becky's pubic area. "The girls in the advert cover each other all the way up here, until there's no skin left bare."

Becky giggled. "And then, they take turns in licking it off each other."

Kevin was so transfixed by the sight of Stella stroking her friend's inner thigh that he was unaware until it was too late that he had started to emit a high-pitched squeak of excitement.

The two girls, realising that Kevin's attention was completely captivated, looked at each other and tried desperately to hold in their building laughter.

Just then, Becky swung her leg back down to the floor.

The look of disappointment on Kevin's face was impossible for him to disguise.

For a moment, the three of them just stood there in silence.

Kevin attempted a feeble apology for not stocking the requested item, but his attention was still firmly fixed on Becky's leg, even though now it was covered once more by her skirt.

Stella slamming her credit card on the counter finally brought him out of his reverie.

"In that case," she announced, "we'll just take this lot."

Chapter Five

WHILE STELLA AND BECKY WALKED MERRILY THROUGH the streets of Huntley, having just had their fun with the hapless Kevin, back in London Jenna slammed the receiver of her uncle's landline back into its cradle and slumped back onto the armchair behind her.

It was the third time since returning home from work that she had attempted to phone the Huntley police station and the third time she had chickened out before the phone started ringing.

Jenna stared at the inanimate object on the table next to her. In keeping with her uncle's eccentricity, it was an old-fashioned tan and brown retro phone from the seventies with a dial on its face. Jenna had managed to find it for him on eBay. She had actually bought it as a joke, but when she'd seen how her uncle's eyes lit up upon seeing it, she hadn't had the heart to tell him.

As she remembered his reaction to his present, Jenna just managed to catch herself before she bit down on another fingernail. Sitting in the traffic on the way home from work, she had managed to absentmindedly rip off a slice of nail from her thumb, which took a piece of skin with it. It was a common trait of hers when she was nervous or pre-occupied, and she knew that it would throb now until the skin grew back.

Hoisting herself out of the armchair, Jenna walked over to the bay window and peered out into the evening sky. The last of the daylight was tinged with a burnt orange hue, which was slipping slowly behind the oncoming darkness. The trees that lined the road swayed from side to side in the evening breeze, sending dying leaves cascading to the ground, ready to be swept away by the next gust.

After a few moments, Jenna closed the curtain and switched on the standard lamp beside her. She walked into the kitchen and switched on the kettle. Her mouth suddenly felt very dry. Having initially arrived home from work, Jenna had checked her uncle's answering machine, and upon seeing that there was no message from him, she had immediately dialled the Huntley police.

But halfway through, she'd replaced the receiver, realising that she was not sure how to start the conversation with whomever answered. She had sat for a moment thinking how best to phrase her concerns before trying again.

This time she waited for the phone to ring twice before putting it down again.

Her opening statement, which she had thought only moments earlier sounded perfectly plausible, suddenly seemed very foolish and not likely to be taken seriously.

For the best part of an hour, Jenna just sat in an armchair, trying to decide how best to convey her concerns to the police without sounding ridiculous or neurotic.

Having now failed for the third time, she decided to have a calming cup of chamomile tea to help compose herself before trying again.

Jenna made her tea and sat in the breakfast nook. While it cooled, she aimlessly played with the spoon in the sugar bowl, making patterns in the white grains until eventually she grew bored and stabbed the spoon down, leaving it sticking up like a lone palm tree on a desert island.

Just then, her mobile erupted into life.

Jenna almost sent her cup and the sugar bowl flying as she jumped up from the table and ran into the living room.

Without checking the screen, she pressed accept.

"Hello," she gasped.

"Hi, Jenna." It was her friend Trisha. Jenna felt her heart sink at the sound of her friend's voice. "I just thought I'd call and see if there was any news."

"Oh, hi, Trish. No, there's no news yet, I'm afraid."

Trish immediately picked up on her friend's melancholy tone. "I take it the police were no help then?"

There was silence on the other end, which Trisha picked up on immediately.

Before Jenna had a chance to answer, she cut in. "You haven't called them yet, have you?"

"No," Jenna sighed.

"Well, why not? I thought you were going to do it the moment you got home if there was no news."

Jenna bit her lower lip. She was starting to feel like a chastised child, but she knew that her friend only had her best interest at heart.

Finally, she replied. "I did try and call them, three times if I'm honest, but I want them to take me seriously, and in my mind, well, I just sound like a complete fruitcake. After all, he's a grown man and entitled to go away if he wants."

She paused for a further moment before continuing. "I just don't want some desk sergeant humouring me to keep me happy and then not doing anything about it."

"But you have to start somewhere." Trisha tried her best to keep the exasperation from her voice. She knew that her friend was extremely concerned for her uncle, which was understandable, but Trisha had always been a proactive individual, and she did not have an awful lot of patience for people who just sat back worrying and waiting for something to happen by itself.

Then, she had an idea.

"Listen, Jen, do you want me to come over and sit with you while you make the call? Hell, I'd even do it for you, but I doubt they'll talk to me as I'm not related to your uncle."

Jenna considered her friend's suggestion for a moment.

Of all her friends, Trisha was the one she would most like to have with her under such circumstances. She had always admired Trisha's strength of personality and often wished that she could be more like her. If she was, she would not still be with Roger, that was for sure.

"Jenna?"

"Sorry, I was just thinking. Thanks for the offer, Trish, but I know I'm being pathetic."

"No, you're not," her friend assured her. "I think that in your mind you've just built this whole thing up to the point where you feel this is your last chance of tracking down your uncle, and if this fails, you don't know what you'll do next."

Jenna realised there was a lot of truth in what Trisha was saying. Even if she had not wanted to admit it to herself, hearing it out loud seemed to make it that much more acceptable in her mind.

"You still there?"

"Yes, sorry, I was just thinking about what you said, and you're right. My uncle is the only family I have left in the world, and he's done so much for me, I just can't imagine losing him right now."

"Well, that's understandable," agreed Trisha, "so would you like me to come over and sit with you while you make the call?"

"No, thank you, Trish. I really appreciate the offer, but I feel I need to start the ball rolling myself. But thank you again, you really are the best friend a girl could have."

Trisha laughed softly on the other end. "Let's not get too

carried away now; you know I wouldn't think twice about stealing Roger away from you."

In spite of herself, Jenna burst out laughing.

It was just what she needed.

"Hey," she replied, once her laughter had subsided sufficiently to allow her to respond, "don't go making promises you don't intend keeping."

They said their goodbyes so that Jenna could make her call.

Trisha made her promise to ring her back if she changed her mind about wanting company, which Jenna was very grateful for, especially as she knew it was a genuine offer.

She decided to make the call using the landline.

She knew that she was probably overthinking the issue, but something told her that with all the junk calls the police probably received these days from untraceable mobiles, it might add some weight of stability to her request if she used the home phone.

To her, it showed that she had nothing to hide.

The call was answered after two rings. "Huntley police, Sergeant Kone speaking." The voice was croaky and a little gruff, although his manner was not off-putting.

Jenna took in a deep breath. "Good evening, my name is Jenna Wilkinson, and I live in London. I am trying to trace my uncle, and I believe he might be staying in your town."

"I see, miss, and when you say trace him, what do you mean, exactly? Has he recently moved to Huntley, or have you just lost touch? I take it from the fact he's your uncle that he's not a juvenile?"

Jenna bit her bottom lip.

She knew before making the call that the hardest obstacle would be the fact that her uncle was a grown man and entitled to go wherever he wanted, for as long as he wanted.

Jenna had to somehow convince the officer that her alarm was genuine.

Chapter 5

"Officer, my uncle is a professor of anthropology here in London. He often leaves on little ventures for the purposes of research and such like, but he always calls me regularly to ensure me he's ok. His call is seriously overdue, and I've tried countless times to call him on his mobile, but my calls go straight to answer phone."

"I see miss, and you're convinced that your uncle was staying here?"

"Definitely, he left me the name of the town before he left."

"But not exactly where he was staying?"

Jenna dedicated a hint of annoyance in the officer's tone. For a moment she was afraid that she had lost his interest. She decided it might be best to stick to facts rather than just her concerns.

"My uncle usually finds somewhere to stay once he arrives at his location. His needs are very simple; it's his work that matters. I appreciate that you probably receive hundreds of missing people calls in your job, but they always say to leave things at least twenty-four hours, and this has been at least five full days!"

Jenna waited on the line, trying to keep her temper steady. There was no point in aggravating the sergeant when she needed him on her side.

From the other end she could hear the sound of computer keys being hit.

After a moment, the officer spoke again. "Right you are then, Miss Wilkinson, you'd better let me have all the details you can, and I'll set it up on our system."

Jenna felt her entire body relaxing.

Her stomach gurgled loudly, probably because of the pent-up anxiety she allowed to build up inside her.

She placed the back of her hand over her mouth, afraid that a burp might be unleashed.

"So," continued the sergeant, "let's start with your details, and we'll go from there."

Over the next twenty minutes, Jenna answered all the officer's questions, detailing as much as she could remember about her uncle and his work, although she was unable to go into too much detail as her uncle was often vague when asked about his latest project.

During their conversation, Jenna's mobile burst into life three times.

Each call showed as being from Roger, and with a certain amount of gratification, Jenna cut off each one before it went to answer phone.

She could just imagine Roger's anger and frustration starting to boil over. Jenna could not remember the last time she had declined one of his calls. He used to be mad enough if they went to answer phone, and she always had to explain to him why when they finally spoke.

But for once, she did not care what Roger thought. This conversation was much more important, and she refused to ask the office to wait while she pandered to her boyfriend's insecurities.

Once Sergeant Kone had taken all the details, he asked Jenna to hold on the line while he made some enquiries.

Jenna waited on the line patiently until he came back.

"Miss Wilkinson."

"Still here," replied Jenna, trying to sound as cheerful as possible.

"Well, miss, the good news is that no one matching your uncle's description has been admitted into hospital in town, nor have there been any unidentified accidents or victims of crime reported."

Jenna heaved a sigh of relief. At least that was a positive result, as far as it went.

Chapter 5

The sergeant continued without allowing Jenna a chance to respond.

"Now, due to the fact that we have no idea where your uncle might be staying, we have no way of checking on his location. I am sure you can understand that there are too many hotels, motels and guest houses to count in Huntley, let alone contact?"

Jenna felt her heart drop. "So there's no way you can put out some sort of 'wanted' notice for him? Someone who works at his lodgings may recognise him and come forward?"

"I'm afraid it's too early for anything like that, miss." The officer's tone was sympathetic, but Jenna still detected a subtle hint of sarcasm. She imagined him raising his eyebrows to a colleague standing nearby, as if to say <u>we've got a right one here,</u> and the thought of it made her want to yell at him down the handset.

But Jenna calmed herself. Officer Kone had probably done all he was authorised to do, and she was grateful that he had least taken the trouble to check the hospital and morgue.

Possibly sensing her despondency on the line, the sergeant tried to offer Jenna some final words of comfort.

"I'm sure that your uncle is perfectly alright, Miss Wilkinson. If he is prone to absentmindedness, as you say, then he's probably just got caught up in his work. You know what these academic types can be like?"

Jenna knew his words were well intentioned, but they were still not very comforting.

"Now, we've got all his details on our system," the officer continued, "and I promise you that if anything comes in, we will be in contact with you immediately, you have my word."

Now that their conversation was coming to an end, Jenna could feel her eyes starting to fill with tears.

She chided herself that she should be satisfied with the fact that her uncle had not come to any harm — at least, not as far as the police knew — and that the desk sergeant had taken her concerns seriously enough to add them to the police database.

Jenna thanked the officer for all his help and apologised if she had been at all brusque with him in the beginning.

Once she hung up, Jenna broke down.

Chapter Six

KEVIN WAS STILL FANTASISING ABOUT WHAT HE wanted to do to Becky and Stella when the bell above the door rang, bringing him out of his reverie.

As he looked up, he saw coming towards him the most beautiful woman he had ever laid eyes on.

She was dressed in a long, flowing, black velvet cape that draped around her shoulders and hung down almost to her feet. Although Kevin could not see any buttons or studs fastening the garment, it somehow managed to encompass her entire body, so much so that he could not tell what — if anything — she was wearing underneath.

Her hair was as black as her cloak, and it hung in a thick, silky mane that cascaded around her shoulders.

Her skin, by contrast, was pale to the point of being almost as white as milk, and even though she wore dark red lipstick and eyeshadow, Kevin surmised that she did not need such camouflage to enhance her natural beauty.

But her most striking feature was her eyes. They were of a sharp green hue and shone like emeralds in a crystal pool, and Kevin found himself completely transfixed by them.

Such was the grace and elegance with which she moved that she seemed to Kevin to almost drift, rather than walk from the door to where he stood.

As the woman approached his counter, Kevin gulped involuntarily, trying desperately to clear his throat before speaking. He wanted his voice to sound strong and in command, the voice of a real man, not a teenage pipsqueak as his mother often referred to him.

But as he opened his mouth, much to his dismay, he could not manage anything more than a high-pitched whine. He was completely overawed by the woman's presence, and he could tell she knew it.

"Hello," she said, tilting her head slightly to one side as if studying him. "My name is Katerina, but my friends call me Kat. I own the little book shop at the far end of town. Perhaps you know it?"

Her voice was soft and gentle, but at the same time it had a husky sensuality about it that exuded seduction.

Kevin barely managed a silent nod in response. In truth, he had noticed the book shop opening a few months earlier, but never having been much of a reader he had not bothered venturing in.

A move which he now regretted.

"Anyway," the woman continued, "I'm thinking of having my flat above the shop redecorated, and I wondered if perhaps you could recommend someone local, in the trade."

Kevin's normally sluggish brain began to whizz at ninety to the dozen.

Had she wanted anything fixed to do with lights or plumbing, he would have been completely out of his depth. But decorating, how hard could it be? A bit of painting, maybe wallpapering, even he could manage that.

"Well, I don't usually advertise because most of my time is taken up with the shop, but I'm quite good at painting and deco-

Chapter 6

rating myself." Kevin tried to keep his voice steady, but he could still feel it starting to quiver.

The woman was only standing a few feet away from him, with only the counter separating them, and the scent emanating from her was almost intoxicating.

Kevin wished now that he had taken the time to have a shower that morning.

He smiled at her weakly.

Her gaze felt as if it were penetrating his body, right through to his very soul.

"Thank you," the woman purred. "I would be ever so grateful if you could come over and take a look. I really am hopeless with such things, and being on my own, I could really do with a big strong man to help out."

Kevin felt his cheeks flush.

<u>Was she actually flirting with him?</u>

It took a supreme effort for him to tear his gaze away from her, but once he managed it, Kevin pretended to check through his register as if looking for a free slot.

Keeping his eyes down, he asked, "When would be best for you to show me what you need?"

The woman placed a slender, well-manicured hand on the counter, close enough that it was almost touching his. She leaned in closer. "I don't suppose you could come over tonight, by any chance?"

Kevin looked up. Taken aback by the closeness of their proximity, he instinctively pulled back.

The movement was not lost on the woman, and she smiled broadly.

"Don't worry," she assured him. "I promise I won't bite."

Kevin tried to laugh off his nervous reaction, but the noise he made sounded more like a snort.

His face grew even redder.

"Shall we say, seven o'clock?" the woman asked hopefully.

Kevin slammed his book and nodded. "Perfect," he muttered.

"I'll look forward to it." She turned with a swish of her cape and began to drift back to the door. As she opened it to leave, she turned back to him. "The entrance to my flat is down the alley at the side of the shop. I'll leave the door on the latch."

With a wink, she was gone.

Seconds later, Kevin dashed around the counter, smashing his knee against the corner in his haste. He rubbed it and swore to himself as he made his way to the door.

He wanted to watch her cross the street and walk towards her shop.

But when he looked out, there was no sign of her!

Once he had locked the shop, Kevin raced up the stairs two at a time to the flat he shared with his mother.

She heard him and shouted out that she fancied a Chinese for dinner and asked him to go to the take-away down the road for her.

Kevin called back that he was going out and that she would have to collect her own dinner. His mother continued to demand that he go, so Kevin slammed the bathroom door to drown out her wailing.

He stripped off and threw his clothes on the floor before turning on the shower.

It always took a few minutes for the water to heat up, so Kevin spent the time productively by checking his complexion in the mirror and taking care of a couple of whiteheads at the side of his nose.

He took his time in the shower, washing his hair twice, as he could not remember the last time it had seen water. He even used some of his mother's conditioner and left it in while he lathered himself all over in shower gel before standing under the hot stream to rinse off.

Once his body was free of soap, Kevin stuck his head under the shower and scrubbed furiously to eradicate every ounce of

Chapter 6

conditioner. Usually, he did not bother with such lavish beautifications, but tonight was special.

He could not get that green-eyed goddess out of his mind, and the more he went over their encounter in the shop, the more he convinced himself that she had indeed been flirting with him.

Of course, he considered she might just be trying it on so that he would offer her a lower price for the work. But in truth, Kevin would have done it for nothing if it meant a chance to spend some quality time alone with her.

After drying himself off, Kevin brushed his teeth and even took a swig from the bottle of mouthwash his mother had in the bathroom cabinet. It had a pungent odour of roses and tasted a bit like strawberries. Kevin hoped that his breath would not smell too <u>girly</u> and put the green-eyed woman off.

His mum had left a pile of clean clothes on the chair in his room. Kevin picked out some clean underwear and his favourite Arsenal shirt, which was just tight enough to accentuate his physique without exposing his ever-growing girth.

There were no clean jeans in the pile, so Kevin chose the pair which smelt the least sweaty and pulled them on.

He opted for trainers rather than his work boots; for a start, they were cleaner, and he surmised they would be easier to remove if things progressed towards the bedroom tonight.

Kevin could feel his stomach starting to churn at the thought of the adventure he was about to embark on, so he forced out a belch to clear it.

The last thing he wanted to risk was releasing wind from any avenue in front of the woman.

He could still hear his mother whingeing on about her dinner from the other room, but checking his alarm clock, Kevin saw that it was already a quarter to seven, so there was no time to waste.

He grabbed his denim jacket and ran down the stairs, not

bothering to call back to his mum as he slammed the front door behind him.

Within minutes, he was standing outside the book shop.

Kevin paused and looked up at the windows of the flat above.

His chest was heaving from the exertion of rushing to his destination, which he realised was totally unnecessary when he glanced at his watch and discovered he was still a few minutes early.

The shop downstairs was in darkness, as he'd expected. Even so, Kevin peered in through the main front window and squinted at the rows of books lining the walls. Towards the back of the shop, he saw what appeared to be a spiral metal staircase. It looked to him to be one of those old-fashioned ornate varieties you often saw in Victorian shops and businesses.

The book shop was indeed, as Kat had told him, at the end of the street. Kevin checked around the far end to see if Kat's front door might be located on the side off the main road, but after the side front window, the nearest doorway led to a different shop, so he made his way back around to the front and around the other side.

The alleyway which led to Kat's front door was unlit, and even with the glow of the nearest streetlamp reaching his side of the pavement, the actual path to her door was in complete darkness.

Kevin waited a moment to try and adjust his eyes to the gloom before he took a deep breath and started down the alley.

After about twenty paces, he saw what he presumed must be Kat's door on his right.

Feeling a sudden presence behind him, Kevin turned around and looked back up the darkened alley, but to his relief there was no one there.

He turned back to face the front door and rapped against the wood with his knuckles.

The door slowly swung inwards.

Chapter 6

Kevin took an instinctive pace backwards before remembering that Kat had said she would leave the door on the latch for him.

As he moved closer and peered inside, he saw a narrow corridor leading to a staircase at the far end.

There were no lights on, either downstairs or above, so Kevin crossed the threshold and called up to announce his presence.

He listened intently, but there was no response from above.

A sudden urge to turn and flee rushed over him, but the thought of the beautiful Kat in her long flowing robe, with those gorgeous green eyes, convinced him to stay put.

Once inside the hallway, Kevin gently closed the door behind him, making sure that he left it on the latch in case he needed to make a quick getaway.

He felt his way along the walls on either side of him as he approached the bottom of the stairs. Once he was at the base, he called up again.

After a few seconds, Kevin saw a shaft of light appear on the upstairs landing, as if a door off that landing had been opened. He heard the soft sound of bare feet crossing the floor and heaved an audible sigh of relief when he saw Kat's silhouette appear at the top of the stairs.

"There you are." She spoke just above a whisper, as if not wanting to disturb anyone else in the property.

"Hi," replied Kevin. He lifted his hand as if to wave to her but realised that in the darkness she probably would not be able to see the gesture, so he let his arm drop back down by his side.

"Come on up," Kat invited him, "I've been waiting for you."

As Kevin began to ascend the staircase, Kat's form came more into focus. By the time he was halfway up, Kevin was convinced that she was naked, although he could not tell for sure due to the inadequate light.

Kevin felt a bulge starting to push against the front of his jeans as he squinted in the darkness to try and ascertain if Kat were indeed naked or if it was merely a trick of the light.

Before he reached the top, Kat moved away and out of sight around the wall.

Kevin continued to climb, his anticipation growing with each step.

As he reached the top, Kevin looked around the corner in the direction he had seen Kat disappear. At the far end of the landing was an open door, and emanating from within was a dim flickering light.

Kevin waited.

"Are you coming in, or what?"

It was Kat's voice, echoing from within the room with the open door.

Not needing any more prompting, Kevin strode purposefully towards the open doorway. All his earlier feelings of apprehension and concern seemed to melt away like wax in a fire the closer he came to the doorway.

Once inside, Kevin was met by the sight of Kat sitting on a large white hearth rug with her back to a blazing log fire. She was leaning back on her elbows, her long hair cascading down behind her and her legs straight out in front of her. They were parted just enough so that Kevin could make out the tuft of black hair between her thighs in the fire's glow.

Kevin could neither speak nor move. He desperately tried to think of something clever to say and even imagined himself as James Bond coming across a similar scene in one of his films. But he had nothing to offer.

He decided that words were no longer necessary. Instead, he would simply undress and take the woman. But yet again, his body refused to obey his brain's command. He could not believe it; here he was, possibly on the verge of the greatest sexual experience of his life, and his body refused to function.

Then a thought struck him!

Chapter 6

This was all too good to be true. What if this woman had some secret agenda for luring him up here?

Perhaps she intended to mug him or beat him up. Well, maybe not her exactly, but her accomplices. She was probably just the bait. Any minute now, a group of men would descend on them and start laying into Kevin.

But what for?

Then he considered that perhaps this was retaliation for something his brother Nick might have done, and as he was in prison and untouchable, Kevin was a likely substitute.

With much hesitance, Kevin turned his gaze away from Kat's nakedness, and he looked back down the corridor he had just walked along. He had not noticed before, due mainly to his excitement at the prospect of what was about to happen, but there were two other doors leading off the corridor.

Perhaps the gang was in there. Waiting for Kat to summon them.

"Something out there more interesting than me?"

Kat's question caused Kevin to automatically turn back to face her.

Realising that she had Kevin's full attention once more, Kat leaned her head to one side so that it was now resting on her shoulder, and at the same time, she slowly positioned her legs a little further apart.

The flames behind her made shadows around the walls and ceiling.

"What are you waiting for?" Kat whispered. "You know you want me."

Kevin felt himself nodding dumbly.

On instinct, Kevin took a step towards the naked woman. Then another, and another. By the third step he started to remove his jacket. He discarded it on a sofa across from where he stood at the other side of the room. Next, he pulled his shirt over his head and disposed of that in the same manner.

"That's better," Kat said, encouragingly. "Now take the rest off and come down here!"

It sounded more like a command than a request, but Kevin found her words all the more enticing as a result.

Trying desperately not to emulate a scene from a carry-on film, Kevin kicked off his trainers and struggled out of his jeans, stepping out of them and kicking them across the room.

When he only had his underpants left, Kevin suddenly felt anxious about his appearance. He looked down at Kat, with her beautiful body and her perfect skin, and realised that once he removed his underwear his overhang would be on full display.

Kevin sucked in his stomach but still felt unable to go all the way.

In the firelight, Kat swept her tongue seductively over her dark-red lips, leaving the tiniest hint of a wet trail. "Please don't go all shy on me now," she intoned. "You can't get a girl all excited and then leave her frustrated, did you never learn manners?"

With that, Kat leaned over and slipped her middle finger in her mouth. After sucking on it a few times, she removed it and slid her hand down between her legs. As she slowly eased her middle finger inside her, Kat threw her head back and moaned softly.

The sight of Kat sliding her finger in and out of her moist cleft was all Kevin needed to spur him on.

He lifted his underpants gently over his growing erection and, like his jeans, kicked them over to the other side of the room.

Kevin strode over until he was standing directly over Kat.

His eyes traced every curve of her gorgeous nakedness, but it was the work her finger was doing that drew his most avid attention.

Kat removed her hand from her groin and leaned forward, gently clasping her fingers around Kevin's protrusion. He closed his eyes and let his head fall back, and Kat carefully began to slide her elegant fingers up and down his growing shaft.

Kevin let out a deep sigh as Kat's lips replaced her hand, closing around his penis and taking it deep inside her mouth. She sucked on him, thrusting her mouth back and forth as her tongue frantically licked the bald head of his erection.

Kevin had never felt such ecstasy.

Both his legs began to tremble involuntarily, and for a moment he felt as if they would no longer be able to support his weight. He leaned forward and placed his hands gently on Kat's shoulders to assist his balance.

Kat's lips and tongue continued to work faster and faster, and Kevin could feel his seed starting to rise. Just when he thought he was about to ejaculate, Kat withdrew her mouth, leaving Kevin quivering on the spot.

He opened his eyes and looked down at her, a pleading, almost pathetic expression on his face.

A cruel smile spread across Kat's face as she guided Kevin down to the rug and made him lie down on his back before she began to kiss and lick him all over. She created a path across his torso with her tongue, while Kevin simply lay back with his eyes closed, moaning softly.

Whenever Kevin tried to raise his arms to touch her, Kat would grab his wrists and force them back to the floor. It occurred to him that she had incredible strength for a woman, but he was far too busy being teased and tormented to give the idea much credence.

Eventually, she mounted him, guiding his throbbing member inside her with her soft hands.

Kevin felt the room start to spin as Kat slid up and down on top of him.

He was totally under her spell and was loving every second of it.

Kevin felt himself starting to reach orgasm.

He bent his knees and tried to thrust up in time with Kat, but there was no strength left in his legs with which to do so. The tingling sensation had grown worse and was slowly making its way from his legs and up through the rest of his body.

Kevin inhaled deeply. He could smell the wood smoke from the fire. He could smell the shampoo used when the rug was last cleaned. He could smell Kat's scent, not a manufactured one from perfume or cologne, but a natural odour of clean skin, soft hair, and just a hint of the perspiration she had built up while she was riding him.

But there was another smell, too.

It was just starting to creep in and assail his nostrils, but it soon turned out to be far more pungent than all the others combined.

Kevin felt Kat's hair brushing his chest and face as she leaned over him.

He kept his eyes closed as he could feel himself about to come. Kevin managed to hold back for a few more seconds in an effort to prolong his pleasure before finally he exploded inside of her.

His entire body spasmed wildly.

Kevin shot up until he could feel every drop squirt out of him.

Once he was spent, Kevin relaxed, breathing heavily.

The odour he had detected just a few seconds ago seemed to be even stronger than before.

Kevin wrinkled his nose.

The smell reminded him of dead animals and rotting carcasses, which he had once experienced when his brother had taken him to meet a friend of his who worked at an abattoir.

Kevin opened his eyes.

He saw Kat above him, her face only inches away.

In the shimmering firelight, her features appeared to have taken on an animalistic quality.

Chapter 6

Kevin blinked several times to clear his vision before squinting up at the mutation before him.

Kat's eyes, moments ago a beautiful emerald green, were now blood red with a pinpoint black iris. Her beautiful white teeth were now the yellowing fangs of a demented dog. Even her hair, black and lustrous seconds ago, had now taken on the appearance of a matted animal mane.

Kevin's first instinct was to throw this monstrous apparition off him, but when he tried to move, he discovered to his horror that he was paralysed from the neck down.

The only movement he was aware of making was as his now flaccid penis slipped out of what moments ago had been the beautiful Kat and slid down to hang loosely across his sack.

The thing above him moved in closer.

Kevin could feel its fetid breath against his skin.

A thin, broad tongue lolled out between the gaping jaws which lines its mouth and hung there, dripping wet saliva onto Kevin's neck and chest.

The werewolf lowered its head and sunk its rotting fangs into the soft skin of Kevin's exposed neck.

The pain was excruciating, but even so, Kevin found himself unable to cry out. It was if his voice, too, had deserted him along with the power in his limbs.

Mercifully, Kevin passed out!

Chapter Seven

JENNA FLIPPED THE INDICATOR LEVER AND EASED over to the left-hand lane of the motorway before crossing over into the slip road for the service station. She thought it best to fill up with petrol as the indicator was nearing the quarter-full mark, and she certainly did not want to end up being stranded in the middle of nowhere.

Also, she needed some strong coffee. Long drives always made her feel sleepy, and considering how restless her night had been, she needed all the help she could get to stay alert.

Having finished her phone call the previous evening with the police sergeant and then crying for the best part of fifteen minutes, Jenna had reprimanded herself for not taking more control over the situation. That was when she had decided on her next course of action, that of driving down to Huntley for a couple of days, or as long as it took, to try and locate her uncle.

She had drawn herself a hot bubble bath and poured herself a generous glass of chardonnay to help her relax and unwind.

Whilst she'd sat in the bubbles, Jenna had called Trish and told her of her plans, asking her to explain her absence at work and to make her apologies for the short notice.

Chapter 7

Trish had been happy to help and mentioned that under the circumstances it was a good thing that Roger was away, otherwise he would have doubtless insisted on accompanying Jenna on her trip.

Jenna had winced at her friend's suggestion, but she knew too that she was correct in her observation. Not only would Roger insist on going with her, but Jenna could just imagine how embarrassing he would be with the police while she was trying to seek their assistance. Roger had never learned that outside of the office, he was no bigshot. In truth, he was nothing to shout about within the office without his <u>mummy</u> behind him.

After her soak, Jenna had changed for bed and packed a small suitcase to allow her the option of staying in Huntley for a few days if the situation called for it.

She'd made herself a sandwich for dinner. She hadn't been particularly hungry, but she knew from experience if she went to bed without anything, she was more likely to wake up during the night.

She had also settled for another large glass of wine to aid her rest.

As it turned out, neither had helped. Jenna had first woken at just after two and lain awake for at least an hour before drifting back off to sleep.

The next time she opened her eyes had been little before four, and once again it had taken almost an hour for her to drop back off. This time she'd decided to read a couple of pages from her latest Harold Robbins to help put her back to sleep.

When her alarm had gone off at six, her whole body had ached as if she had not had any sleep at all. Therefore, she'd made a conscious decision to change her original plan of heading off before the rush-hour started and leave after it instead. Jenna had re-set the alarm for eight, and this time she'd managed to drop back off almost immediately.

When she had eventually awoken at eight, somewhat more refreshed and bright-eyed, she had known that she had made the right decision.

After breakfast and a shower, Jenna had set off for Huntley.

She'd initially programmed her sat-nav to guide her without using any motorways. She had never been a huge fan of driving long distances and tended to keep to the left-hand lane on motorways unless there was someone in front of her going particularly slowly. But even then, she always seemed to end up with some idiot in a massive lorry right on her tail.

Jenna had checked the journey time for her chosen route. The estimated time allowed had taken her by surprise, so she'd decided to re-programme the device for motorway use. Realising how much time she would save, she had resigned herself to being stalked by lorries after all.

Kevin was yanked out of his slumber by the sound of his mum screaming through his bedroom door, telling him that he needed to get up and open the shop.

Ordinarily, Kevin would have either ignored her ranting and turned over for some more shut eye or shouted back that he would wake up when he was ready.

But somehow, on this particular morning, he felt more alert and filled with energy than he could ever remember feeling before.

He sat up in bed and threw the covers back.

Kevin surveyed his naked body as if he were seeing it for the first time.

Although he was sitting up, the ripples of excess flesh which normally collected around his midriff appeared to have been replaced by taut, hard muscle. He sat there for a moment and surveyed the rest of his body. Was it his imagination, or was he suddenly hairier? His skin had a vibrant glow, almost as if he had managed to soak up some sun whilst he slept.

Most noticeable of all was his huge erection.

Kevin often woke up with a hard-on, but now even his penis appeared to have grown in both length and thickness.

I could really do some damage with that! he thought to himself, smiling mischievously.

He considered masturbating but decided not to waste it. Swinging his legs over the side of his bed, Kevin stood up and stretched, yawning loudly.

Walking over to his wardrobe, he took a closer look at himself in the full-length mirror attached to the middle panel.

Besides his toned and sculpted physique, there was something else different about his appearance, and for a moment he could not make out what it was.

Then, it suddenly dawned on him. His complexion was completely absent of any trace of acne. Even upon extremely close inspection, Kevin could not see so much as a trace of his former complaint.

For a moment, he even questioned if he was actually looking at his own reflection. He considered that his mother might have affixed some sort of trick mirror during the night as a punishment for him not buying her dinner for her.

Perhaps she had ordered it online as a joke.

Kevin had seen how those mirrors at the fun fair could distort and deform a person's reflection to make them look extremely fat, or tall, or just plain ridiculous. But this was something else.

Besides, his mother did not have the ingenuity or a sufficient sense of humour to carry out such a task.

He studied his reflection more closely, sliding his hands up and down his torso as if to confirm that what he was seeing was in fact true.

As unbelievable as it seemed, the body in the mirror was his own.

But how could such a transformation take place literally overnight?

He remembered back to when he first hit his teens, how he had suddenly shot up and his mum had had to buy him four different pairs of school trousers in the same year.

Perhaps this was something similar.

His mother's scream broke his reverie.

Kevin quickly dressed and pulled on his clothes. Everything seemed to fit more snugly than it had the day before, but not in an uncomfortable way. He went into the bathroom and splashed some water on his face, admiring his new complexion.

As he brushed his teeth, Kevin could not help but notice how clean and white they looked. He had never been one to take care of his oral hygiene, but there was no evidence of that right now. Plus, they felt stronger, too.

When he walked into the kitchen, his mother was sitting at the table in her dressing gown and slippers, drinking tea and flicking through the morning paper.

As Kevin entered, she glanced up at him, and Kevin could tell from the expression on her face that she, too, noticed something different about him.

He pretended not to notice her quizzical look and proceeded to fix himself some breakfast.

Kevin had always had a big appetite, but this morning he was ravenous. He inspected the contents of the fridge, but nothing really took his fancy. He checked the cupboards and scanned the various boxes of cereal, but again, nothing on offer appealed.

He wanted meat!

Raw, bloody, meat!

Kevin shook his head. He had no idea where this sudden craving had arrived from, but he knew that nothing else was going to suffice.

Chapter 7

He turned to his mother, who by now had gone back to her news article about someone from her favourite reality show or the other, finding out she was pregnant by her boyfriend's father.

"Have we got any steak, or hamburger mince, mum?"

His mother glanced over her shoulders. "What's up with you? Steak indeed, for breakfast. You think I won the bloomin' lottery or sumink?"

She turned back to her article.

Kevin glared down at his mother's back.

He suddenly found himself having to fight an irresistible urge to grab her by the hair and pull her head back, then ripping a huge chunk out of her exposed throat.

Instead, Kevin just grabbed her mug from in front of her and knocked back the contents, slamming the empty receptacle back on the table before storming out.

As he made his way down the stairs, Kevin's mind raced with thoughts of the previous evening. His recollection of events was incredibly hazy, much the same as when he would wake after a night of getting slaughtered with his mates down the local.

But this time, he was positive that he had not been intoxicated.

So why, then, was his memory so bad?

He remembered being in the shop and the two girls flirting with him. But everything after that until he awoke this morning seemed to come in waves, and none of it made any sense to him.

He had a vague memory of a beautiful green-eyed seductress and an open log fire. In his mind he was lying in her arms, and he could feel the soft, welcoming allure of her embrace. An intoxicating odour assailed his nostrils, and Kevin could almost taste the sweet, perfumed warmth of her skin in his mouth.

But it was more like a dream than a recollection of things which took place.

Yet it all seemed so real.

The warmth of her body, the smell of her skin, the touch of her hands as they tenderly caressed his naked body. But most of all those eyes, piercing through him is they had the power to see through to his very soul.

Then suddenly, through it all crashed a memory of snarling, gnashing jaws, slavering spittle over him. The foul stench of fetid breath, overpowering, causing him to want to gag. Burning red eyes, full of malicious hatred, which seemed to view him, for all intents and purposes, as nothing more than a slab of meat, whose only purpose was to serve as course clay to feed its hunger.

Kevin tried to shake the apparitions from his memory as he set about opening for business.

But he knew, without question, that something strange had taken over him.

He was no longer just lumbering Kevin Roop from down the road; now he was so much more.

But the question was what?

Jenna drained the last of her double espresso and disposed of the paper cup in the waste bin behind her seat. For a few moments she continued to stare out of the restaurant window at the car park below, watching cars pull in and out, following their trail back onto the motorway.

The sky overhead had turned to a uniform grey, which threatened rain.

There was a feeling inside her which made Jenna want to stay where she was and wait for the rain so that she could trace the pattern of the raindrops as they streaked down the glass. It was a pastime she had often indulged in as a child on rainy

Chapter 7

weekends, when she found herself sitting in the bay window of her bedroom, curled up with a good book.

That same urge to stay put for a while longer also made Jenna want to turn her car around and head back to London.

But there was no way she was going to give in to that sudden compulsion.

Jenna pushed her chair back and walked toward the stairs that would lead her back down to the main foyer.

On her way out, she stopped at one of the kiosks and purchased a large bag of revels. Comfort food for a rainy day.

As she slid into her seat and slammed the door, the first of the raindrops started to hit her windscreen.

For the rest of her journey the rain hammered down, forcing Jenna to drive below the speed limit due to the poor visibility. Even with her windscreen wipers on maximum speed, she found it difficult to see more than a couple of car lengths in front of her.

Even so, while she dawdled along in the slow lane, other vehicles raced by on the outside, causing Jenna to wonder how their drivers could possibly be able to see where they were going, much less be confident in stopping in time should the need arise.

Having to contend with the hazardous driving conditions, Jenna was relieved when her sat-nav finally instructed her to turn off the motorway at the next junction.

The rest of her journey was mainly on small country roads, several of which were single-lane only, and apart from a couple of irresponsible drivers who insisted on overtaking even though the road signs clearly forbade it, the majority of road users appeared to be content to keep to a far more sensible speed.

Her sat-nav led her directly to the Huntley police station. Once there, Jenna followed the signs to the visitor's car park, and having driven around twice, she managed to locate a space as someone else drove out. She was about as far away from the entrance as it was possible to be, but fortunately the rain had finally petered out. Which, as her umbrella was in the boot along with her suitcase, meant that at least she would not be soaked on her way into the station.

Jenna stayed in her car for a few minutes, pondering how best to proceed.

She knew that the officer she had spoken to the previous evening would not still be on duty, so she would doubtless have to explain everything again to whomever was on the desk, which in a way she preferred instead of them merely skimming over the information Sergeant Kone had entered on the computer and informing her that they were still looking into things.

What Jenna needed to do was convey her concerns face-to-face with someone who would understand and take her present state of distress seriously. She hoped that whoever was in charge would realise that she had not just driven in all the way from London on a whim, merely to be fobbed off with standard response patter.

Jenna jumped in her seat when someone rapped against her side window.

Chapter Eight

Looking up, Jenna saw the face of a uniformed female police officer staring in at her.

Before Jenna had a chance to catch her breath, the officer spoke.

"Is everything alright, madam?" she asked with a practised calmness in her tone.

Jenna realised she could not open the door, otherwise it would crash it into the officer. So instead, she gave the key in the ignition a quarter turn and depressed the switch for her window to open.

As the glass pane slid down, the officer leaned in a little closer.

Jenna surmised she was no older than thirty. She had a ruddy complexion and a mass of blond hair scooped up in a bun. But what surprised Jenna was the size of the woman. Everything about her, from what Jenna could tell, was enormous.

The woman could not have been very tall considering her breasts were almost level with the car window when Jenna first turned to see her, but her uniform shirt was bursting all over as it was forced to contain her immense bulk.

Jenna knew that officers had to undergo vigorous training, both mental and physical before gaining entry to the force, so she presumed that this officer had joined up when she was much younger and fitter.

"Is everything alright, madam?" the officer asked again before Jenna had a chance to say anything herself. Now that she was leaning inside the window slightly, Jenna could smell the pungent odour of raw onion on the woman's breath, and she had to fight an urge to instinctively pull back while making a face.

"Oh, hello," Jenna managed. "I've come to check up on a report I made last night about my uncle. He's missing."

The woman constable considered Jenna's words for a moment while her eyes made a quick scan of the interior of her car.

After an awkward silence, during which Jenna felt unable to speak, the officer nodded and looked Jenna back in the eye. "If you go in there," she indicated with her head towards the entrance, "the desk sergeant will sort you out."

Again, another waft of raw onion assailed Jenna's nostrils.

She thanked the officer, who for no reason Jenna could fathom stayed in position for a few seconds longer before smiling and retracting her head.

Jenna watched the officer waddle across the car park towards a waiting police cruiser.

Jenna threw open her door and leaned out, hoping that the fresh air would clear her senses before she felt the urge to retch.

After a few deep gulps, Jenna closed her window and locked her car. Living in London for so long, she was not so naïve as to believe that her car would be safe if left unlocked, even in a police car park.

She slung her bag over her shoulder and made her way towards the entrance to the police station.

Inside, Jenna waited while a middle-aged man dressed in a

Chapter 8

tweed jacket and a flat hat complained tirelessly to the officer behind the desk about his neighbour encouraging urban hedgehogs into her garden by leaving out food for them, which in turn caused them to inflict havoc amongst his borders in their attempt to make it to her garden.

The officer in charge was clearly bored with the conversation, but he waited patiently for the man to finish speaking before advising him that, as no crime was being committed, it was really not a job for the police to intervene and suggested that the man should perhaps speak to his neighbour to try and reach an amicable solution.

The complainant, obviously dissatisfied with the lack of support he was receiving, shouted something about his council tax as he turned and stormed back out of the door.

Jenna approached the desk and smiled at the officer behind it.

"Sorry about that, madam," he apologised, "can't please 'em all."

Jenna assured him that an apology was not necessary and made some sympathetic noises about being glad she did not have his job.

Her comments made the officer smile, which encouraged Jenna to believe that her opening gambit would be better received now that she had the man on her side.

Jenna gave her details and informed the officer about her conversation the previous evening with Sergeant Kone. While she spoke, the officer found the report on his computer and began to skim-read it, asking Jenna to fill in gaps as he went along.

At the end of their conversation, the desk sergeant stared at Jenna over the rim of his glasses, and before he opened his mouth, she felt sure that she was about to be fobbed off with the old 'doing all we can' excuse.

But surprisingly, the officer sounded more encouraging and sympathetic than she had anticipated.

"There's been a plain-clothes detective assigned to your case," he informed her. "Would you like me to see if he is available to speak to you?"

Jenna could feel her heart lift; this was far more than she had expected.

She thanked the sergeant and waited while he disappeared through the door behind him.

A couple of moments later, he reappeared and handed Jenna a visitor's pass before buzzing her through.

"If you would like to follow this corridor to the end, he's in the last office on the left, and his name is Detective Constable Young."

Jenna thanked the officer again and strode quickly towards the door in question.

There was no name plate on the door, and the opaque glass prevented her from seeing inside, so Jenna knocked and waited.

From inside the room she heard a wooden chair scraping back against bare boards and a thud, followed by someone cursing.

The door was opened by a tall, thin, almost gangly looking man, who Jenna surmised was probably no older than she was herself.

He extended his hand as he introduced himself and invited Jenna inside.

When Jenna walked in, she expected to see the basic office setup: desk, chairs, computer, perhaps a filing cabinet or two. But what she did not expect was to walk into a room which resembled a cleaner's closet more than it did a professional office.

There were masses of cleaning equipment piled in one corner of the room, along with mops and brooms and stacks of paper towels and toilet rolls. Along the far wall stood four

Chapter 8

vacuum cleaners, the upright variety, all with their cables wrapped neatly around their individual brackets. Above those was a makeshift clothesline, complete with four or five overalls draped across it.

The desk in the middle of the room was piled high with files and papers, some of which had already toppled over due to being incorrectly stacked, and there appeared to be even more occupying whatever remaining space in the tiny office they could find, including the only other chair beside the one the officer doubtless used.

Sure enough, Constable Young quickly set about clearing the papers stacked on the chair nearest the door so that Jenna could sit down.

He stood there for a moment having scooped them up in his arms, as if wondering where best to set them down. Eventually, he found a clear space on the floor nearest to the vacuum cleaners.

It seemed ironic to Jenna that, as this was doubtless, or at least had been until very recently, a cleaner's office, it appeared as if it had not been cleaned itself in years.

Dust covered most of the surfaces and rose in little clouds whenever anything was moved.

Young wiped Jenna's chair with his hand before cleaning his palm against his trouser leg.

"Please sit down, Miss Wilkinson, isn't it?"

Jenna smiled her acknowledgement and thanked him for making time for her, as she could see how busy he must be.

Young flung himself back in his chair opposite Jenna's.

Once more, a cloud of dust flew up as he sat down, causing him to cough involuntarily.

"I must apologise for the state of my office," he said, clearly embarrassed. "I only arrived here a couple of weeks ago from London, and as it turned out, they weren't expecting me, distinct lack of communication there. Anyway, this is only a modest-sized station, as you can see, and this was the best they had to offer." He spread his arms around as if to elucidate further.

Young tapped a few keys on his computer pad and rubbed his chin while studying the screen. "I take it you have just driven in from London. Have you heard from your uncle since last night?"

Jenna shook her head. "No, I'm afraid not. The fact is, I've come here mainly because I couldn't stand being so far away and just waiting for news. Even if I just spent some time in Huntley driving around, I'll feel as if I'm doing something to help find my uncle."

Young nodded. "I see, perfectly understandable." He continued checking his screen. "Well, from the look of things, we've got everything we need to instigate a search, but what would be really helpful would be a photograph if you have one, that way we can use it to e-mail the hotels and guest houses in the area. You never know," he looked back at Jenna and smiled, reassuringly, "we might strike gold."

Jenna scanned through her phone until she found a reasonable picture of her uncle, which she forwarded to Young's computer.

"May I ask how long you're planning to stay in Huntley?"

Jenna shrugged. "I don't have a set itinerary as such, I thought I might just play it by ear."

"Do you know where you're staying yet?" Young looked a little embarrassed for asking. "I only ask because if you haven't made arrangements yet, there's a lovely place a couple of miles down the road, it's where I stayed when I first arrived. Lovely rooms, gorgeous food, and if you request a room at the back you get a marvellous view of the woods."

Jenna thanked him and took the details.

Young gave her a business card, apologising as it was an old one from his time in London, as his new ones had not come through yet. But he assured her that his mobile details were still

Chapter 8

correct and that she should feel free to call him whenever she felt the need.

Young walked Jenna back to the front entrance and tried his best to assure her that everything was going to be alright. He promised that he would call her the minute he heard or found anything pertaining to her uncle and asked her not to worry.

There was a sincerity in his voice that Jenna warmed to. Obviously, she knew that he could make no such guarantee, but he genuinely seemed to care about her plight, and when he told her he was going to do everything in his power to help find her uncle, she believed him.

The hotel the officer had recommended was indeed everything he had mentioned and more. It was set in its own grounds, just off the main high street, and it reminded Jenna of an old coaching inn of the type they used to use to film old black-and-white pirate films.

Jenna could not help but feel enchanted by the picturesque décor inside.

All the wood, from the structural supports to the beams that crossed the ceiling, was of a dark, highly polished oak and matched perfectly with the reception desk and various items of furniture strewn around the lobby.

There were brass ornaments adorning the walls, and as she passed by the entrance to the restaurant, Jenna noticed that they were also present around the huge fireplace which dominated the far wall.

She could just imagine snuggling up in front of that on a cold winter's night.

Jenna suddenly wondered if such a magnificent-looking establishment would be out of her price range. So, as there was no one of duty at reception, she had a quick look at the price tariffs advertised on a wooden plaque behind the desk.

Deciding that the fees were completely reasonable, Jenna

rang the bell on the desk, and within a couple of seconds a middle-aged woman appeared from behind a frosted-glass door.

She smiled when she saw Jenna. "Good afternoon, madam," she said pleasantly, "and how may I help you?"

"Hello, I'm afraid I haven't booked, but," Jenna fumbled in her purse and found Young's card, "a friend of mine, Alan Young, recommended you to me."

The woman's face lit up. "Oh, Alan, such a charming young man, yes, he stayed with us when he first moved down here, still pops in for lunch or dinner now and then."

Jenna managed to snare a room with a glorious view of the woodland at the back, and she immediately opened the windows to make the most of the fresh country air.

When she had first climbed into her car back at the station, there had still been a lingering odour of raw onion from the female officer she had encountered upon arriving. So Jenna had driven to the hotel with both side windows open to try and clear the smell.

Having unpacked and placed her clothes in the wardrobe, Jenna made her way back down to reception. The lady behind the counter, who had introduced herself as Audrey, suggested that Jenna might enjoy some coffee after her long drive. It was then Jenna realised how hungry she was, and since the restaurant had finished serving lunch, Audrey suggested some sandwiches to accompany Jenna's coffee, which she gratefully accepted.

When Audrey appeared with Jenna's sandwiches, Jenna took the opportunity to show the hotelier her uncle's picture on the off chance he might have been staying there.

Audrey lifted her glasses, which hung from a band around her neck, and studied Jenna's phone for several seconds before shaking her head and apologising for not recognising him.

This prompted Jenna to give her host a potted version of why she was in Huntley.

Chapter 8

Audrey listened intently, and Jenna could see from the woman's expression that she sympathised with her plight.

Jenna polished off her lunch, and on her way out, Audrey called to her.

"I was just thinking," she ventured, "if you like, I'd be happy to e-mail your uncle's photo around some of the other hotels and inns, here about. I know quite a few of the proprietors due to business."

Jenna knew that D.C. Young had offered to do the same for her, but she decided that enlisting Audrey's help could not do any harm and might even prove advantageous due to Audrey's contacts.

Jenna spent the rest of the afternoon wandering around the town.

Although she did not imagine she would suddenly bump into her uncle coming out of one of the shops, now that she was here, Jenna felt that she had to do something, and sitting alone in her hotel room was definitely not going to help.

Jenna wandered in and out of some of the shops. She visited the local library, as she knew that would doubtless be one of her uncle's haunts if he was still in town.

At each car park she came across, Jenna stopped and scanned the rows of cars, hoping to pick out her uncle's beaten-up old cruiser, but it was to no avail.

By the time Jenna noticed the sun starting its decline, she realised that she had been walking for just over three hours. That and her long drive earlier in the day made her feel ready for a stiff drink and a hot soak.

Chapter Nine

STELLA SURVEYED THE PATRONS OF THE PUB AS HER friend Becky leaned against the bar waiting for their drinks. Their new spot seemed crowded for the middle of the week, and they had both finished their first round before being able to secure a table.

Stella had never visited a pub until she met her college roommate, Becky. Her parents were both tea-total and had always frowned upon those who frequented such places. Stella was their only child. Her parents had wanted more, but her mother had miscarried when Stella was three and had nearly died as a result.

Unlike most similar cases where, after such a tragedy, the parents often over-indulge their first and only offspring, with Stella it was the opposite. There was no overabundance of hugs and kisses in her house. In fact, Stella could never remember a single occasion where she had felt overwhelmed by their affection.

When Stella reached her teens and her mother noticed young boys accompanying her home, both her parents had given her strict instructions that such behaviour would not be tolerated, followed by a lengthy lecture about what happened to young girls who encouraged boys to act in this way.

Stella lived with a tremendous weight of guilt on her young shoulders when she first arrived at St Anselm's because for the first time in her life she felt free of her overburdening parents, and deep down she knew that she should be missing them more than she was.

But that all changed when she met Becky.

Becky was a true free spirit, adventurous and wild and seemingly unaffected by anything from her past.

A past that Stella would subsequently discover most people would be unable to recover from.

Becky was the youngest of five. She was a late child, and all her elder siblings were boys. They had grown up in an overcrowded two-floor council flat in south east London on an estate with prostitutes and drug dealers on virtually every corner.

Becky's father had left when she was still a baby, and Becky's mother eventually had taken up with a window cleaner called Stan Benning who spent more time out of work than in it.

It had been a volatile relationship, and Becky grew up to the sound of constant arguments, usually about money, or the lack thereof.

Becky's eldest brother left home as soon as he was old enough to join the army, and the next two in line both moved away when they found partners, so she remembered very little about any of them. Her one guiding light had been her big brother Martin. Being the closest to her in age, Martin was the one who, more often than not, would babysit for her and was the only one of her brothers who ever seemed to have a smile and kind word for her.

As the others had all started to leave home, there was more room in the pokey flat, and eventually both Martin and Becky had had their own bedrooms.

As a child, Becky had often had nightmares, and she would

creep into Martin's room and crawl under the covers next to him until she fell back to sleep.

With their mother working three different jobs and Benning always either at the pub or the betting shop, Becky and Martin grew as close as any brother and sister could be.

Becky excelled at school in most subjects, due mainly to Martin's encouragement and assistance with complicated homework topics. He was always the first, and sometimes only, one that Becky would want to show her test results to, especially when she had earned a gold star for her efforts.

Regardless of the tumultuous relationship between her mother and Benning, along with the constant rows and slamming doors, Becky was as happy as any child could be, all thanks to Martin.

But Becky's life changed beyond all recognition the first time Benning sneaked into her bedroom during the night and raped her.

She had only been twelve the first time it happened, and because of Benning's threat to slit her throat as well as her mother's and Martin's if she said anything to anyone, Becky had kept her ordeal to herself.

After it happened, as she continued to do from then on after each assault, Becky had waited for her stepfather to go back to bed before she took herself off to her brother's room and snuggled next to him to fall back asleep.

Over time, Benning's visits grew more and more frequent, each accompanied by the same threat should Becky divulge their little 'secret.'

Martin soon began to suspect that there was something wrong, but even he never suspected the depraved depths their stepfather had sunken to. Therefore, he put his little sister's moods down to the fact that she was entering her teens and her body and perception of life were changing.

Then one day, Martin had dropped a bombshell on his little

sister. He announced that he had been accepted into university in Leeds, and he would be moving away.

Becky had been inconsolable.

She'd wept uncontrollably and pleaded and begged Martin not to leave her.

There had been tears in her brother's eyes, too, as he had explained to Becky that this was possibly his only opportunity to make something of himself, and even though he assured her that they could keep in touch via e-mail and mobile, Becky was too distraught to even contemplate life without her big brother being there for her.

Out of sheer desperation, Becky had finally told Martin the truth about what Benning had been doing to her. Her brother had turned red with rage and told Becky they had to go to the police immediately to report him. But as they were about to leave, Benning returned from the pub, drunk as usual and belligerent with it.

When Martin had confronted him with Becky's accusation, Benning had laughed in his face and tried to grab hold of Becky, who was cowering behind her brother at the top of the stairs. A struggle had ensued, and Benning had managed to throw Martin head-first down the stairs, where he had come to rest at the bottom with his neck broken.

Becky had rushed to her brother's side, but he was already dead by the time she reached him.

Realising what he had done, Benning had made a run for it, and Becky's mother had discovered her daughter cradling her dead brother's head in her lap when she returned from work several hours later.

Benning had pleaded self-defence for Martin's death and denied categorically ever touching Becky. Fortunately, the jury had not believed him on either count, and Benning had been sentenced to life in prison.

Becky's mother had had a nervous breakdown, which saw

her being sectioned for her own safety, and young Becky had been taken into care, where she'd stayed until leaving for St Anselm's.

Stella always took great strength from her friend's capacity to cope with whatever life threw at her, especially after such a tragic start.

Their move to Huntley and the dream of starting their own business had all come from Becky, and Stella was more than happy to be guided by her friend.

As Becky arrived back at the table with their drinks, she winked at Stella and indicated over her shoulder with a nod of her head. "I think we're about to be chatted up," she informed her friend, "are you up for the challenge?"

Stella immediately blushed and glanced past her friend. Sure enough, there were two men striding over towards them from the direction of the outer bar.

"Do we have to?" Stella whispered under her breath.

"Not if you're not in the mood," replied Becky reassuringly.

"Do you want to?"

Becky shook her head and took a sip of her wine. "Not fussed, leave them to me."

The two men took up their positions on either side of the girls. As there were no spare seats available, they both crouched down to bring them level with the two friends.

"Alright, ladies," started the one closest to Becky, "couldn't help noticing that you two were all alone, so my friend Pete and I thought you might like some company."

The one named Pete smiled broadly towards Stella.

"Thanks all the same, lads, but we're ok by ourselves, thanks." Becky spoke in a friendly manner but with an underlying accent of authority.

"Come on now," said Pete, "we're only trying to be friendly, what harm can it do?"

Becky turned on him. "Do you boys have a problem with

understanding the word no?" She kept her unblinking gaze fixed firmly on Pete.

After a moment's silence, Pete straightened, followed by his friend. "Your loss," he said, clearly embarrassed by the rejection.

As the two men walked away, the girls heard one of them say, "Fuckin' lesbians."

The two girls looked at each other and burst out laughing.

They clinked glasses and took another drink.

"Yours wasn't up to much," suggested Becky.

"Cheers," replied Stella, "but you know how I pick 'em?"

Becky placed her glass back on the table. "Don't I just," she said with a laugh. "Remember that bloke during our first year, you know, the one with the bad breath who really reckoned himself?"

"Oh, god, Mickey Edgell, crikey, I'd almost forgotten about him."

"How could you," insisted Becky. "I can still see him running down the street in my lime-green nightshirt."

The two girls suffered another fit of giggles as they remembered the incident.

Edgell had been the first boy at college to ask Stella out, and at first, she had thought that he was a very polite, well-mannered and considerate partner. But after a couple of months he had begun to pressure Stella into sleeping with him. At the time, Stella had been still a virgin, and although a part of her had wanted to lose it so that she would fit in more with the rest of the girls in their crowd, she had started to hear rumours about her boyfriend that caused her concern.

Campus gossip had seemed to indicate that Edgell was definitely a 'love 'em and leave 'em' kind of bloke, and Stella was not prepared to risk her virtue for the sake of someone like that. So she had decided to break up with him, but that was when her problems really started. Edgell could not take rejection, and he had started a campaign of spreading lies around that they had already slept together and that Stella was some kind of clingy, needy freak who insisted that Edgell become her life-long companion.

Even though those closest to Stella had known the truth, it soon had become obvious from whispers of overheard conversations in the student bar that some believed Edgell's version of events.

Then, Becky had had a plan.

One evening, dressed in her shortest skirt and tightest top, which accentuated her pert breasts, Becky had come onto Edgell in the student bar. She had always known that he fancied her by the way she sometimes caught him looking at her when he came over to pick up Stella.

She'd flirted with him, outrageously, until he finally fell into her trap and suggested that the two of them should go back to his rooms.

Claiming that Stella had gone home for a family emergency, Stella had persuaded Edgell that their rooms would be quieter and more discreet.

Once back at the girls' place, Becky stripped down to her bra and panties, encouraging Edgell to discard his clothing, until she had him down to his boxer shorts. Kissing and fondling him, Becky had managed to manoeuvre Edgell back onto her bed, while she carefully removed his last item of underwear.

Becky could see that he was already fully excited, so she had reached into a drawer in her bedside cabinet and removed a foil packet, from which she removed a condom.

Edgell had been too lost in the moment to notice that the foil container was already open when Becky removed its contents, and he lay back with his hands behind his head as she expertly slid it down over his rigid member.

As Becky had set about removing her own underclothes, Edgell had started twitching and shuffling around on the bed.

Then he had begun complaining that the condom did not feel right and that it was causing him to itch.

Becky had assured him that it was because she had chosen a ribbed variety to afford herself more pleasure and that he just needed to lie back and enjoy the ride.

As Becky had begun to straddle him, Edgell finally began to relax.

Just then, the wardrobe door had flown open, and Stella had stepped out, dressed in a flowing white nightgown with her hair all matted and straggly and a vacant stare on her face as if she were looking through the pair on the bed, rather than at them.

She'd had one hand behind her back as she approached the bed, and as she drew closer, she'd brought it around to the front, revealing a long carving knife clutched in her shaking hand.

Becky had immediately begun to make excuses for her predicament, pleading with her friend to forgive her. But before she'd had a chance to placate her friend, Stella plunged the knife into her belly.

Becky had gasped and clutched the spot where the knife had gone in. She'd toppled off the fear-stricken Edgell and slid off the bed onto the floor.

As Stella had switched her attention to her ex-boyfriend, Edgell, now free of the weight of Becky on top of him, had scrambled backwards, pummelling his legs against the mattress as if he was riding a bike. Once his head had reached the headboard, he'd pushed himself up until he was almost in a standing position, holding one hand out in front of him as if to keep Stella at bay, while stuttering through his tears about Becky having forced him into bed against his will.

Stella had kept her blank stare focussed on him as she lifted the carving knife above her head. "I thought you loved me," she'd said, almost mechanically, "and now you've broken my heart, so I must take yours!" With that, she had lunged forward towards the stricken Edgell, bringing the knife down in an arc, just missing his side by inches.

Edgell had screamed and thrown himself off the bed, narrowly avoiding the fallen Becky, who was writhing and moaning on the floor, still clutching her belly.

As Stella had retrieved her knife and raised it once more, Edgell had made a dash for the bedroom door. He had not bothered to stop to collect any of his clothes but instead grabbed what he believed was a tee-shirt draped over a chair on his way out.

Stella had let out a wail as she'd stumbled after him, but Edgell had managed to make it through the door and out into the communal corridor before Stella could catch him.

Once the door had slammed shut behind him, Stella had helped Becky off the floor, and they'd both rushed to the window to wait for Edgell to emerge from the main entrance.

Becky had slipped a large tee-shirt over her head to cover her modesty.

After a moment, they'd heard the main door being flung open, and seconds later Edgell had come into sight wearing the lime-green shirt he had grabbed from Becky's room.

The two girls had both been in fits as they watched the half-naked man running down the path, passing several bemused students on his way.

Once Edgell had moved out of sight, Stella had wrenched the wig from her head. "I'm glad to be rid of that thing," she'd announced to her friend, "it itched like crazy."

Becky had winked at her. "Not half as much as Johnno will be itching tonight."

Stella had looked at her friend, a puzzled expression on her face. "How do you mean?"

Becky had grinned. "Before I went out tonight, I filled that condom I put on him with itching powder; he'll be up half the night scrubbing it all out."

Chapter 9

The two had girls laughed together until their sides hurt.

Now that the story had resurfaced in the pub, their laughter came again, this time witnessed by curious drinkers.

Once their laughter had subsided, Becky lifted her glass. "Besties forever," she announced.

Stella raised her own glass, and they clinked.

Chapter Ten

Jenna's bath really helped to relax her, and her walk around the town had given her quite an appetite. She initially considered ordering a sandwich in her room but at the last minute decided that she would prefer something hot.

Just as she was about to leave the room, her mobile rang. Janna grabbed the phone and looked at the screen, hopeful that it might be D.C. Young. She was also afraid that it would be Roger calling to find out when she would be coming back to London.

The last thing she wanted right now was to get into an argument about what she was doing. For one thing, Roger would keep her on the phone for so long Jenna was afraid she would miss the last serving for dinner.

The previous evening, after she had spoken to the desk sergeant, Jenna had returned Roger's calls. She had not been in the mood to explain to him about her sudden plan to leave for Huntley the next morning but had known that if she did not call him back then he would keep trying all night until she answered.

Fortunately for her, she had only reached his answering

Chapter 10

machine. So she'd left him a quick message that she was going to bed and that she would call him later.

Now that she came to think about it, it was a little odd that he had not called her yet to find out why she still had not contacted him. Generally, if they were not in each other's company, Roger needed to know where she was and who she was with.

Jenna surmised that, for once, he must be otherwise engaged.

She saw from the screen that it was Trisha calling. She was disappointed that it was not Young, but no news was good news, and it least it was not her boyfriend.

"Hi, Trisha." Jenna slumped down on the bed to take the call.

"Hey, hon, how're you doing?"

It felt good to hear the comforting voice of her friend. Until this moment, it had not occurred to Jenna that she was so far away from home, and other than Young, she did not know anyone, and then she had only met him once, and that had been hardly a social visit.

"I'm fine," Jenna replied, not sure if she was trying to convince herself or her friend more. "I went to the local police station when I arrived and met with the detective in charge of my uncle's case."

"What was he like?" asked Trisha, showing genuine concern. "Did he seem as if he was taking it seriously, or do you think he just fobbed you off?"

"No, he seemed really genuine. He promised to keep me informed of any developments, and he promised to make some calls to all the hotels and guest houses where my uncle might have booked in to see if he'd been there. He even recommended the one I'm staying at."

"Is it nice?"

"Lovely, actually. It's more like an inn than a hotel, judging by the décor, but it really feels homey, and the proprietor was very welcoming when she found out that Detective Young had recommended the place to me."

"Well, that's something. I was afraid you might end up at some miserable guest house where you'd be stuck in a tiny room all day waiting for the phone to ring."

Jenna laughed. "Yea, me, too. But after booking in I took myself around the town, just on the off chance I might bump into my uncle."

"But no luck?" Trisha surmised.

"Nah, but it's only day one. So how are things back in London, has Roger returned from his trip yet?"

There was a slight pause on the other end.

"Trisha?" Jenna checked that they had not lost their signal.

Finally, Trisha responded. "Has he not called you yet?"

"No." Jenna detected a slight note of concern in her friend's voice, and she immediately felt that something was wrong. "Why, what's up?" Jenna suddenly had a thought. "Oh, Christ, he hasn't been in an accident or something?"

She immediately felt guilty that she did not want to speak to him earlier.

"No, nothing like that," Trisha assured her.

Jenna heaved a sigh of relief. She had enough on her plate for now with her uncle to worry about; the last thing she needed was a guilt trip over Roger.

"Listen." Trisha sounded apprehensive as if she were afraid to continue their conversation.

"Trisha, what's up, you're really starting to concern me now?"

Jenna heard her friend release a long breath on the line.

"Ok," she began, "I wasn't sure how to tell you, but I have to, nonetheless. Do you know that new temp we've got in accounts, the one with the bright pink hair who wears the skirts that are almost short enough to be classed as a belt?"

Chapter 10

Jenna was puzzled. "You mean the one with the squeaky voice who sounds like a cartoon mouse when she speaks?"

"That's her," Trisha confirmed. "Well, today I was in the toilet and she came in with one of the other girls, and I heard her say that she and Roger spent the night together."

"What!" Jenna had not been sure what her friend had to reveal, but she was certainly not expecting this. "Are you sure she was talking about my Roger?"

Jenna heard it as soon as the words left her lips.

My Roger!

Recently, all she could think of was how to dump him, and now, suddenly, he belonged to her.

"Oh, yes," Trisha assured her, "it was your man, alright. She was boasting about how they snuck out to a hotel behind your back and how he wanted them to make it a regular thing."

"I can't believe it! He was supposed to be on a business trip! His mother arranged it!"

"Sounds like she must have been in on it, too. Either that, or her son just lied to her and made out he was going."

Jenna could feel the anger rising within her.

Roger was a lot of things, most of them bad, but she had never considered him the type to two-time her behind her back.

"Did you see him at work today?" Jenna asked, still trying to make some sense of what her friend was telling her.

"No, according to the slut, he was too worn out to come in, so she left him at the hotel."

"I don't believe this!" Jenna said incredulously. "That fucking little weasel didn't even have the balls to break up with me first, and do you remember how he reacted that time when I tried to break up with him?"

Trisha had never heard her friend swear before.

It almost sounded funny coming from her mouth.

"Oh, yes, I remember," Trisha confirmed. "I know that it might not be much of a consolation, but at least now you have a perfect excuse to dump him without feeling guilty, so, silver linings and all that."

"You're right," Jenna agreed, "and what's more, if the little shit threatens suicide or any other crap like that, I'm going to call his bluff, and to hell with the consequences."

"Good for you." Trisha sounded relieved. "To be honest, I was a little unsure about whether to tell you or not, I figured you had enough on your plate what with your uncle and all. But then, I decided if our roles were reversed, I would definitely want you to tell me, so here we are."

"You're a true friend, Trisha, and I owe you for this," Jenna reassured her. "When I think of how much time and energy I've wasted on that creep, arrgghh, it makes my blood boil."

Trisha laughed. "Sounds like you need a drink."

"You're not wrong there," Jenna agreed, "in fact, as soon as we're finished, I'm going straight down to the bar to celebrate."

"That-a-girl."

The restaurant stopped serving food at nine, and by the time Jenna made it downstairs it was almost a quarter past.

Jenna felt her tummy rumbling as she watched the dining patrons polishing off their meals. She considered asking the waiter if there was any chance of still ordering, but she decided against it. She had worked in a restaurant for one summer when she was at university, and she still had not forgotten how tired she was at the end of a shift.

She was sure that the staff would not appreciate having to stay back to cook and serve another meal when they were probably counting down the minutes until they could go home.

Jenna opted for a packet of cheese-flavoured crackers and a bag of crisps at the bar instead.

She ordered herself a large vodka and tonic.

Chapter 10

The barman raised his eyes when she tossed it back in one hit within seconds of him placing it in front of her.

"Tough day?" he asked.

Jenna held her hand in front of her mouth, afraid for a moment that she might belch from the sudden reflux caused by the liquor going down too fast.

Once she was sure she had it under control, she smiled back at him.

"That could be the understatement of the week," she replied. "Same again, please."

This time Jenna carried her drink and her snacks over to a booth near a window.

As she laid them down on the table, her mobile rang. Checking the screen, she saw that it was Roger. Her first vodka was already starting to take effect, and Jenna was just about in the mood to give him a piece of her mind.

But remembering where she was and the fact that she was in earshot of several people, Jenna cancelled the call instead.

She switched her phone over to silent mode and smiled to herself as she slipped it back into her handbag. The mere fact that she was not going to answer him would be enough to send Roger into overdrive.

For now, that thought was enough to keep Jenna satisfied until she was ready to let him have it properly.

Jenna ate her snacks and sipped her drink while she glanced around the bar at her fellow drinkers.

Most of them appeared to be couples enjoying their evening. There were a few single men dotted around the place, mostly middle-aged, wearing suits, which she presumed made them businessmen relaxing after a hard day of doing whatever it was they did to make their money.

She noticed a few of them glancing in her direction, so Jenna made a point of not making eye contact. The last thing she needed right now was having to fend off unwanted advances.

To her dismay, she noticed one of the men shaking his empty glass in her direction as if to catch her eye. It was obvious to Jenna that he was offering to buy her another drink, and she was afraid to ignore him in case he came over to try in person, so she smiled and shook her head firmly.

The man, obviously not the type to give up so easily, slid his chair back and straightened his tie before striding towards Jenna's table.

She could really do without this right now.

Jenna did not wish to be impolite, but she hoped that the man would take a definite 'no' for an answer and leave her alone.

Just then, as if in answer to a silent prayer, Jenna saw Young enter the bar from the foyer. He obviously had not seen her and was striding towards the other side of the bar when Jenna called out to him and waved him over.

The man who had offered her a drink was already halfway across the room when Jenna called out to her saviour. Realising the situation, he changed direction and made his way over to the bar.

Jenna wondered if the gratitude she was feeling by Young saving her was revealed in her expression as she greeted him.

"So, you took my advice, then?" Young asked as he reached Jenna's table.

Jenna smiled. "How could I not, the landlady was so impressed when I mentioned your name, she gave me the best room in the place."

"With a view of the woods?"

Jenna nodded and drained the last of her drink.

"Here, please let me get you another." Young held out his hand for her empty glass.

Jenna had not considered having more than two, especially on a virtually empty stomach, but still she found herself accepting Young's offer.

"Vodka and tonic, please." Jenna smiled. "But just a small one."

She decided she would make this one last until she was ready for bed.

After a few moments, Young returned with her vodka, which looked suspiciously like a large measure to Jenna. "Are you trying to get me tipsy," she said through furrowed brows, pretending to be angry. "I said a small."

Young blushed immediately. "Yes, so did I, but I think the barman was on automatic."

Young placed his pint in front of a seat opposite Jenna.

They clinked, and Young took a long swig, downing almost half the glass in one go.

"You obviously needed that," Jenna observed, taking the merest sip of her drink.

Young nodded. "It's been quite a day."

"Your desk certainly appeared to be overflowing with files when I came in; are you just desperately understaffed, or is the crime rate in Huntley that bad?"

Young smiled. "Not exactly, it's a bit of a long story."

"I'm all ears." Jenna relaxed back into her seat, as if to demonstrate she was eager to hear his tale.

"Well," he began, "I think I might have mentioned that I came down from London, and somehow due to a mix-up in communication, the Huntley squad were not expecting me. Well, for a start, it appears they do not like Londoners, added to which, I am on a graduate scheme, and this is my first promotion, whereas all the other officers in Huntley worked their way up through the ranks, so they feel as if I haven't earned my stripes as yet."

"You look a little old to be on a graduate scheme!" The words left Jenna's mouth before she could stop herself.

The two double vodkas were starting to do their work.

She slapped her hand across her mouth. "I am so sorry," she

mumbled through her fingers. "That came out far ruder than I intended."

Young shrugged and took another gulp of his ale. "That's ok," he assured her, "and what's more, you're right. I joined the force in my mid-twenties after going from one uninspiring job to another. I didn't even mention my degree when I joined, but it somehow came up in conversation one day when I was with one of the fast-stream inspectors, and he virtually had a word in the right ear without even letting on to me until it was all done and dusted."

Jenna nodded. "You could have said no, though."

"Yes, but to be honest, I was becoming a little tired of working shifts, patrolling some of the dodgier parts of town in the pouring rain, so when the opportunity arose, I think I just grabbed at it for a change."

"And then they sent you here?"

Young raised his eyebrows. "Did they ever!"

"Is it really that bad? You could always transfer."

Young pulled a face. "True, but to be honest I refuse to be cowed down by bullies." He held a hand up. "I'm making it sound worse than it is. I can handle a bit of stick, and besides, I've only been here five minutes, so I don't think it will look good if I put in for a transfer so soon."

"So, you decided to tough it out?" Jenna took a swallow, allowing one of the ice cubes in her glass to slide into her mouth. She crunched down on it, feeling the cooling liquid slip down her throat.

"Yep," answered Young. "You saw the office they generously gave me. They've put me in charge of unsolved crimes going back over the last year."

"So how did you end up with my uncle's case, he's only been missing a short while?"

"To be honest, I think one of the other officers assigned it to me because they couldn't be bothered to take it on. Missing

Chapter 10

persons, unless it's a child, tend to be passed over by those with ambition in the force. They are not always given the attention they should."

Young immediately regretted his words. He could see the expression of concern on Jenna's face, and he realised he should have been more diplomatic.

"I'm sorry," he said, "I didn't mean to sound so insincere. Sometimes being in this job can make you a little too matter of fact when you speak. It's something they warn you to look out for during training."

"That's ok." Jenna tried to sound convincing as she glanced down at the remaining ice cubes floating in her glass. "I suppose it's not likely to be the case of the century. It's just that it is so unlike him to stay away for so long and not keep in touch."

Young slipped his hand over Jenna's arm.

She met his gaze.

"Believe me," he said, "I promise I will give your uncle's disappearance my full attention."

He sounded reassuring, and Jenna was comforted by the earnestness in his tone.

She smiled back at him.

Just then, her mobile began to vibrate in her bag.

Jenna ignored it.

"Shouldn't you get that?" Young asked, pointing at her handbag.

Jenna sighed. "No, I can guess who it's from, and I'm not in the mood right now."

"But it might be from your uncle."

Jenna knew that was too much to hope for, but she could see Young's point, so she hastily unzipped her bag and grabbed her phone.

It was Roger again.

Jenna cancelled the call and replaced her mobile back in her bag.

When she looked up, she saw a very elegantly dressed woman sauntering towards their table. It was quite obvious the woman was making directly for them.

Young immediately picked up on Jenna's stare.

He turned around just as the woman reached their table.

"Hello, Alan, fancy seeing you here!"

The woman spoke as sophisticatedly as she was dressed.

Young jumped out of his chair, bumping his thigh against the edge of the table and almost knocking over both their glasses.

At first glance, Jenna estimated that the woman was in her late thirties. She was dressed in a long, flowing evening gown, the type worn by woman who are attending some sort of big opening or gala event.

He hair was a deep red colour, which Jenna suspected was highlighted to cover any greys from peeking out. It was swirled around on top of the woman's head with a few loose strands strategically placed to hang down by the side of her face.

Jenna had to admit to herself, the woman was stunning.

Young was clearly embarrassed by the woman's sudden appearance in the bar.

"Oh, hello, June, how are you?" Jenna could hear the nervousness in Young's voice.

"So-so, you know how it is," replied the woman, keeping her gaze fixed firmly on Young's face. "Aren't you going to introduce me?"

"Yes, of course." Young tried desperately to keep his voice under control. Jenna could not help but wonder what sort of hold this woman had over him, and she hoped that he would explain all once they were alone again.

Young turned to Jenna. "Jenna Wilkinson, this is June Le Vant,"

The woman cast a momentary glance towards Jenna, turning back to face Young before either of them had a chance to acknowledge the other.

There followed a moment's awkward silence, which Jenna felt unable to break, under the circumstances.

Eventually, Young took the lead. "Were you and your husband dining here tonight, or are you just stopping in on your way back from somewhere more elegant?"

June threw back her head and laughed. "Oh, Alan," she almost drooled, "always the joker, you know I never come here with him." She leaned in towards Young as if to whisper in his ear without Jenna overhearing. But when she spoke, her voice was still loud enough for them both to hear. "Too many loose tongues around here, darling."

Young, realising the closeness of proximity between the two of them, suddenly pulled back. The gesture was not bold enough to make it obvious to anyone else in the bar who might be watching. But June certainly received the message loud and clear.

Turning on her heel, June walked away from their table. "Have fun, kids," she called back over her shoulder as she left.

Young waited until she had left the bar area before he slumped down in his chair.

His cheeks were stained red, and Jenna could see from his expression that he was not happy about the other woman's intervention.

He grabbed up his glass and drained the last of its contents in one go.

"Join me for another?" he asked, holding up his empty glass.

Jenna knew that she dared not.

But something inside her was curious to know the story of June Le Vant.

Jenna opened her handbag to find her purse. "My round," she said.

"No, please, I'm still in the chair," replied Young. Before Jenna had a chance to object, he was already on his way back to the bar.

While Young was buying their drinks, Jenna's mobile vibrated. She took it out and checked, but it was only another call from Roger.

Evidently, his little temp was not keeping him amused.

Jenna cancelled the call and replaced her mobile.

When Young returned with their drinks, Jenna did not have to press him for information. For some reason, he seemed willing to unload without needing persuasion.

He sat down and placed Jenna's glass in front of her.

"When I first came to Huntley," he began, without prompting, "I had just come out of a long relationship, I won't bore you with the details. So, I was sitting here one night, having a nightcap when this rather elegant-looking lady came and sat beside me and offered to buy me a drink." He looked over his shoulder to ensure that June had indeed left. "As you might have guessed," he continued, turning back to face Jenna, "the lady in question was June. We really hit it off, one thing led to another, and she joined me for the night in my room. It was all a bit fast, but I was at a low ebb and hadn't been here long enough to know anyone, so it seemed a good idea at the time."

Young paused for a moment, taking a sip of his fresh pint.

"But something went wrong?" Jenna interjected, not wanting to sound inpatient but still allowing her curiosity to get the better of her.

Young shrugged. "She told me the next day that not only was she married, but dating younger men was a hobby of hers, one which apparently her husband approves of. I told her straight away that such an arrangement was not for me, and after a few choice words, she finally left."

Jenna leaned forward. "Has she been stalking you ever since?"

Young laughed, in spite of himself. "No, no, nothing like that, she just kind of 'turns up' every now and then, usually when I've popped in here for a nightcap."

Jenna was not convinced.

However, she could not be sure if it was the alcohol making her suspicious.

"Do you think that she follows you from the station?" she whispered.

Young shook his head. "I doubt it," he hypothesised, "I don't think she's wired that way. But she did tell me that she often comes here for her little trysts, so it could be nothing more than coincidence."

After they both finished their drinks, Young left, promising Jenna that he would be in touch with her the following day, regardless of whether he had any news concerning her uncle.

Jenna was glad.

There was something about Young that made her feel safe in his company. She wondered if it was just the fact that he was a police officer or if it went deeper.

She hoped it was not just the alcohol making her feel that way.

Before she turned in, her mobile shook into life once more.

Yet again, it was Roger.

Jenna considered answering this time. She was certainly in the mood for a good argument, and this might be the best opportunity to dump him once and for all.

But she decided such an argument could wait until she was sober enough to really enjoy telling him where to go.

So she switched off her phone and went to bed.

Chapter Eleven

KEVIN TOSSED AND TURNED ON HIS BED, UNABLE TO make himself comfortable enough to get back to sleep.

He had had the weirdest of days, and he still had no idea why.

All morning in the shop Kevin, had served his customers as usual, in his monosyllabic manner, paying little regard to their questions and enquiries, offering the bare minimum of courtesy in return for their custom.

He ignored the remarks made by some who muttered under their breath about his rudeness and instead, once he had taken their money, returned to the magazine he had been reading.

By midday, Kevin was ravenous.

He closed the shop and strolled down the high street towards the fish and chip shop, where he usually purchased his midday meal.

But somehow today, something was different.

Kevin knew instinctively that from today, his usual fare would be nowhere near adequate enough to satisfy his craving.

Instead he walked past the chip shop and on down the high street until he reached the butcher's.

Chapter 11

The second he stepped inside the door, Kevin's senses were filled with the succulent aroma of raw meat.

He could almost feel himself salivating at the thought.

He bought a huge bag of braising steak, which was on special offer, and carried it back to his shop. As he walked back up the street, it took all his control to resist the temptation to rip open the bag he was carrying and devour the raw meat in full view of all those out shopping.

Instead, he quickened his pace until he was once more safely within his own premises.

With his back to the main door, Kevin opened his bag and began to grab huge handfuls of raw steak, shoving them into his mouth as if his life depended on it.

He was not concerned by the blood dripping onto his shirt while he ate. All that mattered was to kill off this all-consuming hunger that had been building since morning.

Once his feast was over, Kevin turned the plastic carrier bag inside out so that he could lick any remaining morsels of meat or blood left behind in the creases of the bag.

Once he was satisfied there was no more left, Kevin lurched over to the shop counter and lay on the floor behind it to take a nap.

When he woke later that afternoon, Kevin felt completely refreshed and ready to take on the world. He walked into the back room, which housed — amongst other things — a toilet and sink, and he stuck his mouth under the cold tap and stayed there until his thirst was finally quenched.

Kevin spent the rest of the day in the shop as usual, but he found himself being far more engaging with his customers than was his norm.

He felt alive.

Possibly for the first time in his life.

By the end of the day, Kevin was exhausted, and having locked up the shop he took himself upstairs to his bed.

He fell asleep almost immediately and dozed fitfully, dreaming about hunting wild animals and ripping the flesh from their bodies with his bare teeth when he caught them.

During one such dream, Kevin found himself walking through what appeared to be an abandoned graveyard, surrounded by moss-covered tombstones and overgrown foliage. In the moonlight Kevin could see carrion spread around the floor in different stages of dilapidation.

Some appeared to be so fresh that blood still flowed from the rips and tears made to their torsos, while others were no more than skeletons covered by a thin veneer of skin.

Kevin felt no fear as he strolled amongst the cadavers.

In fact, he felt as if he belonged.

Further on, he came across a young lamb tethered to a tree.

The poor creature cried out in terror as Kevin approached it, as it tried in desperation to free itself from the rope that bound it.

As Kevin came up to the tiny lamb, he reached down to grab it. But to his horror, the hand which he saw in front of him was not his own but one covered in coarse, rough hair, with long, talon-like fingers encrusted with dirt and blood.

He pulled back his hand to inspect it more closely, and to his horror he realised that it resembled some kind of animal's forepaw, rather than a human hand.

Kevin sat up in bed, bathed in sweat.

"Are you going to just lie there all evening, or are you going to go out and get me chips; me fry-up's almost ready!"

His mother stood in his open doorway, dressed, as was her usual state if she did not plan on going out, in her towelling dressing gown and floral house slippers, her hands planted firmly on her hips.

For a split-second Kevin felt a rush of heat flood his head.

His vision seemed to blur as a red mist covered his eyes as he focussed on her slippers.

He remembered as a child how on countless occasions, and usually for no proper reason, he had felt the sting of his mother's slipper against his naked backside, over and over again as he squealed in pain.

The sudden memory of all those undeserved beatings gave Kevin the urge to leap forward and rip his mother's throat out.

But after several deep breaths, the feeling passed.

"Well?" his mother demanded. "Are you goin' for me chips or what?"

Kevin flung himself off his bed and stood up to leave. It appeared that he had lain down without first removing his boots, so he checked his pocket for change and strode towards his mother, who was still blocking the doorway.

Before she had a chance to move out of his way, Kevin barged past, treading on her foot with all his weight as he turned on the landing.

"Ow, yer stupid bugger, that's me bad corn!"

Kevin looked back to see his mother hopping on one foot, her ungainly frame jiggling and bouncing as she attempted to grab her injured foot with her hands.

For a moment, Kevin believed that she was about to lose her balance and tip over the bannister, which would send her crashing to the hallway below.

He found himself holding his breath in anticipation.

But at the last second his mother righted herself and caught the top of the post for support.

Kevin was disappointed, but he could not help but smile. "Sorry, didn't see yer there."

Having brought back his mother's chips, Kevin went into the bathroom to take a shower. As he soaped himself under the warm spray, he felt as if his body had been covered with an invisible layer of skin, which made him feel as if he was not actually touching his own body.

As he rubbed himself down, Kevin was also bemused by the

extra muscles that seemed to bulge through his skin whenever he moved or flexed them.

After his shower, Kevin stared at himself in the bathroom mirror, thrilled by his new physique and, especially, his clear complexion.

He felt too wired for bed, so he decided he would go out and maybe grab a pint somewhere. He considered calling some of his mates but then decided that he preferred to be alone.

As he was about to leave, his mother called to him from the sitting room.

"Oy, where are you off to all of a sudden?"

Kevin stayed where he was on the landing outside his room.

The red mist was starting to descend once more, and Kevin clenched his fists and tried to calm himself before he did something he might later come to regret.

"Well, come in 'ere when I'm talkin' to yer, yer rude sod!"

Kevin strode purposefully towards the sitting room.

His mother was lying back on the sofa, the remnants of her late-night feast still evident on the table before her. In the background the television was blaring some reality show about young people who lived in London. Kevin had watched it a couple of times with his mother, but he had soon become bored with the concept.

"So where are yer off to?" his mother demanded. "It's gettin' late, an' yer still need to open the shop tomorrow."

Kevin bit his tongue. "I'm just going out. I won't be long."

"Yer ain't 'ad any tea," she observed. "There's still some chips left if yer want 'em."

"No thanks, I'm not hungry." Kevin began to turn to leave when his mother broke into another of her constant rants.

"I don' know what's wrong with you these days, 'alf the time yer walk about like yer in some bloody daze, yer never tell me nothin', come an' go as yer please, this ain't a bloody 'otel, yer know!"

Chapter 11

Kevin could feel his nostrils flaring, the rage inside him building slowly.

He tried to concentrate on the new odours his increased sense of smell now perceived.

Besides the disgusting remains of his mother's meal, he was able to home in on the unmistakable aroma of her cheap perfume and underneath that the natural smell of her body odour, which forced itself through her usual sanitary line of defence.

But the strongest and most pungent odour by far was the sweet-sticky smell of her sex. It assailed his nostrils, almost as if he had his face shoved between her legs.

The mere thought disgusted him.

After all, she was his mother!

But for some reason, that no longer mattered. Kevin's initial feelings of revulsion quickly subsided, and he actually felt himself growing aroused by her scent.

His mother was still complaining about his lack of responsibility towards her, but Kevin could barely hear a word.

In his mind, he leapt forward and without a word lifted his mother across the sofa and lifted her nightie, forcing himself inside her while ignoring her screams of pain and anguish.

Kevin wiped the back of his hand across his mouth.

A wet trail of saliva spread across his hand.

His breathing was now coming in short, sharp bursts, his chest and shoulders lifting with the effort.

Before he turned to attack his mother, Kevin ran out of the room and down the stairs.

Once he was out in the street, he bent over and took in several deep lungsful of the night air.

He felt repulsed at the thought of what he had just stopped himself from doing, and yet, at the same time he could not deny the massive erection which was pushing against the denim of his jeans.

He began to walk.

He needed to think.

What he really needed to know was what was happening to him.

Kevin walked on through the town, ignoring the curious looks he received from passers-by. He kept his head down and tried to walk with purpose, but the truth was his entire body was starting to ache, and his joints were growing stiffer and more tender by the second.

Eventually, he reached the woods on the outskirts of town.

By now his head was throbbing, and every movement ached.

Kevin found a deserted patch surrounded by a clump of trees, and he slumped down on the grass to relax.

Within seconds, Kevin had fallen asleep.

In his dream, Kevin saw an apparition drifting slowly towards him until it finally materialised into the form of a naked woman.

It was Katerina.

Upon recognising her, the events of the previous night all came flooding back to him.

Katerina appeared to drift around him, never actually making physical contact, although Kevin could feel his body tingling as if she were stroking him with her long fingernails.

Kevin tried to move, to reach out and touch her gorgeous body, but in his dream, he discovered he could neither move nor speak.

As she drew closer, Katerina's once beautiful eyes took on the form of red pools of swirling fire that seemed to draw him ever closer to them, as if he were being sucked into the gaping maw of a volcano.

Finally, Katerina spoke to him. But not with words; her mouth did not even move.

Even so, Kevin could hear her words quite clearly and distinctly.

Chapter 11

Katerina explained that they were now a part of each other, mind, body and soul, and that he existed merely to carry out her bidding. Kevin understood and agreed with her, and although his mouth could not form the words, she still seemed to understand his willing compliance.

As a reward, Katerina floated over him, and although his body was without feeling, he could sense her impaling herself on him and riding him until he orgasmed.

Kevin sat up abruptly.

He was alone in the woods, and his entire body was bathed in perspiration.

He sat there for a moment, breathing deeply. The remnants of his dream and his copulation with Katerina were still vivid in his mind.

The sky was dark, and the moon was on the rise.

The wind picked up and whistled through the trees surrounding him, but Kevin did not feel its chill. If anything, he appeared to be growing warmer from the inside.

He forced himself up and stood there for a moment in the shadowy gloom.

His whole body felt strange, alien almost.

The heat inside him felt as if it was spreading throughout his torso and on through his limbs, raging like a blacksmith's brazier.

As the temperature grew unbearably hot, Kevin could no longer help himself. He fell to his knees and began tearing off his clothes, as if by doing so he would somehow manage to release the furnace within, allowing it to dissipate into the night air.

But once he was completely naked, he realised to his horror that there was no escaping his torment.

Kevin rolled around on the ground, back and forth, slapping his hands against his body like a man whose clothes were alight.

He started to cry out in frustration.

But the noise that emanated from his mouth was not one he recognised.

Chapter Twelve

STELLA HELD OPEN THE PUB DOOR FOR HER FRIEND while Becky fumbled with her jacket buttons.

"Thank you, slave," Becky joked as she passed through the open doorway.

Stella swung her foot and gave her friend a sharp kick to her behind as she walked past her.

"Ow," Becky yelped, rubbing her cheek where she had just been hit. She staggered out onto the tarmac parking area, swinging her arms around in a caricature of someone about to collapse from the force of an unexpected blow.

Stella laughed at her friend's antics. "Serves you right, Graham, you old cow."

She slammed her hand across her mouth as she noticed two middle-aged men approaching from her left. They were close enough to have heard her insult to her friend, and from their facial expressions, they were enjoying the show.

Stella could feel her cheeks reddening.

She looked away when one of the men winked at her, then she unconsciously turned back to face them, just in time to see the other one blow her a kiss.

Her face now completely beetroot, Stella turned and moved quickly to her friend's side.

"Did you see that?" Stella asked, still in shock.

"See what?" Becky shrugged. "They were just being friendly."

"Friendly! Dirty old men!"

Becky laid her hand on Stella's shoulder. "I do believe you're growing fussy in your old age, Braithwaite."

"Yuck!" Stella squirmed.

"Should we go back inside?" Becky enquired, trying desperately to keep a straight face. "Who knows, it might be our lucky night."

Stella turned to her friend, staring at her in astonishment. "Are you serious?" she demanded.

Becky could not keep a straight face anymore and let slip her mask.

Stella playfully moved forward to slap her friend again but this time gave her ample time to move out of the way.

"You're incorrigible," Stella chided her.

"Hey, no calling me names I can't spell."

The two friends linked arms and made their way out of the pub car park and on towards the centre of town to catch their bus.

The night air felt cold against Becky's legs, and she began to regret not opting for tights like her friend instead of just a skirt. As they turned the corner at the end of the road, a fierce wind whipped down for the woodland at the other end of town, making both girls shiver and huddle closer together.

As they walked down the high street, the night wind penetrated both their defences. Neither of them had anticipated such cold conditions as it had been a particularly warm day, and now that they were out in the open, the high street offered them no barrier against the chill.

Chapter 12

Both girls zipped, tucked and buttoned everything they could before tucking their hands under their armpits as a last resort.

"I thought alcohol was supposed to keep out the cold," Stella remarked.

"Perhaps we didn't have enough," reasoned Becky, "fancy going back for a night-cap?"

"Please tell me that's just a bad joke?" said Stella, trying to stop her teeth from chattering as she spoke.

Becky shrugged. "It was just a thought."

There was no one else waiting at their bus stop, so the two girls took a seat on the plastic bench and tried to shelter from the wind behind the glass panel.

They waited for what seemed like ages, talking absently to try and take their minds off the cold.

The electronic information board was out of action, so Stella checked her phone, having downloaded the application for local transport when they first arrived in Huntley.

"Oh, you are not going to believe this!" she cried.

"What?" asked Becky, rubbing her bare legs in an effort to bring back her circulation.

"According to this," continued Stella, "our bus has been involved in an accident, and the next one is over half an hour away!"

"You have got to be kidding, seriously!" Becky did not try to disguise the irritation in her voice. "Well, there's no point just sitting here and freezing, shall we call for a cab?"

"Good idea," Stella agreed, swiping through her call list for the local mini cab company.

Becky listened in while Stella was speaking to the dispatcher, and she was not encouraged by her friend's half of the conversation.

"What did they say?" Becky asked as Stella disconnected the call.

"Forty-five minutes," Stella answered dejectedly. "Half their drivers are off sick."

"Oh, man!"

"The woman told me they had been passing some of their fares over to the only other cab company in this 'one-horse' town, but they are a lot smaller than this one, and apparently they have told them they cannot deal with any more calls for at least another hour."

"Terrific, this just gets better by the second."

"We could always go and wait in the cab office," suggested Stella, "at least it would be warm."

Becky considered her friend's proposal for a second. "But it's way over the other end of the high street; we could be halfway home by then if we walked it."

Stella sighed. She knew Becky was right. They had walked into town before, and the journey had taken them less than half an hour.

But then, the conditions had been more conducive to a gentle stroll than they were tonight.

Becky hopped off the bench and began stamping her feet to try and re-start her circulation. "Come on," she said, "it looks like it's either walk or freeze."

Stella moaned softly.

Becky went over to her and held out her hand. When Stella took it, Becky helped her friend to stand. "Come on, the longest journey starts with a single step and all that," she offered encouragingly.

Reluctantly, the two girls began their task.

The cold wind seemed intent on fighting them every inch of the way.

As they reached the edge of town, Becky suddenly had an idea.

She stopped in her tracks.

"What's the matter?" asked Stella, looking around her for a reason for her friend's sudden change of heart.

"You know," Becky speculated, "if we carry on this way, it's going to take us, what, twenty to twenty-five minutes."

"So?" Stella remained perplexed.

"But if we cut through the woods, once we're over the main hump it's less than ten minutes down the other side, and we're home and dry."

"Are you nuts, woman?" Stella could not initially be sure if this was just her friend's sense of humour or if she genuinely thought it was a good idea. "We can't go tromping through the woods in the middle of the night, there aren't even any lights to guide us!"

Stella was adamant this idea was not going to be given the chance to take flight.

Becky turned to her. "Look, we're talking about cutting our journey time in half, surely that's worthy of some consideration, under the circumstances?"

Stella could still not believe what she was hearing. "And what should we do if we end up being attacked by some maniac wielding a huge knife?"

Becky spread her legs and held out her fists. "You seem to forget I am a black belt in karate, hi-ah." With that, she began to imitate someone performing martial arts, although it was obvious to anyone looking on that there was no power behind her moves.

"You took two lessons on campus because they were free," Stella interjected, trying not to laugh at her friend's behaviour. "You couldn't karate your way out of a wet paper bag, and we both know it."

Becky gave up on her demonstration. "Come on, Stella," she implored, "this isn't London. There aren't murderers lurking behind every corner. This is the sticks — people still leave their doors open. It'll be perfectly safe."

Stella bit her bottom lip. She knew that there was sense in what her friend was saying, but it did not allay her fears altogether. The countryside had its fair share of lunatics, too.

She turned and looked out over the entrance to the woods.

The path that led from the street, which they would have to use if they decided to go along with Becky's plan, disappeared into darkness a couple of hundred yards in. From here, it seemed to Stella that a mist was starting to descend over the trees in the distance, which would make the journey even less inviting.

She turned back to her friend.

"Please?" Becky was using her best pleading voice. "I'm freezing."

"Me, too," countered Stella.

"Pretty please, with jam and sprinkles?"

Stella let out a massive sigh. She surmised that she should have known better than to try and win an argument once Becky had made up her mind.

"Dammit, Graham, you'll get us killed one of these days."

Becky let out a triumphant whoop. She knew that she had won.

She linked arms with her friend, and together they set off into the woods.

Kevin peered out from under his makeshift shelter behind a line of bushes.

He watched as the two women began to enter the woods.

He lifted his head and sniffed the air, drinking in the unmistakable aroma of the women.

Licking his lips with his elongated tongue, Kevin felt the sharp edges of his razor-like fangs. He had been deemed worthy by his wolf-mistress to make his first kill, and he could feel the anticipation welling up inside him as his taste for human flesh increased.

By the time the two women had crossed the flat ground that led to the trees and the steep incline, Stella was beginning to wish that she had stayed firm and insisted that they stick to the high street.

True, it was less windy with the trees and bushes acting as natural barriers, but there was something spooky about these woods after dark. The mist had grown measurably thicker since they entered the wooded area, and now it resembled fog more than just evening mist.

They climbed the hill in silence, save for the sound of their laboured breath.

As they reached the summit, the way before them appeared longer than Stella had remembered from their last visit.

"Isn't this fun?"

Stella was immediately taken aback by her friend's words. But, as she opened her mouth to answer, she saw in the dim light that Becky was grinning, and Stella knew immediately that her friend was only joking to try and lighten the mood.

Stella wondered if she, too, was starting to believe they had made a mistake.

Even so, Stella felt her friend's observation demanded a reply.

"The trouble with you, Graham, is that…ow!"

Stella stumbled, and before Becky could reach out and grab her, she had collapsed to the ground, holding her foot.

Becky crouched down beside her friend. "Are you alright?" she asked, and there was genuine concern in her voice.

Stella rolled around on her back. "Not really," she answered, not making any attempt to disguise her sarcastic tone.

"What happened?"

"I stood on something, it felt like a tennis ball, and I lost my balance."

"Do you think you can stand?"

"I can try. Give me your hand."

Becky braced herself against the woodland floor and grabbed hold of her friend's offered hand. She took the strain, and Stella pushed away from the floor using her uninjured leg for support.

Once she was standing, Becky asked, "How does it feel? It's not broken or anything, is it?"

Stella placed her weight on her wounded foot and tried to support herself on it.

"Ow, it really hurts," she informed Becky. "But I don't think it's broken."

Becky moved around Stella and placed her friend's arm across her shoulder. Placing her other arm around Stella's waist, she tried to alleviate some of the pressure on Stella's weakened joint.

"If I support you like this, will you be ok the rest of the way?"

"I hope so; if not, you're going to have to carry me."

Becky laughed. "Fat chance, Braithwaite, I'll just leave you here for the foxes."

They continued on their way, although their progress was now somewhat slower.

"This is all your fault, you know," Becky muttered.

"What do you mean by that?" replied Stella, sounding hurt.

"Well, if you hadn't insisted we come through the woods, this would never have happened."

Stella lifted her hand off her friend's shoulder and gave her a light slap across the side of her head.

"Ow!"

"Any more observations you'd care to make?" asked Stella, in the most peevish voice she could command.

They both heard the sound of something large moving through the foliage to their left.

Becky, still supporting her friend, tried to turn first to see what it might be, but before she had a chance, something struck them from behind, sending them both sprawling forward onto the ground.

Stella smacked her head on something very hard as she landed. Her head immediately began to spin, and a sharp pain shot across her temple.

She could hear Becky screaming, but the sound was muffled as if something was covering her mouth.

Fighting the pain, Stella managed to turn herself over onto her back.

She lay there for a moment with her eyes tightly shut against the pain.

Just then, she felt two large hands clasp her shoulders and force them down, followed by what felt like a hefty pair of legs straddling her.

Stella opened her eyes and found herself staring into the face of the most hideous creature she had ever seen. The head was covered in shaggy, unkept hair that bristled out in all directions.

The mouth appeared elongated, more like a dog's, with a huge black snout at the end.

The lips were pulled back, revealing a mouth ringed with huge jagged fangs, with the tongue lolling out between them, dripping saliva on her from above.

But worst of all were the eyes!

The red orbs glowed like the tips of hot pokers just removed from a brazier.

From somewhere deep within the creature's throat, Stella could hear a low, guttural growl, which froze her blood.

Stella tried to scream, but no sound escaped her lips.

The warm, fetid breath emanating from the beast assailed her nostrils and made her want to gag.

Stella watched as the beast surveyed her. The thick brows above the thing's eyes knotted together in a menacing frown, as if it were about to strike.

Stella tensed her body in anticipation of the attack.

As if out of nowhere, a scream emerged from the darkness as Becky went careering into the beast, almost managing to topple it off her friend.

The beast let out a ferocious roar, which seemed to echo throughout the woodland surrounding them.

With one mighty paw it reached back and grabbed Becky by the neck, lifting her high off the ground and holding her there, choking and spluttering, as if deciding on her fate.

Seeing her friend in such peril, Stella tried to move herself from underneath the beast, but it held her fast with its sturdy thighs. Stella swung a punch at the beast, but although she made contact with the thing's chest, her effort had no effect.

Becky's eyes began to bulge as the creature squeezed the life from her. She could already feel each breath becoming harder to take, and her vision was growing hazy.

With the last of her strength, Becky grabbed hold of the beast's wrist with both hands and tried to wrench it from her. But each time, all she felt were the thing's claws digging ever deeper into her neck.

Finally, the beast swung Becky across the footpath as if she were no more than an empty soda can.

Becky's body hit a tree with an ear-cringing crack, and her lifeless body fell to the floor in a crumpled heap.

Filled with rage, Stella began screaming as she pounded the beast with both fists, swinging wildly. She was no longer concerned with her own safety, for she accepted that there was no escape. But she wanted to hurt the beast for what it had done to her friend.

The beast allowed Stella to continue with her onslaught until she was too fatigued to continue. Then, with one swipe from its mighty paw, Stella was almost knocked unconscious.

In her semi-conscious state, Stella could feel the beast

Chapter 12

ripping away at her clothes, making huge gashes in her skin in its haste.

Once she was completely naked, the beast spun Stella over and mounted her from behind. The pain was excruciating, but Stella found herself unable to cry out.

She had nothing left to fight with.

Stella felt a fresh stream of tears welling in her eyes. She opened them and through her blurred vision could see the scrunched heap of human flesh and bones which had, until recently, been her closest friend.

Stella prayed that she would soon join her friend before the beast had a chance to violate her further.

But her prayer was not answered.

Chapter Thirteen

JENNA OPENED HER EYES. THE SUNLIGHT STREAMING in through the windows of her hotel room informed her that it was morning. She stretched her arms above her head and yawned loudly before sitting up.

The sudden movement caused the room to swim around her for a second.

Jenna closed her eyes and placed her hands over them. She could feel a faint throbbing behind her temple, and she recognised the all too familiar traits of a hangover.

Remembering the evening before, Jenna surmised that her condition was no doubt down to a lack of food as well as the double vodkas she had put away.

Eventually, Jenna found the energy to swing her legs out from under the covers and to prop herself upright with her legs hanging off the bed.

Her headache was building, so Jenna searched through her handbag for some aspirin to help take the edge off it before it took command.

She took a bottle of cold water from the mini-bar and swal-

Chapter 13

lowed two of the tablets, washing them down with several gulps.

Gazing down at the coffee- and tea-making facilities the hotel provided, she decided to try a strong coffee before her shower.

While the kettle boiled, Jenna retrieved her mobile from her handbag. It was switched off. She could not remember doing it but presumed she must have at some point during the evening. When she turned it back on, it immediately buzzed into life.

She tried to focus on the small screen, and eventually she saw that Roger had tried to call her fifteen times since the previous evening.

There were several messages waiting, so Jenna made her coffee before retrieving them.

Each one was from Roger, as she'd suspected, and Jenna placed her hot coffee on the bedside table as she lay back and listened to them.

Roger was clearly miffed that she had not accepted any of his calls, and with each subsequent message his tone grew more outraged, demanding that she call him back immediately.

Jenna checked her menu and saw that Roger had been calling her right up until three in the morning.

In his final message, Roger had threatened to drive down to Huntley himself to make sure that Jenna was not in the arms of another man.

Jenna immediately regretted ever telling him where her uncle was, but at the time, she could not have foreseen the present situation.

She tossed her mobile on the bed and sat up to grab her coffee. She took it over to a large glass set of doors that led out onto a veranda and opened one before venturing out in her bare feet and taking a seat on one of the metal chairs provided.

The cool morning air certainly helped to clear her head.

As Jenna sipped her coffee, she could feel the tablets beginning to work.

She felt very calm and at peace, considering her reason for being in Huntley, and she wondered how much of that had to do with the unexpected drinking buddy from last night.

Young had certainly been good company, and the evening had drifted along nicely until they were disturbed by that awful Le Vant woman.

Jenna placed her feet on the table and sat back to finish the last of her coffee. She had certainly made it strong, and it was just what the doctor ordered.

She sat there for a while listening to the sounds of the early morning wildlife outside her door and considered whether she should call Roger back before or after breakfast.

Knowing him as she did, Jenna knew that Roger's threat to drive down after her was merely idle nonsense. But even so, his voice on the phone was starting to sound more unhinged with each subsequent message.

Jenna checked the time on her phone. It was a few minutes after eight, so she knew that Roger should be awake by now. Although, as he had stayed up so late calling her, perhaps he was still asleep.

Jenna rubbed her eyes and forehead with her palm. The sudden recollection of what Trish had told her about Roger and the temp made her realise that she did not care whether he was awake or not. She could feel her anger rising within her, and now felt like the perfect opportunity to put Roger straight.

She lifted her feet off the table and went back into the bedroom.

Jenna considered calling from inside, just in case the conversation grew heated; she did not want her fellow residents to hear her side of the conversation.

But, on the other hand, Jenna decided that no matter what was said, she was going to keep her cool. Roger could rant and rave all he liked; she was firm in her resolve. This was finally it, the moment she told him where to go and to hell with the consequences.

Jenna took her phone out onto the veranda and hit Roger's number.

"Hello," Roger answered within two rings. He sounded drowsy, as if the call had woken him from a deep slumber.

"Hello, Roger, it's Jenna." She kept her tone business-like, detached to the point of being cold.

In the background, Jenna could hear the sounds of objects being knocked over, some even hitting the wooden floor of Roger's bedroom.

She heard him curse and imagined him fumbling with his dressing gown as he tried slipping it on whilst still holding the phone.

He had once told her that he could not speak to anyone on the phone unless he was dressed. Being naked, even though the other party could not see, made him feel too vulnerable.

Jenna waited for him to organise himself.

"Where are you, are you still in that Huntley place? What's going on?"

Jenna took a deep breath. "Yes, I'm still here. The police are investigating the disappearance of my uncle, so I'll probably be here for a while."

"Disappearance!" Roger almost sounded as if he were about to break into a fit of laughter. "Surely that's a little presumptuous, isn't it?"

His tone was the usual condescending one he preferred to use whenever he thought he was right and everyone else was wrong.

Jenna had heard it more often than she cared to admit.

"Well, the police don't seem to think so." Jenna could feel her anger rising and took a couple of deep breaths to keep herself calm.

She was determined that she was going to stay in control of this conversation, no matter how it ended.

"Oh, come on, they're probably just pandering to you because you're a pretty woman alone in a strange town. They won't actually do anything about it. It's more than likely they're humouring you until you go away."

That did it for Jenna.

"Frankly, Roger, I don't much care for your opinion." Jenna kept her tone steady, although underneath, the fire was raging.

"What!" Roger was clearly taken aback by Jenna's words. "Jenna, I don't care for your tone." He was almost whining.

The time had finally arrived, and Jenna was ready.

"How was your 'business' trip?" She placed extra emphasis on the word 'business.'

"My…my trip was fine, thank you."

Jenna could hear the sudden alarm in his voice.

"How was your companion? Did she manage to type up all the minutes in good time?"

There was silence on the other end.

Jenna could feel herself moving in for the kill.

"Listen, Roger, I know all about you and that little tart of a temp, so let's not insult each other by making excuses. We're done!"

Jenna heard Roger draw a sharp intake of breath.

"Done, what do you mean done? Listen, I don't know what you're talking about. What temp?"

Jenna sighed. She should have expected he would not go down without a fight.

"The one with the pink hair who resembles 'My Little Pony' that you spent the night with while you were meant to be on a business trip. Ring any bells?"

"What! No! Who's been spreading idle gossip? I'll have them sacked!" Roger was blustering like a schoolboy who had been caught out peeking through the window of the girls' changing room.

Jenna had to think fast.

The last thing she wanted was to land Trish in hot water, and knowing Roger, he was definitely vindictive enough to try and make life not worth living for her at the office.

She had to steer him off course.

"She's been boasting about it all over the office, Roger. You obviously did not explain the etiquette rules of an affair with the boss's son adequately."

"Ridiculous, I…I can't imagine what's got into the girl. I'm phoning the agency this morning, she'll have to go, I can't have temps spreading malicious rumours about senior staff all around the office."

Jenna could tell from the authority seeping back into his voice that Roger felt he had handled the situation admirably.

In his mind, he could get rid of the girl and just deny anything took place, and everybody, including Jenna, would believe him without question.

Jenna waited a moment before answering.

She was determined that this situation was not going to be left unresolved. In truth, she did not care that Roger had had an affair, or indeed the fact that he had lied to her about it. The most important thing was that he had given her an excellent reason to end their relationship, and Jenna was not about to let the opportunity pass.

"Stop lying, Roger. I know you slept with her, and quite frankly I no longer care. You can sack her if you want, but we both know it was you who instigated the liaison, so why don't you just be a man for once and accept the responsibility?"

"Alright, alright," Roger spluttered, "but it meant nothing to me. I've been under a lot of stress lately, and you've been so preoccupied with your uncle's disappearance that I was feeling unappreciated, so I spent the night with someone who really cared about my problems, for once."

Jenna could not believe what she was hearing.

After taking a moment to process what he was saying, she kept her composure and took another breath before responding.

"Roger, I want you to pack up all my things and leave them on my desk at work. I will collect them when I return."

"You can't leave me!" It sounded more like a demand than a plea. "You know what I'll do if you dare leave me. This isn't a threat; I'll go through with it, and you know I will!"

"No, you won't, Roger, you've got too much to lose. Your fancy job, the cars, the money, the all-expenses paid holidays. Let's face it, when it comes down to it, you're just a spoilt little rich boy who always wants things his own way."

"How dare you speak to me like that! I'm your senior director, you have to show me respect!"

Jenna sighed. "Respect needs to be earned, Roger. You may be my senior, for now, but you're no longer my boyfriend, so get used to it!"

"I'll kill myself!" Roger exploded, the old threat resurfacing. Obviously, he realised that it was his last vestige of a chance to win the argument.

"No, you won't, Roger." Jenna stayed firm. "Now pack up my stuff and leave it on my desk. I'll return your keys when I get back. Goodbye, Roger."

Jenna could hear Roger postulating all manner of irrelevant details down the phone as she pulled it away from her ear and disconnected the call.

After her shower, Jenna took herself down to the restaurant for breakfast.

She had switched her mobile over to silent after terminating her call to Roger, and now that she looked at the screen, Jenna could see that he had tried to call a further three times since then.

Chapter 13

There were also two messages from him, which she deleted without listening to them.

The breakfast area of the restaurant was only about half full when Jenna arrived. Before she had a chance to sit down, Audrey appeared by her side and shooed away one of the waitresses so that she could take her order personally.

Although Audrey tried to talk her into tucking into a full English, Jenna opted for cereal and toast and black coffee.

While she waited, Jenna scanned her fellow diners.

There was a group of four pensioners at the far end excitedly discussing their planned activities for the day. Jenna presumed that they were two couples who clearly enjoyed each other's company.

A couple of tables over sat an extremely emaciated-looking young man wearing a business suit clearly cut for someone larger than him.

Jenna watched him from the corner of her eye. He seemed to have a nervous twitch, which reared itself every couple of seconds.

To Jenna's right sat a rather corpulent lady, also dressed for a business meeting. She studied reams of papers spread out on her table while she absentmindedly stuffed sausage and egg into her mouth, oblivious to the fact that there was egg yolk dribbling down her chin.

The last group appeared to be a man and his wife with their two young children, a boy and a girl. The couple seemed preoccupied with their newspapers, while the children, who Jenna estimated must be between six and seven, sat in silence with their empty plates still in front of them, swinging their legs back and forth under the table.

"There you are now, my lovely," said a beaming Audrey, placing Jenna's breakfast on the table. "Now, you are quite sure I can't interest you in our full English? Our chef does a lovely full English: eggs, bacon, sausage…"

"No, really," Jenna cut her off in mid-sentence, "thank you, this will be just fine."

Having accepted defeat, Audrey began to busy herself by instructing the waitresses to ensure that everyone had everything they needed.

Jenna poured the milk over her muesli and began to eat.

At one point, she caught the eye of the young boy sitting with his parents and sister. Jenna gave him a crafty wink and smiled to herself as he seemed to blush before turning away.

After breakfast, Jenna went back to her room. She brushed her teeth and collected her handbag and jacket before leaving.

She intended to spend the day exploring the town in the vain hope that she might see her uncle or perhaps find a hotel or inn where he might be staying. She surmised that the town probably boasted a museum or two and that there was always the chance that her uncle was visiting one of them.

When she handed in her key at reception, the girl behind the counter barely had a chance to take it from her before Audrey appeared from the kitchen and walked around the main desk as if to escort Jenna from the building.

Once outside the foyer, Audrey began asking Jenna what her plans were for the day.

She put it down to her overactive imagination, but Jenna had the distinct impression that Audrey was not merely being curious but was pumping her for information.

Jenna kept her voice light and her answers equally unspecific.

When the moment presented itself, Jenna made her excuses and left Audrey to walk to her car.

As Jenna drove out of the car park, the husband of the couple with the two young children emerged from the foyer and came and stood beside Audrey.

Neither acknowledged the other's presence as both of them focussed on Jenna's car as it disappeared around the corner.

"Are you sure it's her?" It was Audrey who spoke first without turning to look at the man beside her.

The man nodded. "It is her!" he replied convincingly.

Audrey's lips creased into a fraction of a smile. "Then we must be prepared," she answered before turning and retracing her steps, followed by the man.

Chapter Fourteen

JENNA SPENT THE REST OF THE MORNING AND THE best part of the afternoon venturing through the town visiting every hotel, motel and guest house that she could find. Several of the larger ones, it appeared, had already been contacted by the local force, which gave her a good feeling knowing that Young was not fobbing her off and that a real investigation was ongoing.

It was exhausting work. It seemed as if every second or third large house in the town had been converted into a guest house. The one positive thing was that there was always someone in residence when she called, so at least she did not need to concern herself with the prospect of revisiting the same area again.

By mid-afternoon, Jenna was feeling tired and hungry.

Not wishing to return to her hotel just yet, she parked up near a quaint little tea shop and went in to sample their cream tea. After her morning's labour, she felt she deserved a little pick-me-up.

While she ate, Jenna gazed out of the restaurant window at a book shop across the road. Jenna had always been an avid reader since childhood, but unlike most people of her generation, she preferred the feel of real paper between her fingers, rather than the convenience and simplicity of a Kindle or similar device.

Jenna was never without a book, although now she thought about it, her latest novel was probably still sitting on the nightstand at Roger's flat, if he had not decided to throw it away in a fit of juvenile rage. That would not have been completely alien to his nature.

Jenna wondered for a moment how safe the clothes she had at his place would be.

She recalled an occasion when she had been due to attend a university reunion, and she had made the mistake of informing Roger that her old boyfriend from campus would be there. Roger had insisted on accompanying her, but Jenna had stood firm and told him that other halves were not invited.

When she had emerged from the shower to change, she'd discovered that Roger had cut the dress she had bought especially for the party into ribbons.

As Jenna had laid into him, Roger had just sat slumped in a chair and sulked, refusing to even hold her gaze. In hindsight, Jenna knew that she should have walked out on him then and there. But, like a gullible fool, she had accepted his grovelling apology when it had come, as well as his promise to reimburse her for double the cost of her new dress.

While she ate, Jenna noticed a group of old women gathering outside the tea shop. It was obvious to her that they fully intended to come in, but for some reason they chose to loiter just outside the door for a while, blocking the pavement.

"Can I get you anything else?" The waitress's appearance brought Jenna round from her reverie.

Jenna smiled. "No, thank you, that really hit the spot."

The waitress noticed Jenna's attention being drawn to the group blocking the doorway. "Don't worry," she laughed, "they're not about to rob the place. We offer a group discount for OAP's twice a week from three o'clock, they're just some of our regulars waiting for the town bell to strike the hour."

Jenna paid for her cream tea and left a generous tip for the friendly waitress.

As she opened the door to leave, she heard the town hall clock begin to strike the hour. As if on cue, the group of old dears rammed in through the door, almost sending Jenna flying off her feet.

Jenna stood there in wonderment as the last of the ladies swept by without so much as a 'pardon.'

She walked over to the book shop and gazed in through the window.

From what she could tell, there did not appear to be anyone on duty at the counter, and for a moment Jenna supposed that it might be closed for lunch. But then, remembering the lateness of the hour, that did not make sense.

She walked up to door and gave it a gentle push. It opened without much resistance, and a tiny bell jangled above her as she ventured inside.

Jenna waited for a moment just inside the door for an assistant to appear. But when after a while none did, she decided to start browsing, presuming they must be somewhere in the back.

The shop had been fitted out with rows upon rows of dark wooden bookshelves, some of which were floor to ceiling. Jenna wondered how anyone could reach the books on the higher shelves, but then she noticed the matching wooden ladder on wheels hiding in the corner. It was similar to the type often found in libraries, with a platform at the top encased by railing.

In the middle of the floor stood an ornate iron staircase, which spiralled up, Jenna suspected, to another floor. At the top there was a thick iron chain across the entrance, with a sign stating, 'No Entry.'

Jenna passed by the sections for romance, drama and thriller and made her way towards the horror section at the end. She reached out towards a Richard Laymon novel that caught her eye when she suddenly heard footsteps on the iron staircase.

Jenna looked over. The feet she saw descending the staircase were shod in black ballet-style pumps, with laces that crisscrossed up past the ankles. As the woman the feet belonged to came into view, Jenna took a sharp breath. She was stunning.

She was wearing a skin-tight, black, leotard cat suit, which accentuated her incredibly toned body. Her hair was of a lustrous black and fell around her shoulders, bouncing as she walked, like one of those models in a shampoo commercial.

From behind, she reminded Jenna or Yvonne De Carlo from the Munsters. But as the woman turned to face her at the bottom of the staircase, she saw that unlike the character from the show, who had always been made up to appear pale and tragic, the woman had skin like porcelain, as well as a beautiful tan.

Katerina smiled and held Jenna in a firm gaze for a moment before walking towards her. "I'm so sorry to have kept you waiting, may I help you with anything?"

The woman's voice had a slight accent to it, which Jenna could not quite place, but she imagined it to be eastern European. It also had an almost hypnotic quality to it, which caused Jenna to make a conscious effort to tear her eyes away from her momentarily before she could reply.

"No, thank you, I was just browsing, if that's alright?"

Katerina stopped within a couple of feet of Jenna. "Of course, please take your time, and let me know if you require my assistance."

Jenna smiled back, but she felt unable to move until Katerina turned away and walked over to the main counter. She found Katerina's presence mesmerising, almost intoxicating. From the way she sashayed across the room with such poise and grace,

Jenna felt sure that she must have studied ballet or gymnastics at some time.

Jenna had always been a confirmed heterosexual, and she had never so much as experimented whilst at university, but she felt as if Katerina could have swayed her on the spot with just a word or even a nod of her head.

She felt her cheeks flush at the thought, so Jenna quickly turned back to face the shelves, just in case the owner noticed from across the floor.

After checking out a couple of other titles, Jenna opted for the Laymon she had first picked. The back cover described the story as being about a group of female friends who go camping in the grounds of a deserted haunted hotel, only to find out that far from being deserted, there is a knife-wielding maniac lurking in the grounds.

Jenna did not consider herself to be an avid reader of horror fiction. But every so often she craved the excitement of a good scare, and having read Laymon before, she knew that he could deliver.

She held the book in her hands for a while, steadying herself before approaching the woman, as if she was afraid Katerina could somehow suss out what she had just been thinking.

Jenna steeled herself with a deep breath and made her way over to the counter.

Just then, she heard the bell above the door tinkle, and when she glanced over, she could not believe her eyes when she saw June Le Vant enter the shop.

The two women stared at each other for a moment, and then realising the ridiculous nature of the situation, Jenna offered a polite smile. June reciprocated, half-heartedly, before she walked around the shelves that separated them and disappeared behind the staircase.

"A friend of yours?" Katerina enquired as she rang up Jenna's purchase.

Jenna smiled as she reached into her purse for the money. "A brief acquaintance, you might say." She kept her voice low, not wanting June to hear her.

Katerina placed Jenna's book in a plain paper bag. "You should enjoy that," she informed her, "it kept me up a few nights, I can tell you."

From this proximity, Jenna could not help but notice that Katerina was not wearing a bra under her leotard, and the firm, tight buds of her nipples were pushing relentlessly against the thin fabric.

When she looked up, Jenna could tell from the expression on Katerina's face that she had noticed her admiring her breasts. She felt her cheeks flush again but attempted to act as if everything was normal. "Thanks," she replied, almost grabbing her purchase from the counter where Katerina had placed it. "I'll look forward to reading it."

As she turned to leave the shop, Jenna could not help turning to see if June was still out of sight. Instead, she saw the woman glaring at her over the top of one of the bookcases adjacent to the staircase.

She decided to pretend she had not seen her, after all, and left.

As Jenna slammed the door to her car shut, the first spots of rain hit her windscreen.

She turned on the ignition and flicked the arm for the wipers to swing into life.

Looking back at the shop through the rain-splattered side window, she could see the figure of June standing at the window with her hands on her hips, watching her.

It was too far for Jenna to be able to make out the expression on the woman's face. But somehow, she doubted it was one of affability.

June Le Vant watched intently as Jenna's car pulled away from the kerb. All she could think about right now was the possibility that she and Young had spent the night together after she had seen them cosying up in the hotel restaurant.

Ordinarily, she had never been the jealous type. But Young stirred feelings within her that she had long thought were too deeply buried to ever risk surfacing again. She had slept with dozens of men, both before and after her tryst with Young, but he was the first man she had ever considered leaving her husband for.

Her marriage to Arthur had been a farce for more years than she could remember. In truth, she had never actually found him physically attractive, but he was rich and very well connected socially, and without any appetite for honest toil herself, he had seemed a good catch.

Fortunately for her, Arthurs's appetites in the bedroom were few and far between, and June had mastered the art of using her hand to make him ejaculate under the pretence of arousing him for sex.

That and his frequent business trips, which allowed her plenty of opportunities to obtain her pleasure elsewhere, afforded the marriage an element of congeniality, if not raging passion.

When Young had suddenly turned into a choirboy at the revelation that she was married, June had been prepared to leave things as they were. But over time she had grown more and more attracted to the policeman and had even caught herself stalking him from a distance without his knowledge.

She hated the fact that Young made her feel so vulnerable. With all her other sexual partners, she was the one in charge. She called the shots, and she decided how, when, and if they were to meet. But Young, without realising it, had a power over her that she could not overcome.

In fact, she had made her mind up only recently that she was going to snare him, no matter what, even at the cost of her luxurious lifestyle, and then, lo and behold, she had caught him with Jenna.

Well, if that little strumpet thought she could just waltz in and snatch her man away without a fight, she had another thing coming.

June could feel the tension inside her growing. She knew that her concern for Young and Jenna's relationship was making her anxious, and she tried to calm herself down by scanning the shelves and waiting for one of the titles to grab her attention. She picked out one she had not read before, but after scanning the cover for a while she realised that a book was not going to relieve the conflict raging within her. Plus, all this thinking about Young was making her feel rampant. She needed relief. Preferably from Young, but if that was not possible, a stiff drink and her middle finger would have to suffice.

June replaced the book she had been examining and turned to leave the shop.

Without realising that Katerina had somehow manged to creep up behind her, June almost stepped on the woman in her haste to leave, just managing to halt in mid-step as she turned.

"Oh, I am sorry," June mumbled, "I didn't realise you were there."

Katerina smiled at her. "It's these pumps," she indicated towards her feet, "they make me feel like a cat-burglar sometimes."

June laughed in spite of herself. She was not normally the type to bother with inane banter with strangers. But Katerina certainly had a way about her that intrigued June to the point of no longer being in such a cast-iron hurry to leave.

"Did you change your mind about the book?"

"Yes," June replied, almost feeling guilty for leaving empty-handed. "I think I'm just feeling a little too frustrated at the moment to consider a good book."

"I see," Katerina agreed sympathetically. "Would it by any chance have something to do with the woman who just left here?"

June was shocked by the woman's presumption. She spoke as if they were old friends instead of complete strangers. She was just about to remonstrate with the woman when June saw something in her eyes that completely threw her off her guard.

Until this moment, June had not noticed the piercing emerald-green hue of the woman's eyes, not to mention the way they almost seemed to convey the feeling that she could read your innermost thoughts.

Instead of rebuking the woman in her usual manner of righteous indignation that she saved for such occasions, June found herself wanting to confide in this stranger and bring her into her confidence.

"How clever of you," June replied, feeling a little like a rabbit caught in oncoming headlights. "Was I really that obvious?"

Katerina shrugged. "Not really, it's just that working in here gives me plenty of opportunities to study people and their reactions. I suppose it has become a bit of a hobby of mine over time."

June smiled. It took a supreme effort to tear her gaze away from the woman's hypnotic stare, but she finally managed it.

But it was only for the briefest of moments. June found herself studying the woman's incredibly well-toned figure, accentuated as it was by her apparel.

By the time her eyes reached Katerina's again, she felt completely captivated.

"Listen," Katerina enquired, "is it too early for you to enjoy a cocktail? I have all the makings upstairs, and I can feel the need to close early coming on."

"Lovely," June agreed without taking the time to consider the offer.

Chapter 14

After locking the front door, Katerina led June up the spiral staircase to her flat above.

Once inside the living room, June relaxed on the large leather sofa in the middle of the room, while Katerina mixed their drinks.

"So, do you fancy dishing the dirt on what's going on with you and that other woman?" Katerina made her enquiry sound to June as if she had nothing to lose and everything to gain by confiding in her new companion.

"Well, it's silly really, but last night I saw her out with a man whom I have recently discovered I've fallen in love with."

Katerina raised her eyebrows as she carefully poured the contents from a glass jug into two cocktail glasses. "I see, and dare I ask how he feels about you?"

June sighed. "Oh, he's already made it clear to me that I am not on his radar. But then..." June felt it necessary to elucidate further, as she was beginning to sound, even to herself, like a desperate woman. "He only said he wasn't interested because I am already married."

"Ahh, that can put a spanner in the works."

"Fact is, I've decided to divorce my husband if it is what I need to do to get him back. But before I had a chance to tell him, I caught the two of them getting very cosy last night."

Katerina nodded her understanding of the situation and gave the drinks a final stir.

When she carried the two glasses over to her guest and handed her one, June glanced at the striking aquamarine liquid swirling the ice cubes around the surface and placed the glass under her nose to ascertain its contents.

The aroma that hit her nostrils was by no means unpleasant. But June could not upon first impression decipher what it was.

Katerina sat next to her guest and held her glass up to clink.

"What is it?" asked June, automatically raising hers in a similar fashion.

Katerina gazed deeply into her eyes. "It's something special, and it's very good."

They touched glasses, and both drank in unison.

Unlike Katerina, who merely took a sip of hers, June found herself tipping her head back and draining her glass in one. The bright liquid slipped down her throat so easily, it hardly seemed to her as if it contained any liquor at all.

Having emptied her glass, June set it on the side table to her right.

She could see from Katerina's expression that the woman was amused by her behaviour, and although she felt slightly embarrassed by it, June could do no more than smile back.

June closed her eyes and savoured the delicate combination of flavours as the drink began to warm her from inside. She could almost feel the liquid coursing through her body, leaving her with a slight tingle, which was not at all an unpleasant sensation.

June felt her entire body relax, as if all the tension, stress and strain caused by her obsession with Young was being drained away.

Her body began to feel weightless, as if she were floating in a dream.

Such was her trance-like state that she did not feel her shoes being removed, nor her stockings and panties being slowly slipped down her legs.

When June finally opened her eyes, she saw Katerina standing over her, naked.

June smiled up at her dreamily.

Although she could see the woman quite clearly before her, through her drink-induced state, it appeared as if Katerina was wearing some sort of skin-tight all-over suit made from a wispy, fur-like material.

Either that, or the woman had suddenly sprouted hair all over her body.

Chapter 14

June attempted to laugh at her own joke, but she discovered she no longer had control over her mouth.

Staring up at the naked woman before her, June became acutely aware, even through her intoxication, that her companion's features were in fact undergoing some form of transformation.

As she tried to focus, June envisaged that Katerina's facial features had altered quite dramatically, to the point where she now appeared to have grown a muzzle, complete with elongated fangs that protruded from it quite significantly.

Katerina's dazzling green eyes had also changed, and now they seemed to have turned a deep red in colour, with a gaze of pure malevolence emanating from them.

June managed to blink twice, but the effort drained her of what little strength she had left. She looked up at the creature, which moments before had been the beautiful Katerina, and she could feel an urgent hammering of panic deep within her.

But she was completely paralysed and unable to respond to her growing concern.

The creature crouched down between June's thighs and sniffed at the wet mound of pubic hair before it. Slowly, it opened its gaping maw and released its elongated tongue, which proceeded to slither and slide into June's moist cavern.

Despite her current state, June could still feel the probing tongue enter her, and within seconds she experienced the greatest orgasm of her life.

June's mind raced against itself. She knew that she was in the grasp of some terrible entity which, no doubt, meant her nothing but harm, and yet she still felt the desperate urge to buck and thrust her hips to increase her pleasure.

June could feel herself starting to climax once more.

Although she had allowed countless men to enter her in the past, as well as some battery-operated toys she had experimented with, nothing had ever brought her this much pleasure in such a relatively short space of time.

Unable to react or respond, June decided to give herself over to the creature.

She could feel the room starting to spin, and an overall weightlessness overcame her, making her feel as if she were floating in space, unfettered by gravity, and completely at one with nature.

The pleasure she was receiving began to spread from the nucleus of her vagina to every part of her inactive body. All her nerve endings suddenly came alive in a mass orgasmic explosion, as if the probing tongue of the beast had somehow managed to stimulate every erogenous zone within her simultaneously.

June felt sure she was about to die from the overwhelming experience.

But she no longer cared.

Chapter Fifteen

THE HARSH TONE OF THE PHONE ON HER NIGHTSTAND roused Jenna from her doze. She raised herself onto one arm, letting the Laymon novel slip down her chest and settle on the bed.

Jenna grabbed the handset. "Hello."

"Hello, dear, sorry to bother you." It was Audrey's jovial voice on the other end. "I've got Alan on the line. He says he's been trying to reach you."

Jenna rubbed her eyes. "Oh, I see, thank you, Audrey." She moved into a seated position to take the call.

There was a click on the line.

"Jenna, it's Alan, are you alright? I've been trying to reach you for ages, is your phone off?"

It was. Having received another barrage of calls from Roger on her drive back from the bookshop, Jenna had switched her mobile off to give him time to get the message. Although, in truth, she doubted very much that he would.

"Yes, sorry about that, work's been calling non-stop, and I wanted a rest." For some reason, and she was not exactly sure why, Jenna did not want to tell Alan the real reason her phone was off. Even though lying made her feel decidedly guilty.

"Oh, ok." Young accepted her lie without question. "Well, I may have some good news. I think we might have located the place where your uncle has been staying. All those calls paid off after all."

Jenna felt her heart skip a beat. "Really, where? Has anyone been down there yet? Is he there?"

"No, in fact I am just about to leave now. I've spoken to the landlady on the phone, and unfortunately, she hasn't seen him for over a week. But she wasn't concerned because she told me he had informed her that he might be away for some time during his stay."

Jenna felt her spirits tumble.

It was good news that Young had located her uncle's hotel, but the fact his landlady had not seen him for so long was definitely a bad sign.

"Where is it?" Jenna asked. "Give me the address, and I'll meet you there."

There was a pause on the line.

"Alan, are you still there?"

"Yes," sighed Young, "look, the thing is this is part of my investigation, and protocol dictates that I cannot take a civilian with me to interview a witness. I'm really sorry."

He sounded it, too.

"Alan, please, I won't get in the way, but this is the first break we've had since I lost track of him. Please, I just want to talk to her, she might remember something he said about where he was going."

"I know." Young tried to sound sympathetic. "That's the reason I need to interview her, it's all part of my job. Don't worry, I know all the questions to ask." He was desperately trying not to sound patronising, but he needed to make Jenna understand that he did this sort of thing for a living.

There was another silent pause.

"I'll tell you what," Young offered, "why don't I come down and see you after I've spoken to her? I promise I will tell you everything pertinent."

Jenna brightened at the idea of seeing him again. But she really wanted to go with him. Seeing her uncle's room and the familiar paraphernalia he always carried with him on these jaunts would make her feel closer to him, and right now, she needed that.

"What do you say?" Young asked somewhat hesitantly.

"Is there no way you could take me with you?" Jenna's voice was almost pleading, and she was not ashamed of using all the tools left in her arsenal.

Young made a whining noise on the other end, which Jenna could tell immediately meant that he was about to cave in.

She waited a moment, then she waded in with her final assault.

"Tell you what," she suggested, "how about after we visit his hotel, we find a nice quiet bar somewhere so you can let me buy you a thank-you drink?"

She heard Young sigh in surrender. "If my governor ever finds out, he'll have my guts for garters, I hope you realise that?"

"Well, then we'd better keep this as our little secret. I'll meet you in the car park downstairs." Jenna did not want to give Young a chance to back out. "I'm already looking forward to our drink."

They agreed to meet in fifteen minutes.

Jenna thanked Young again and waited for him to cut off the call.

Just as she was about to replace her receiver, Jenna heard another click on the line, as if someone else had just replaced their receiver before her.

She wondered for a moment if perhaps Audrey had been

listening in on their call. Jenna decided that she did not really care for her landlady. Too nosey by far!

Jenna brushed her hair and applied a fresh coat of makeup. She only ever used a light foundation and lipstick unless she was going out somewhere special, but for tonight she decided to make an extra effort and raided her makeup bag.

She changed into a summer dress with a plunging neckline, which accentuated her breasts, and opted for a pair of courts with kitten heels to complete the look.

Jenna grabbed a cardigan in case they were out late and slung it over the handles of her handbag.

As she opened her door to leave, the sight of the young boy she had winked at that morning at breakfast, standing directly outside her door, gave her a start.

Jenna's key slipped from her grasp and fell to the floor.

"Oh," she cried, "you made me jump."

The young boy did not respond; he merely stood there looking up at her with a dull glaze over his eyes.

As he was blocking her way, Jenna bent down to retrieve her key, hoping that her movement might act as a signal for him to back away.

But as she bent down to grab her key, the boy's arm shot out, and his hand closed over one of her breasts.

Jenna was taken aback, and she did not react immediately.

For a moment, she remained in a crouched position while the boy squeezed and fondled her breast, keeping his eyes fixed firmly on hers.

Regaining her composure, Jenna shot up, and the boy's hand fell away.

Before Jenna had a chance to reprimand him, the boy turned and ran along the corridor, finally entering a door at the far end on the left.

Jenna settled herself and locked her door behind her.

As she walked down the corridor, she considered letting the

Chapter 15

matter go, as the boy was only young and probably unaware of how uncouth his actions were. But as she reached the door he had disappeared behind, Jenna decided that a quiet word with his parents might prevent any future such episodes.

Jenna knocked, and after a couple of seconds the door was opened by the boy's father.

He was clearly shocked to see Jenna standing there, and she wondered if perhaps he had been expecting someone else.

"Yes, may I help you?" the man asked. His voice was formal and not at all friendly.

Jenna opened her mouth to speak, but all at once, she was struck by the ridiculous nature of her reason for knocking.

The man stared down at her. His eyes conveyed an almost menacing sense of superiority, which Jenna found quite unnerving.

"I'm sorry to bother you," she began, "and I realise that what I am about to say may sound completely ludicrous, but may I speak to your son a moment?"

The man's frown deepened. "My son!" he barked. "What on earth for?"

Jenna took in another deep breath.

She realised that she was going to have to stop beating around the bush and get straight to the point.

She cleared her throat before continuing. Just being in such close proximity with this man was causing her to feel distinctly fatuous. "Well, to be honest with you, I am afraid that your son just assaulted me."

Much to her surprise, the man burst out laughing.

Jenna could feel her anger rising. "Look, I am not in the habit of making false accusations, especially against young boys. I know it might seem ludicrous, but I am telling you what happened!"

The man stopped laughing, and his expression grew serious and foreboding once more. He manoeuvred himself so that he blocked the frame of the door and planted a fist on his hip. When he spoke again, he did so with all the righteous indignation of a Victorian patriarch.

"And just how, pray, did my six-year-old son assault you, madam?"

Jenna gulped. "He was waiting for me outside my door, down there," she indicated along the corridor, "and when I bent down to retrieve my key, which I had dropped by accident, he grabbed hold of my bosom and squeezed it."

As she spoke, Jenna could feel her hand automatically reaching for her breast.

She let it slip back down to her side, not wishing to draw attention to her cleavage.

"Nonsense!" the man declared.

Jenna had had enough of the man's condescending tone.

"Look, why don't you just bring your son to the door and ask him? I'm sure that he would not dare to lie to you."

The man's brow furrowed.

He opened his mouth to reply, but just then, a woman's voice called from behind him.

"Stanley, what's going on? Who is that at the door?"

The man moved back to allow his wife to take up a position beside him in the doorway.

Jenna immediately switched her attention to the woman, hoping for a little sisterly support, even though her complaint was about the woman's son.

"I am sorry to bother you," Jenna began, her tone lowered to help get her point across. "But as I was just trying to explain to your husband here, your son assaulted me in this corridor outside my room."

The woman turned to her husband. "What's she talking about, Stanley?"

The man merely shrugged his shoulders in a manner which

conveyed that he was at a loss to understand what Jenna was talking about.

Jenna kept her focus on the wife. "Your son was waiting for me when I came out of my room just now. He gave me such a start that I dropped my key, and when I bent down to retrieve it, he grabbed my bosom!" Jenna felt a little more awkward each time she retold the story, but she hoped now that the wife had heard it, she would at least take her seriously.

"I'm sorry, but when did you say this happened?" The woman kept her voice calm and in control.

"Just a few minutes ago," replied Jenna, finally feeling as if she was getting through.

The woman looked up at her husband, and then back to Jenna.

"But that's not possible," she stated confidently. "Both our children have been watching television with us for the last half an hour, at least."

The woman sounded perfectly sincere, although Jenna could not believe what she was hearing.

Before Jenna had a chance to answer, the man ushered his wife back inside the room.

"So, as you can see," he stated, indignantly, "you are obviously mistaken. Now if you don't mind, we need to prepare for dinner."

With that, he closed the door before Jenna had a chance to respond.

For a moment, Jenna stood outside the door, perplexed.

The man had been a complete arse, as far as she was concerned, but his wife at least had seemed genuine, and yet, she insisted that her son had not left the room when Jenna knew that she was not mistaken.

Shaking her head in disbelief, Jenna made her way downstairs to meet Young.

As expected, Audrey was waiting at reception when Jenna passed.

"Hello, dear, are you off out for the evening? Going anywhere nice?"

Jenna felt the sudden urge to turn on the woman and inform her that she was all too aware that she had listened in on her call.

But instead, she decided to hold her temper and shot back a perfunctory, "Yes, thanks," as she continued making her way out.

Young was already waiting, leaning against his car.

He opened Jenna's door for her, and she noticed how his eyes took in her appearance.

After the incident upstairs, Jenna was pleased that her efforts had not been in vain.

They chatted amicably on route to the boarding house where her uncle had stayed.

Jenna considered telling Young about the incident with the young boy and his parents but decided against it. She was happy to put the entire unpleasant business behind her and focus on the meeting with her uncle's landlady.

Mary Cranley was waiting outside in her front yard when Young pulled up.

Jenna estimated the woman was probably in her late sixties or early seventies, and she smiled as she greeted the new arrivals and welcomed them to her home.

Jenna noticed there were no signs or plaques outside to suggest that the house was, in fact, a guest house, and she found that a little odd. But she was determined to heed Young's subtle warning in the car that he would be the one asking the questions.

After refusing the landlady's offer of refreshments, she took them both up to the room she claimed Jenna's uncle had occupied.

Chapter 15

The house was a large, Victorian, terraced building, and the room they were shown was remarkably spacious, with solid wooden furniture, which included a writing desk and chair in the far corner.

Jenna immediately recognised her uncle's battered old suitcases sitting beside the writing desk.

She felt a sudden jolt of melancholy at the prospect that she may never see her uncle again.

Young behaved completely professionally in his gentle questioning of the old woman. It was clear to Jenna that he did not suspect any foul play, at least not by her.

There was a raft of papers in a folder on the writing desk.

Jenna immediately recognised her uncle's handwriting when Young started to sift through the jottings.

The old woman appeared to be genuine enough, at least as far as Jenna was concerned. She answered all of Young's questions openly and honestly, without hesitation. She, too, seemed legitimately concerned for Jenna's uncle's welfare.

Having been through the room thoroughly, the three of them made their way downstairs to the woman's spacious living room.

"Has the professor ever stayed with you before?" asked Young as they took their seats.

"No, I'm afraid not, but he seemed a very nice gentleman, and as he was a recommendation, I was only too happy to accommodate him."

Young scribbled in his notebook as she spoke.

"When you say a recommendation, could you be more specific?"

"Well, yes, you see, I make it a point only to rent out to retired gentlemen, or at least those of a certain age, and then, only one at a time. I don't do this for financial gain. I am independently comfortable, you see."

"Is that why you don't advertise your business?" Young asked.

Jenna was pleased he had noticed the lack of signage outside.

The old woman laughed heartily. "Oh, I don't see this as business, young man," she replied. "It's more of a calling for me. I enjoy looking after elderly gentlemen and giving them that extra special attention that I find lacking in most large establishments."

Young continued scribbling. "And when you say the professor was a recommendation, do you remember from whom that recommendation came?"

"Certainly," the woman answered brightly. "It was Professor Pudelko. He's stayed with me on several occasions over the years." She turned her attention towards Jenna. "I believe they know each other from the university."

"They work together?" asked Young, not looking up from his notebook as he checked over his details.

"Yes, at least, I think so." The woman gazed into space as if seeking confirmation. "I'm sure that's what Professor Pudelko told me."

Young turned to look at Jenna. "Is there anything you'd like to ask?" he offered, smiling.

Jenna smiled back before she turned back to the landlady.

"Do you by any chance have the contact details for this Professor Pudelko?"

Young raised his eyebrows. That was a good question, and he knew he should have thought of it first.

The old lady shook her head. "I'm so sorry, my dear, I don't. You see, like all my gentlemen, he calls me when he wants to book a stay. I never need to contact them."

"You don't take a credit card number or anything to secure the booking?" Young interjected.

The old lady laughed. "No… No, I'm sorry, officer, I don't have anything to do with credit cards. Nasty, expensive things. I was brought up to believe that if you can't afford it, you can't have it."

Jenna took out her phone. "Would you mind taking my mobile number, just in case you hear anything or my uncle turns up? I just want to know he's ok."

"Of course, it'll be my pleasure." The old woman rose from her seat and made her way over to a bureau, from which she pulled out a leather-bound book. She turned the pages until she found the right space and picked up a pen from a pot in front of her. "Go ahead, young lady, I'm ready."

Jenna recited her mobile number slowly as the woman wrote it down.

Young gave the woman one of his cards in case she thought of anything after they left.

The old woman hugged Jenna at the door and told her what a lovely gentleman her uncle was and that she hoped nothing had happened to him.

Jenna hugged her back and thanked her.

She could feel the tears starting to roll down her cheeks as she walked back to the car.

Chapter Sixteen

Reginald Le Vant turned his company BMW into his driveway. Switching off the engine, he removed his glasses and rubbed his tired eyes. It had been a long conference with a three-hour drive at the end of it.

He was looking forward to a large scotch, a hot bath, a hot meal, and then bed.

After four days in London, Reginald was glad to be home.

He refused to make the daily drive from Huntley to London, as time spent on the motorway, to him, equalled wasted time he could have been using dealing with his business.

His lifestyle suited him. He actually enjoyed being a guest in a swanky hotel, especially as it was tax deductible. But it was still nice to come home to the relative peace and quiet of Huntley, a lovely home, and a beautiful wife who seemed to appreciate his lifestyle as much as he did.

If not more!

Having a reliable spouse was essential to anyone in business, as far as he was concerned, and June certainly knew how to play the part of the glamourous hostess to perfection.

In many ways, their marriage created the perfect situation for

Chapter 16

both of them. Arthur loved being in business, even if some of the meetings he had to attend were long and boring. He loved the social life in London when he stayed there, especially the attention he received from the escorts he hired.

In his mind, London prostitutes were the best and by far the most professional.

When they'd first married, their sex life had been routine at best and lacklustre at worst. But then, Reginald had not chosen June as a sex partner. Several of his colleagues had proven that when you chose a wife for her sex appeal, the chances were that she would soon become bored with playing the homemaker and part-arranger. Then before you knew it, you were knee-deep in a divorce, which could virtually strip you of all your hard-earned money.

No, June knew the score.

Arthur suspected that she had 'men-friends,' but he was happy to turn a blind eye, so long as she continued to play her part in their relationship.

Arthur felt in his pocket for the small velvet box he had placed there earlier. It held a pair of gold and emerald earrings he had purchased for June in London from her favourite jeweller on Bond Street.

Although he knew his wife could order anything she wanted online, making the effort with such gestures was still important, so far as he was concerned.

When Arthur opened his front door, his nostrils were suddenly overwhelmed by a strange odour which resembled raw meat.

The light in the kitchen was on, so he presumed that June was preparing their dinner. Presumably they were having some form of roast this evening, which June had not yet placed in the oven.

"I'm home," Arthur called out as he placed his briefcase on the hall table.

There was no response!

Arthur walked into the kitchen, expecting to see his wife, glass of wine in hand, busily dressing the meat. But instead, when he entered the room there was no sign of her.

On the wooden cutting board, Arthur found the source of the smell that had met him at the door. Dumped on the large board was a plastic carrier bag full of what appeared to be miscellaneous cuts of red meat, some of which had started to leak blood onto the counter.

Arthur wrinkled his nose.

From this distance, the stench was almost overpowering.

Where the hell was June?

Arthur searched downstairs, moving through the dining room, living room, study and conservatory, but his wife was nowhere to be seen.

He wondered if she had forgotten something from the shop and darted out to fetch whatever it was, leaving the raw meat on the side.

But when he checked the garage, June's car was parked inside, as usual.

Arthur made his way back to the hallway and stood at the bottom of the stairs.

"June," he called up. "Are you up there?"

Again, there was no reply.

The lights upstairs were off, but as Arthur could not imagine his wife ever leaving the house on foot, he decided that perhaps she was in the bath with candles all around her and her headphones on.

It was certainly a reasonable proposal, all else considered.

Arthur flicked the switch at the bottom of the stairs for the landing light.

The upstairs remained in darkness.

He tried it several times but without success.

Groaning, Arthur began to climb the stairs.

When he reached the top, the bathroom door was directly in front of him.

There was no sign of any light emitting from under the jamb, but Arthur decided to err on the side of caution and gently knocked on the door.

Receiving no reply, he entered. The room was in darkness with no evidence of anyone having taken a bath recently.

Feeling frustrated now, Arthur made a sweep of the upstirs, calling to his wife as he went. Each light switch he tried failed to work, and he now suspected that perhaps the trip-switch under the stairs had been activated.

Probably as a result of June overloading the system with her myriad of electrical gadgets and gizmos, he surmised.

Arthur decided to check the last few rooms for his wife before going back down to investigate the fuse box.

When he reached their master bedroom, he could see that the light was off in there, too, and seeing that the entire circuit was not working, he did not bother to try the switch as he entered the room.

To his surprise, June was standing at the far end of the room, gazing out of the window.

It took a moment for Arthur to recover from the shock of seeing his wife in the room.

"June, what are you doing? I've been calling and calling you since I came in."

The bedroom curtains were drawn open, and although it was dark outside, a nearby streetlight cast an eerie shadow where June was standing.

"Hello, darling," June purred. "I've been waiting for you."

For a moment, Arthur strained to focus his eyes on his wife.

Somehow, she seemed different.

As he walked closer a few steps, he realised that she was naked.

"June, what are you doing? Come away from there, the neighbours will see you!"

Arthur grabbed hold of the counterpane from the bed and walked around with it, intending to throw it around his wife's shoulders to shield her nakedness from possible prying eyes.

As he reached June, he lifted the coverall towards her.

"Don't!" she demanded. The harshness in her voice caused Arthur to take a step back. His wife did not usually speak to him in such a manner, and Arthur was beginning to feel a little suspicious of her behaviour.

For a moment, Arthur stayed put, unsure of what to do or say next.

After a few seconds, he could bite his tongue no longer.

"Look, June," he began, trying to summon up the same tone he used with his subordinates when they were underperforming. "I don't know what's going on here, but…"

Before he could finish, June spun around to face him.

In the shadowy darkness, Arthur could not make out his wife's features, but still, something seemed odd about her appearance.

"Don't be cross, Arthur, I just thought it might be fun to make love with the curtains open. We never make love with the curtains open."

Her words shocked him.

Not just her words, but her voice, too. She sounded seductive, almost bewitching. It reminded Arthur of how the prostitutes in London spoke when they wanted to wheedle a bit more cash out of him.

They hardly made love at all these days, much less in such an adventurous manner.

Arthur wondered if his wife had been watching some of the dodgy channels they had access to with their latest contract, or perhaps she had been visiting one of those alleged sex therapists that seemed to be popping up all over the place these days.

Either way, he was definitely not in the mood

As far as he was concerned, if June was suddenly feeling frustrated, she could use one of the vibrators she kept hidden under the bed in that old suitcase of hers.

Arthur decided that he needed to put a stop to this nonsense, once and for all.

"June, I don't know what has got into you, but for goodness sake, get a hold of yourself, and stop with the Marta Hari act!"

June took a sudden step forward, bringing her face only inches away from her husband's.

Without meaning to, Arthur took an instinctive step backwards, forgetting for the moment that their bed was directly behind him.

Losing his balance, Arthur crashed back onto the bed.

In one swift movement, June jumped on the bed and straddled him, pinning him to the mattress with a strength Arthur had never witnessed her having before.

As she lowered her face towards his, Arthur reeled back at the sight of his wife's features.

Her entire face had changed. It had somehow grown distorted and twisted and now appeared to resemble that of a large canine, rather than a woman.

June's eyes glowed bright red, like a poker just removed from a fire.

They bore into Arthur's with a ferocious hunger that caused him to try and pull back, but his efforts were without success.

June had him trapped beneath her.

The grip of her thighs was so tight that Arthur could not even manage to free his hands.

"Isn't this fun, darling?" June spoke with a voice that sounded unlike her own.

She opened her mouth and began to laugh, revealing two sets of razor-sharp fangs.

The stench of his wife's fetid breath from such close proximity reminded Arthur of the raw meat he had discovered in the kitchen.

Arthur opened his mouth to scream, but before the sound could leave his lips, June sank her enormous fangs into his neck and ripped out his vocal cords.

Jenna and Young poured over her uncle's scribblings for over two hours but achieved very little. Their task was not made any easier by the scruffy, almost indecipherable handwriting which seemed, to Young, anyway, to resemble ancient hieroglyphics as opposed to modern English.

They sat in a corner booth of a pub they'd discovered on the way back from Mary Cranley's house. They had chosen this particular booth because it was away from the main bar and had a large wooden table now covered with the contents of the file they had discovered in the professor's room.

From what they were able to ascertain, Jenna's uncle had come to Huntley to study some form of ancient cult. He'd mentioned spending hours scouting the local woods, mostly during the night, and links he had discovered between Huntley and an historic cult dating back to before medieval times, which apparently had the power to transform men into beasts.

The writing was littered with drawings and sketches, some of which depicted pentagrams with unrecognisable symbols embedded within them.

The individual pieces of paper did not appear to be in any specific order, which made trying to comprehend them even more difficult.

Finally, Jenna gave in. "This is hopeless," she sighed, pushing herself back from the table and lifting her glass to her mouth. She took a long swallow and allowed one of the melting ice cubes to slip past her lips. She played with it between her tongue and the roof of her mouth as she stared blankly at the littered table.

Young dropped the papers he had been holding, letting them fall where they wished. "Well," he said, trying to keep a cheerful tone, "I suppose your uncle was a doctor, if not a medical one, so he was entitled to have poor handwriting."

He could tell by Jenna's lack of appreciation that she was not in the mood for jokes.

The two of them sat there in silence for a moment.

Then, he had an idea. Turning to Jenna, he asked, "What about that colleague of your uncle's the landlady mentioned, do you think it might be worth me speaking to him? Perhaps he has some idea about why your uncle was down here to start with."

Jenna's eyes opened wide. "That's not a bad idea, Sherlock." Her words could so easily have sounded patronising, but instead, Young could tell that she genuinely approved of his idea.

Young flicked through his notebook until he found the man's name.

"Professor Pudelko," he read out for Jenna's benefit, "did your uncle ever mention him to you?"

Jenna shook her head. "No, but then to be honest, we hardly ever spoke about his work or his colleagues."

Young nodded. "If he's from the same university, he must be on their website."

"Way ahead of you this time," Jenna replied, already skimming through Google.

Young smiled to himself. The fresh excitement in Jenna's tone was a welcome change. Since he had picked her up from her hotel, Young had suspected that something was bothering her, but he did not want to pry, so he decided to let Jenna tell him what it was in her own time.

Her spirits had lifted a little when they first encountered her uncle's landlady, but once it became clear that she had very little to offer them by way of information, Jenna's mood grew melancholy once more.

"Here he is!" Jenna exclaimed excitedly. "Professor Marius Pudelko, he teaches folklore and mythology, apparently." Jenna skimmed through until she found a picture of the academic. She enlarged it to cover her screen before showing Young.

The picture showed a smiling, bald man with huge tufts of bushy grey-black hair on the sides of his head and a matching moustache.

Jenna quickly scanned his profile, but to her dismay, there was nothing specific to link him to her uncle.

Not surprisingly, the only contact details were to the university, and Jenna surmised that it was way too late to try calling now. It would have to wait until the morning, but at least it was a fresh direction.

On a whim, Jenna found the link to her uncle's university profile.

The sight of his warm and friendly, smiling visage brought a single tear to her eye.

She wiped it away absentmindedly before it had a chance to stream down her cheek.

The action was not wasted on Young, and he moved in closer and put his arm around her shoulder, giving her a tender squeeze.

Jenna turned to him and smiled.

For a moment, their eyes locked before Jenna took the initiative and leaned in for a kiss.

Young responded without hesitation.

They decided to stay at the pub for dinner. It was getting late, and as Jenna did not want to eat at her hotel, it saved them trying to hunt down a restaurant.

During their meal, Jenna's phone vibrated into life.

Chapter 16

She checked the screen, and naturally, it was Roger, so she terminated the call without answering.

Young looked at her. "Nuisance caller?" he asked.

Jenna shook her head. "No, not exactly, just someone from work I'd rather not get into a conversation with right now."

She felt bad for the lie, but she was not about to allow Roger to ruin their meal, and disclosing everything to Young here and now would definitely kill the mood.

To make sure they would not be disturbed, Jenna switched her mobile off and replaced it in her handbag.

She smiled at Young. "Out of sight," she said cheerily.

When Young dropped Jenna back at the Grange, they kissed and held each other in his car before he walked her to the main door.

Young did not ask if he could accompany her upstairs, and Jenna did not offer. But as she made her way upstairs, their evening gave Jenna a sense of happiness she had almost forgotten existed.

As she approached the room of the couple with the little boy, Jenna almost felt as if she should remove her shoes and creep past. But she checked herself for being stupid and carried on to her room without interruption.

So much had happened this evening, the incident with the little boy and his parents seemed to her as if they had taken place days, instead of hours, ago.

Once inside her room, Jenna switched her phone back on.

As she suspected, there were several messages from Roger waiting.

She slumped down on her bed and kicked off her shoes. She was feeling drowsy and certainly not in the mood for another showdown.

The problem was, she knew that Roger would not give up so easily. He was like a spoilt brat who could not have his own way, and as much as she refused to pander to him, she did not want to have to keep her phone permanently switched off whenever she was with Young.

Sooner or later, it would become a little too obvious that she was hiding something.

Sighing, Jenna cancelled the outstanding messages.

She was too tired for an argument and far too happy to allow Roger to spoil that.

Chapter Seventeen

When Jenna awoke the following morning, her first thought was to call her uncle's colleague and try and find some answers. But when she glanced at her phone, she discovered it was only seven thirty, and she realised that it was too early to bother trying.

Instead, she decided to call Roger and demand that he stopped harassing her. But even as she began to scroll through her contacts, Jenna realised that phoning him was probably not the best idea.

For one thing, it would give him an excuse to plead with her for forgiveness, and she really did not want to hear his whiny voice this early in the morning.

Instead, she opted for a text. Short, succinct, and above all, leaving no room for ambiguity.

Roger, please stop calling me!
I do not wish to see you again!
I have nothing more to say to you!
Goodbye!

The minute Jenna pressed send, she made her way to the

bathroom and took a long, hot shower. The pumping water helped to clear her head and let her focus on the day ahead.

Whilst under the hot stream, Jenna could hear her mobile ringing. She knew that it had to be Roger in reply to her text, but she had already decided that whatever his reply was, she was not interested.

After drying herself off, Jenna checked her phone, and sure enough, Roger had left her a message. Jenna cancelled it without bothering to listen to what he had to say.

Once she was dressed, Jenna went down to breakfast.

While she ate, the family with the boy who had fondled her came into the restaurant. Upon seeing her, the father guided them towards a table at the far end of the room.

Jenna watched them as they made their way to their table.

The little boy turned back and looked straight at Jenna, but his mother, upon noticing, quickly scolded him and made him turn back.

Jenna decided to concentrate on her newspaper instead of bothering with them.

There was no sign of Audrey this morning, which was a blessing. Jenna was not in the mood for listening to her inane banter. Now she thought about it, it did seem odd that the hotelier had not pounced on her the previous evening when she'd arrived back at the hotel.

Perhaps, Jenna surmised, Audrey had finally taken the hint.

After breakfast, as it was still too early to call the university, Jenna sat out on her balcony and went through her uncle's papers once more. In the dazzling sunlight of a new day, she hoped that she might make more progress in deciphering his handwriting than she and Young had the previous evening. But she soon gave up in frustration and placed the papers neatly back into their folder for safekeeping.

Checking the time, she saw that it was almost nine o'clock.

Chapter 17

She could wait no longer. The phone on the other end rang three times before it was answered.

"Good morning, West Central University, how may I help?" The female on the other end sounded bright and professional, which Jenna took to be a good sign.

"Yes, I was wondering if you could please help me, my name is Jenna Wilkinson, and I'm the niece of Professor Gerald Cross, one of your lecturers."

"Yes, madam."

Jenna realised now that she should have made a mental note of what she intended to say before calling. She needed to convey her urgency at wanting to speak to her uncle's colleague without sounding too desperate in case the receptionist took her for an annoying student trying to bother one of their faculty.

"I was wondering if by chance I could speak to a Professor Pudelko?" Jenna turned the file over where she had made a note of the professor's name. "You see, he's a friend as well as a colleague of my uncle's and…well, I really need to speak to him."

There was a pause on the other end.

Jenna could hear the woman breathing down the phone while she contemplated Jenna's request. From her own experience, Jenna knew that the majority of lecturers in universities had specific hours in the week where they were willing to speak to students, and anything outside those hours was strictly taboo.

Finally, the woman responded. "I'm afraid we do not give out lecturers' personal numbers, but I can patch you through to his office number if you would care to leave him a message?"

Jenna sighed. She should have realised that this would be the best offer she was likely to receive.

"I wonder," she ventured, "would you happen to know if the professor is in today? I only ask because if he's not, I'll be waiting by the phone all day for a reply I'm not likely to receive."

"Just a moment, I'll check for you." The line switched to classical music while Jenna waited. After a few moments, the woman cut back in. "Sorry to have kept you. He is due in today. He has two lectures this afternoon, so he should receive your message at some point."

It was better than nothing.

"Thank you," replied Jenna, "in that case, would you please put me through to his office?"

"Certainly." The line switched back to the music for a couple of seconds before a gruff male voice with an eastern European accent came on the line.

Jenna waited for the bleep and quickly explained who she was and the fact that her uncle was missing. She repeated her mobile number twice into the phone before the machine cut her off.

Jenna sat there for a while thinking.

She could feel the anxiety of the situation starting to form a knot in her stomach, and she knew that she was not going to be able to just sit around all day waiting for the professor to return her call.

Jenna called Young.

When he answered, he sounded genuinely happy to be hearing from her.

Jenna decided not to waste any time.

"Hi," she said, "how do you fancy a trip to London?"

Once he had overcome his initial shock at the request, Jenna explained to him about her call to the university and the fact that she knew Pudelko would be there that afternoon.

Unlike Jenna, Young considered it more prudent to wait for the professor to get back to her himself, but he soon realised that Jenna had made up her mind, and he had the choice of either going with her or leaving her to go alone.

Chapter 17

Eventually, he gave in. "Ok," he declared, "you win, I've just arrived at the station, and I need to check in with my guvnor, so I'll pick you up in about half an hour, ok?"

Jenna was more than pleased that Young had agreed to accompany her.

For one thing, she really did not want to face a drive into London and back again by herself. Added to which, she thought that if Pudelko was reluctant to speak to her for some reason, then the added weight of Young's authority might be just what was needed to persuade him otherwise.

After all, he had not sounded like the most approachable individual over the phone.

An hour into the drive, Jenna's mobile went off.

Presuming it was Roger again, she almost cut off the call without looking, but fortunately for her, she glanced at the screen first and saw that it was an unknown number.

"Hello," she said hesitantly, thinking it was probably from one of those annoying telesales companies.

"Oh, good morning, may I please speak with Miss Jenna Wilkinson?"

She recognised the voice from the answering machine.

"Speaking, is that Professor Pudelko?"

"Yes, it is, you are Gerald's niece?"

Jenna felt a sudden wave of relief flow over her. The fact that the professor had called her back so soon was certainly a good sign, to her, and he sounded friendlier now than he had on his voice message.

Without holding back, Jenna launched straight into her reason for contacting him.

"That's right, professor, I am really concerned about my uncle. He appears to be missing, and I was wondering if you might be able to shed any light on where he might be."

There was a slight pause before the old man continued.

"Where are you now, Miss Wilkinson?"

"Well, actually, I'm on my way to the university now. I'm driving down from Huntley, where I've been staying whilst trying to find out what's happened to my uncle."

"I see, well, in that case, I will leave some papers at reception for you to read before we meet. I have a couple of lectures to give this afternoon, but I should be finished by about four o'clock. Is that convenient for you?"

"That will be fine, thank you so much, professor, I really appreciate you taking the time to speak to me."

They reached the university a little after one thirty. Parking was horrendous, and after driving around several times trying to find a spot, Young suggested that he wait in the car while Jenna went in and retrieved the papers the professor had left for her.

While he was waiting, a traffic warden approached him. Young dropped his window and flashed his badge, which the warden eyed suspiciously before grunting to himself and continuing on his way.

Jenna emerged from the reception a few moments later clutching a manila envelope under her arm.

They decided to try and find somewhere in the vicinity where they could sift through the documents whilst waiting for the professor to finish his lectures.

Eventually, Young found an NCP car park a couple of streets away from the university. The lunch-time crowds were in full swing, but luckily, they came across a sandwich bar with tables large enough for their venture.

Having ordered their food, Jenna began to spread the papers, which were all photocopies taken from various books, across their table for them to examine.

From the headings of each sheet, it appeared as if the copies had been taken from three separate books: Copenhien's Forgotten World, the Chillicoathe Encyclopaedia of Arcane Knowledge, and European Witch Trials of the Sixteenth and Seventeenth Century.

Jenna and Young exchanged glances as they each picked up a sheet and began to read.

Jenna's sheet was entitled: Tribes of the Moon. It described how an explorer named Hissaner discovered the tribe whilst on an expedition in China at the turn of the twelfth century. The article described how the explorer and his team observed the tribe's ritualistic dances from a safe distance and how after several hours certain members of the tribe appeared to sprout thick black hair all over their bodies.

The article included what purported to be actual diary entries made at the exact time Hissaner and his team witnessed the spectacle. It mentioned how the tribe seemed to possess boundless energy, and after several hours of them dancing without stopping, their movements were still filled with fervour and verve.

The explorer then went on to write that as time passed, some of the tribe began to crawl around on all fours and that their chanting grew low and guttural.

By this point, several members of the team had expressed their concerns about what they were witnessing, and more than half had already decided to leave.

It was at this point that Hissaner made a decision that resulted in catastrophe.

Jenna read the passage out to Young, keeping her voice low so as not to attract any unwanted attention.

"I ordered one of the less reluctant members of my party to invade the
 gathering, although in my defence, this was purely for scientific
 interest, to ascertain how they would react to an outsider joining their
 party.

Nothing could have prepared me for the result!

Before my man had reached the outskirts of their camp, he was detected, and attacked in a most frenzied manner.

The group set upon him like a pack of wild animals, and before any of us had a chance to use our rifles to scare them off, they had ripped my colleague apart with their bare hands, and began to devour him."

They looked at each other in shock.

"What do you make of that?" Young enquired.

Jenna shrugged her shoulders. "No idea," she replied.

"What relevance do you think it has to your uncle's work?"

Jenna bit her bottom lip. "None, I hope."

They continued to read in silence. All around them the tables were slowly vacated as office workers and passing trade went back about their business after lunch.

Eventually, there was no one else sitting within four or five tables' distance from Jenna and Young. This privacy encouraged Young to read out one of the entries he had just finished, taken from the book on witchcraft.

"During the fifteenth and sixteenth centuries, the belief in witches and werewolves reached epidemic proportions throughout Europe, resulting in those accused being either burned or hanged, usually without a proper trial.

Over time, it was believed that those whom the devil had marked
for his own, he would first make mad. So, it was not unheard of that
those who suffered from common medical ailments, might well
be deemed a witch or werewolf, and dealt with accordingly."

Young expelled a long breath through his teeth before continuing to read.

"In France alone, over 30,000 cases appertaining to those
accused of being werewolves were documented between 1520 and 1630. All of which ended with the accused either being hanged or burned alive."

There then followed a list of some of the more well-known cases throughout history.

"In Dijon, 1573, Gaston Gillis was burned at the stake after a
couple of sheep belonging to a neighbouring farmer were found
with their throats ripped out. Gillis had an ongoing dispute with
his accuser over some pasture, but this evidence was not submitted
at his trial.
In 1598, a half-wit named Rolland St Jacques was found cowering

under a bush by a gang of vigilantes who were hunting a wolf seen in the vicinity. Due to his unkempt appearance, and the fact that dried blood was found encrusted under his fingernails, St Jacques was strung up by the men from the nearest tree.

In Bordeaux in 1608, a young boy named Gerard Jeanier exposed himself to several children in the village. When asked why he had done so, he apparently replied that he had made a pact with Lucifer, and that he had been turned into a werewolf.

At his trial, Jeanier described in graphic detail stories of how he had captured and eaten several children he had found alone in his father's field.

He also told of an incident when he broke into a cottage in the next Village during darkness, and stole away a baby from its crib, which he later sacrificed to his master.

Upon investigation, it was reported that a baby had indeed been snatched during the night whilst the parents slept, so because of his age, it was decided that he would be confined to an asylum.

But one night, about a week after his confinement, his guards were alerted by a horrific scream, and when they came upon the scene, they discovered young Jeanier crouching over one of the other inmates, ripping flesh from the man's neck with his teeth.

In their panic, the guards shot him dead. Their reports later stated that, at the time of discovery, Jeanier no longer resembled human form, and instead had taken on the guise of a wolf.

However, they also reported that upon killing him, his body changed back into that of a human child."

When Young finished reading, he turned to Jenna. She could tell immediately what he was thinking, but he hesitated before he began to speak.

"Remind me again what field your uncle is in?"

Jenna sighed. "Anthropology...or so I thought. He's never mentioned any interest to me in witches and werewolves, or any of this stuff."

"But there must be a reason Pudelko has given us these articles to read," Young concluded. "Do you think it's possible he and your uncle were carrying out some kind of investigation into cults, or...I don't know, satanic covens, or something?"

Jenna scratched her head. "If he was, then this is the first I'm hearing about it. But my uncle was a serious scholar, an academic, not some nutcase scouring the countryside like some modern-day Van Helsing. He wouldn't get mixed up in nonsense like this!"

Young pondered over the remaining papers before them. He reshuffled those they had already read into a separate pile. There appeared to be almost as many still to read as they had already finished with.

Young checked his watch. There was still an hour before they had to meet with the professor.

"Shall we continue, we still have time?" he asked, deciding it was best to put the ball firmly in Jenna's court.

Jenna pouted. "I really hope that when we speak with the professor, he can shed some serious light on all this. Please, god, don't let him be a fruitcake."

Young laughed, holding his hand over his mouth.

The sight of him caused Jenna to smile. It felt good.

"Tell you what," Young suggested, "how about I get us a refill, then we finish off these last pages. After all, the professor did go through the trouble of collating them for us. Let's just hope when we meet him, it will all make sense."

Jenna nodded and slid her empty mug across the table to him.

"Fingers crossed, eh?" She smiled.

Chapter Eighteen

JENNA AND YOUNG CONTINUED TO READ THE REST OF the reports supplied by Professor Pudelko. By ten to four they had finally finished the last article, so they set off to meet with the lecturer.

They waited in the foyer of the university until Pudelko came to collect them.

When he arrived, Jenna was surprised by his appearance. From the sound of his voice on the phone she had imagined a tall, slim man with wavy black hair. But instead, the professor was a short, stout individual who was completely bald on top, with tufts of wild grey hair at the sides of his head and a drooping moustache, which made him appear to Jenna like a circus strongman from years gone by.

His glasses were wire-framed and sat perched on the end of his nose.

After introductions were made, he signed them in at reception and took them up to his office.

Once inside, Pudelko closed the door and invited them both to sit down.

The tiny office was decked out with wall-to-wall bookshelves buckling under the weight of textbooks. There were even a couple of piles of them stacked in a corner of the room.

The professor took his seat behind his desk and offered them both a drink, which they declined.

"So," began Pudelko, "I take it you have read through the items I left for you?"

Jenna nodded, holding up the file. "We have, professor, but to be honest, I'm a little bemused as to the relevance concerning my uncle."

The professor nodded. "Of course, I understand. I presume that your uncle never mentioned me before?"

"I'm sorry, he didn't." Jenna felt a little awkward at her admission, so she quickly added, "But to be honest, we hardly ever discussed his work at home."

Pudelko leaned forward on his desk, looking directly at Jenna.

"I am sorry to have to inform you of this, especially as we have only just met. But I have a strong feeling of foreboding that your uncle, my great friend and colleague, may have met with foul play."

At this remark, Young moved forward in his seat. "Can you be a little more precise, professor?"

When they had met at reception, Jenna had merely introduced Young as a friend. They both agreed that revealing his actual involvement might make Pudelko wary of telling all he knew.

"You are, I take it, familiar with your uncle's field of expertise?" Pudelko asked, switching his gaze back to Jenna.

"Yes, he's a PhD in anthropology," replied Jenna.

The professor nodded. "Yes, that's quite right, but over the years his passion has become the main focus of his research, and unlike many colleagues in the field, he was also willing to write and lecture on his findings and observations."

Jenna was starting to grow confused. "I'm sorry, professor, what 'passion' are you referring to, exactly?"

Pudelko scratched his head as if he was searching for the right words to use. "Let me explain, my field of expertise is mythology and folklore, that is what I lecture on here at the university. For several years now, your uncle and I have been involved in research that has delved into some ancient cults that, if legend is to be believed, thrived on the notion of werewolves actually existing."

Jenna and Young turned to each other, each wearing an expression of disbelief.

When they turned back to face Pudelko, he was already holding his hands up, as if expecting a barrage of questions.

"Please," he began, "let me start at the beginning, perhaps then this might all make some sense to you both."

They settled back in their chairs, waiting for the professor to begin.

"Several years ago, I was sent some information from a colleague of mine concerning a lost tribe known as the Lycanas. They were originally mentioned in some ancient scrolls from Africa some three hundred years before the birth of Christ. All records of them disappeared, or were lost, until 500 AD. After that, they seemed to vanish once more without trace, until the twelfth century, when they were rumoured to be existing somewhere in the orient."

Pudelko reached down and opened his desk drawer, extricating a large, blue ring binder. He began to turn the plastic folders within the binder slowly and carefully until he found what he was looking for.

He slipped a folded piece of paper out of its sleeve and opened it up on the desk so that they could all see it.

It appeared to Jenna and Young to be a hand-drawn map.

"It was right about here," Pudelko pointed to a small patch of land, no bigger than a pound coin, "on this tiny island in the

Caribbean that my colleague discovered evidence of their existence."

Pudelko looked up momentarily to ensure that both Young and Jenna were following his tale.

Satisfied that he had their full attention, he continued. "You see, this tribe were originally part of an ancient order of moon worshipers. From what little was documented about them, they were a fairly harmless bunch to begin with. No human sacrifices or anything of that nature. That was until approximately five hundred years ago, when one of the elders decided he was going to make a pact with the devil."

Jenna felt herself gulp unintentionally. She was not at all happy with where this story was leading, but she knew she had to persevere, as the professor was their only viable link to what might possibly have become of her uncle.

"Legend has it," continued Pudelko, "that the elder ventured up into the mountains, and there he was actually visited by the prince of darkness himself, who turned him into a wolf. It was written that he returned to the tribe and proceeded to bite certain members, who themselves then transformed into wolves, and devoured those amongst them who had initially objected to their elder's pact with the devil."

The professor cleared his throat. All this talking after completing two lectures earlier that afternoon had obviously left him feeling dry.

He opened a drawer on the other side of his desk and removed a half empty bottle of whiskey, placing it on the desk.

He looked at his guests. "Are you sure I can't tempt either of you to a small Scotch?"

They both declined politely.

Pudelko grabbed a coffee cup from the cabinet behind him and poured himself a large measure. He took a drink and held his hand over his mouth as he belched quietly.

"Oh, excuse me." He looked at Jenna, clearly embarrassed.

"Now, where was I?" He continued to turn over the plastic sheets in his folder until he found the one that he was looking for. "Ah, here we go, now, according to the findings my colleague unearthed, over time these Lycanas made their way throughout central Europe, laying waste to entire communities. They developed the ability to change their forms from human to wolf at will. Until finally they merged more in the guise of what we might consider werewolves, that is to say, half human, half wolf."

Once again, Jenna and Young caught themselves looking quizzically at each other. The professor appeared to be completely forthright in what he was telling them, and yet, it still sounded too far-fetched to either of them to be taken seriously.

"Professor," ventured Young, "I've heard of this disease before, where someone thinks that they can turn themselves into a werewolf. But it's a medical condition, isn't it?"

The professor nodded. "You are correct, my boy," he commended him. "What you are thinking of is lycanthropy, which is indeed a disease of the mind which has been well documented over the years. I believe that some of the articles I gave you mentioned various cases throughout history."

Jenna nodded. "Yes, usually about some poor demented creature who confessed to being a wolf, even though it was probably all in their minds."

"Well, lycanthropy is not to be confused with what I'm talking about here!"

Both Jenna and Young looked shocked.

"Lycanthropy is a condition which still exists today, but in every modern documented case, there is no evidence that the sufferer actually transforms him or herself into a wolf. You see, it all takes place in their fevered imaginations."

"So, are you saying that this tribe, these Lycanas, did not suffer from this condition, and that they had the power to turn themselves into wolves at will?" Jenna sounded far sterner than she had intended, but she was growing tired of hearing about cults and werewolves and was beginning to think that this journey had been a waste of time.

Pudelko placed his elbows on the desk. He removed his glasses and rubbed his eyes several times before replacing them.

"All I can tell you for definite is what I know. This is all based purely on research and documentation, but naturally, there has to be a certain amount of speculation thrown in. After all, a lot of what we know, or think we know, is the result of tales being told and re-told over generations, so we must accept that a modicum of hearsay will creep in."

Young placed a comforting hand on Jenna's. He could tell from her tone that she was growing impatient with what the professor was telling them.

More to the point, there was still no correlation between what the old man was saying and the disappearance of her uncle.

"Professor," Young began, "please forgive me if I sound like a non-believer, I realise that this is your area of expertise, but nothing you have told us so far seems in any way connected to Jenna's uncle's disappearance."

The old man nodded his understanding. "Have either of you ever heard of the village of Monk's Hood?" he asked, looking from one to the other.

They both shook their heads.

"It was a small village in rural England back in medieval times. The name Monk's Hood is another name for the poisonous plant wolfsbane, which in those days people believed only grew during a full moon during harvest time and that it's appearance signalled an imminent attack by werewolves."

"And someone named a village after it, charming," Jenna chimed in.

"And with good reason," replied Pudelko. "You see, about

three hundred years ago, Monk's Hood was considered by many to be the nucleus of devil worship and satanic masses in England. The villagers themselves, those that were unlucky enough to live there, would not venture out after dark for fear of being attacked and sacrificed to Beelzebub."

"And was there any evidence of such rituals taking place?" Jenna asked.

"Why, yes," replied Pudelko, "in fact, due to the reputation of the area, anyone who believed themselves to be a servant of the devil congregated there to join with other like-minded individuals, to pledge their loyalty to the dark one."

"So, what happened?" Young asked, hoping this was leading somewhere.

"One night, the local baron who owned the land grew so fed up with his holding's poor reputation that he gathered together a band of about forty soldiers and leading men of the cloth, and together they rode into Monk's Hood and attacked and killed anyone they caught holding any kind of ritualistic gathering. Once the carnage had ceased, the baron led the churchmen through the village so that they could bless the ground and exorcise any evil that might be present. In time, the baron built a church for the village, and eventually more people began to live and work there, and it thrived."

"So where is this village now?" asked Jenna. "I've never heard of it."

The old man smiled knowingly. "That is because the villagers decided to re-name the village after the baron who had saved them, and his name was Huntley!"

Young sat up in his chair. "What, you mean the town I live in used to be this Monk's Hood village?"

"That's quite correct," answered the professor, "and what's more, my colleague's research led him to believe that the Lycanas were planning to set up a commune there, which is why, I'm afraid," he turned to Jenna with an apologetic expression on his face, "your uncle was visiting the town to gather evidence which we could present at the next Royal Society meeting."

"But…That doesn't prove anything," Jenna stated, clearly exasperated. "Just because my uncle went on this wild goose chase of yours, you can't be sure this tribe even exists."

Pudelko removed his spectacles and placed them on the desk.

"You're perfectly right, my dear," he offered sympathetically. "But from the information my colleague sent me, I can only conclude that the threat of their existence is extremely likely. Your uncle was certainly convinced of their presence; that's why he agreed to go down there to investigate."

"And what about this colleague of yours who sent you all the information? Why didn't he go down and investigate it himself?" Jenna demanded.

Pudelko shifted uncomfortably in his chair before answering.

"Unfortunately, my dear, I lost contact with my colleague several weeks ago. I very much fear that he, too, has become a victim of the Lycanas."

Chapter Nineteen

JENNA DID NOT SPEAK ON THE WAY BACK TO THE CAR. Young concluded her mind was probably trying to cope with Pudelko's summation that something bad had happened to her uncle.

Deep down, he suspected that Jenna had already considered the possibility, but having heard it directly from the professor obviously gave the idea more gravitas.

As they were about to cross over to the car park, Young slipped his arm around her shoulders and gave Jenna a gentle squeeze. She turned to him and gave a half-smile of thanks, but he could tell her mind was elsewhere.

As they drove out of the car park, Young indicated right and waited for a gap in the traffic to allow him to join the flow. The early evening traffic was already growing heavy, and he envisioned a slow journey back to the motorway.

Just then, Jenna shot out her hand and placed it on the one Young had hovering over the gear stick.

"Sorry, Alan," she began, "do you mind if we head over to the flat first? There are a couple of things I'd like to get before we head back to Huntley."

Young smiled. "No problem, which way from here?"

Jenna guided him to her uncle's flat.

As they turned into her street, Jenna's heart dropped.

"Oh, no, I don't believe this!" She did not try to hide her disappointment.

"What's the matter?" asked Young, searching for a convenient space to park.

Jenna buried her head in her hands.

She had recognised Roger's car the moment they turned the corner.

Her mind raced.

Would it be better to drive on and just head back to Huntley, she wondered? After all, Roger had not seen them. He would not know Young's car, so there was no reason for him to pay it any notice. They could just keep on driving, and that would be the end of it.

For now, at least!

Jenna knew that she should have realised that he was not going to be that easy to get rid of, especially after the last time she attempted it.

But this was the last thing she needed, having just received the terrible news from Professor Pudelko.

Young began to slow down as a vacant space came into sight.

Jenna grabbed his wrist. "I'm sorry, Alan," she stammered, "there's something I need to tell you before we go in." She gazed down the road past her uncle's place. "Look, there's a space further up, could we please park there instead?"

Young was confused by her sudden request, but he acquiesced without questioning her.

Jenna glanced through her fingers as they drove past Roger's car, just to make sure he was inside. Sure enough, she made out his form behind the wheel. He was looking up at the window of her bedroom.

She had never given him a key to her uncle's place, and now she was more grateful for that fact than at any time in the past.

Roger had asked on more than one occasion, but Jenna had remained firm, claiming that as it was not her place, she did not feel right giving out spare keys. He'd seemed to accept the situation once he discovered that no one else had one, either.

Jenna did not dare tell him that she had given one to Trish in case of emergencies.

Young pulled into the new spot and killed the engine.

He released his seatbelt and turned to face Jenna.

"Is everything ok?" he asked, not attempting to disguise the concern in his voice.

Jenna sighed deeply. "I haven't been completely honest with you, Alan, and I'm afraid now is not the best time, but my hand is sort of being forced, so I need to come clean."

Young tried not to look overly concerned, but he could not disguise his disappointment.

After their kiss the previous evening, Young had hoped that something more serious might develop between them. He knew in his heart that, technically, he should not become involved with someone attached to an investigation, but under the circumstances, he had been willing to risk it.

Now he knew that Jenna was about to reveal that she was married. Or possibly engaged to her childhood sweetheart. Or maybe she already had kids from a previous relationship, and that was what she had been keeping from him.

Of the three possible scenarios, the third one sounded the most promising.

So, what if she did have children?

It was not the ideal scenario, but if he was serious about entering into a relationship with Jenna, then he should be able to accept her as she was, family and all.

It was odd that he had only realised in the last few minutes that he was serious about wanting to be with her.

But he knew he had to keep himself guarded, just in case the situation really did involve either of the first two scenarios he had considered.

"Go on," he replied calmly, "I'm listening."

Jenna took a deep breath.

She told Young all about Roger, making sure that she emphasized the part about breaking up with him and informing him that she never wanted to see him again.

As she spoke, Young could feel his insides relax. Things were nowhere near as problematic as he had led himself to believe.

When she had finished her story, Jenna looked at Young to try and ascertain his response.

The look in his eyes told her everything she needed to know.

Jenna leaned in towards him, and Young met her halfway.

They kissed like excited teenagers after a first date.

Once they parted, Young asked, "So how do you want to play this?"

Jenna tuned to look behind her. She could just see the edge of Roger's car sticking out. She wondered for a moment how long he had been sitting there waiting for her to return.

Considering she had told him that she was staying in Huntley, she had never imagined finding him here, otherwise she would have probably just told Young to take her back to her hotel instead.

But a part of her was glad that Roger's presence had forced her into revealing the truth to Young.

She certainly felt better for it.

The question now was, as Young asked, how did she want to play this out? Driving off and heading back to Huntley was a coward's way of doing things. Although it would solve her present dilemma with the minimum of fuss.

But Jenna was tired of letting Roger rule her existence, and it seemed obvious to her now that she would have to face him sooner or later.

Chapter 19

Far better, she thought, with Young by her side.

"Come on," she said, giving Young a final peck. "Once more into the breech, and all that."

They crossed the road together, hand in hand. It was Jenna who had reached out to grab Young, and he was happy to follow her lead.

They were already halfway up the stone steps that led to the front door of the block before they heard Roger calling out to Jenna from behind.

They stopped and turned around.

"Jenna, what's going on here!" Roger demanded, looking at their linked hands. "I've been trying to call you for days, who the hell is this?"

"This is…" Before Jenna had a chance to complete her sentence, Young whipped out his warrant card.

"DC Young, Huntley police," he stated in his firmest, most professional police tone.

The sight of his identification, and his introduction, made Roger halt in his tracks. He eyed Young's ID card suspiciously for a moment before looking back up at him.

"Oh, I see." Roger cleared his throat. "Well, thank you for your assistance, officer, but I'm here now, so if you don't mind…"

Roger climbed another step towards Jenna, purposely avoiding Young, who stood firm as he replaced his warrant card in his inside pocket.

As Roger was about to reach out for Jenna, she took a step back so that she was now behind Young.

She placed her hand on his shoulder.

"Roger, let's not make this any more awkward than it already is. You know full well why I haven't returned your calls. I think I made my position quite clear on the phone."

"But you haven't given me a chance to explain," Roger whined, holding out his hand towards Jenna. "Perhaps if we just went inside and talked, we could clear up this entire mis-understanding."

"There is no misunderstanding, Roger!" Jenna snapped, still using Young as a shield between them. "Now I want you to go, please, just leave me alone!"

"But honey..." Roger went to take another step up towards Jenna, but this time Young moved to block his path.

"I think the lady has asked for you to leave!" he stated, staring directly into Roger's eyes.

"This is nothing to do with you, now move out of my way or I'll report you to your superiors!" Roger's voice was wavering slightly, but his demeanour was one of someone who was still in charge.

Young was not prepared to allow Roger any more slack.

He took a step down so that they were now only one step apart.

"If you do not do as the lady requests right this minute, I will arrest you for harassment!"

Roger began shaking with rage and indignation.

His eyes grew to the size of bowling balls and seemed to Jenna as if they might actually pop out of their sockets.

"How dare you!" Roger stormed. "Do you realise who I am?"

Young raised his eyes to heaven. He had lost track of how many times he had heard those very words during the course of his duty.

Some of the neighbours had come out of their properties to see what all the commotion was about, and several bystanders had started to gather across the street.

This was the last thing Jenna wanted, and she could feel herself trying to sneak behind Young to conceal her identity.

"My mother knows the Chief Constable!" Roger continued, somewhat taken aback by Young's lack of concern at his earlier threat.

"What's more," he continued, trying desperately to puff out

his chest, "you're out of your jurisdiction, officer, you have no authority here!"

Roger's voice was rising in both volume and pitch, which did nothing to aid Jenna's attempts to remain undetected. As she watched, she could see more curtains twitching as their owners' inquisitiveness became too much to bear.

Young laughed at Roger's suggestion. "Oh, really, so you think when an officer of the law is outside of his remit he would just sit back and allow a crime to take place?"

Roger snorted several times as if trying to think of a suitable answer.

"Now, I am going to say this only once more," confirmed Young, his unwavering gaze still directed at Roger. "If you do not do as this lady requests and move away from here, right this minute, I will have no option but to slap my handcuffs on you, in front of all these lovely people," he gestured with his hand to elucidate to Roger that they now had an audience, "and drag you down to the local station for the evening."

Roger turned his head both ways to see what Young was alluding to.

When he saw the crowds gathered, his cheeks flushed crimson.

He knew his mother would never approve of him causing such a scene, and if he ended up having to call her to release him from a cell… It was too much for him to even contemplate.

He turned back to face Young.

Looking past him, he tried to offer Jenna one of his most practised pleading looks, but he could tell that she was not about to break this time.

He looked back at Young.

Roger waved his index finger at the officer. "Don't think for a moment that this is over!"

Before Young had a chance to retaliate, Roger spun around and walked down the stone steps towards his car.

He stared directly at a couple across the road from his vehicle before climbing in. "Yes?" he demanded.

The couple turned to each other, and the man said something that made the woman laugh and slap him on the arm.

Roger slipped in behind the wheel and drove off without looking back.

Jenna could feel the embarrassment seeping into her cheeks.

She reached out for Young's hand and pulled him after her as she made her way up to the front door.

Once inside, she pulled Young towards her, and they both held each other for a moment.

When they broke apart, Young said, "Sorry about all that. He doesn't take no for an answer, does he?"

Jenna kissed him on the lips. "Please don't apologise, he needed putting in his place. Now maybe he'll get the message and leave me alone."

They climbed the stairs to her uncle's flat.

Jenna was sure that she heard some of her neighbours' doors being closed as carefully as possible as they made their way up.

While Jenna packed herself some fresh underwear and clean clothes, Young made them both a strong coffee to fortify them on the journey back to Huntley.

Once they were back on the motorway, all thoughts of Roger and his outburst seemed far behind and long ago, and Jenna was grateful for that.

While they drove, Jenna reached behind to the back seat and retrieved the cardboard folder Pudelko had given them as they left his office.

He had stated that the contents included some more information on the cult her uncle was investigating, and he had graciously asked Jenna to let him know if there was ever anything that he could do for her.

His kind word had softened Jenna's resentment against the man for sending her uncle on this mission in the first place, and she had taken his offered hand and promised him that she would inform him if she heard anything from her uncle.

She could tell from his expression that the old man was truly sorry for any harm that might have befallen his colleague, and Jenna had been sure that she could see a tear forming in the corner of the professor's eye as he spoke.

As it was already growing dark, Jenna could not make out enough of the text contained in the photocopies within the folder to read them in their entirety. But she was still able to make out some of what was written, especially those articles which were in a clearer font.

While she sifted through the contents, Jenna and Young talked aimlessly about what they should do for dinner.

Suddenly, Jenna sat up in her seat and held out a stack of papers in front of her, as if she was trying to distinguish what was on them from the dim light outside the windscreen.

Young kept his focus on the road ahead.

The motorway was fairly busy, and he was already wary of some of the drivers in front of him who appeared a trifle overzealous when it came to the use of their brakes.

"What's the matter?" he asked, glancing quickly over at the papers in Jenna's hand.

"I know this woman!" Jenna stated confidently. "I'm sure I've seen her in Huntley."

Young was tempted to pull over onto the hard shoulder so that he could see who Jenna was talking about. But he decided to keep going, as it was not life or death that he looked right at that moment.

"Who is she?" he asked, his focus back on the cars ahead.

Jenna shook her head. "I can't be a hundred percent sure; this is a very poor-quality print, but I'd swear the woman in this picture runs a little book shop in town. I popped in there the other day to take cover from the rain."

She was about to mention that she had seen June Le Vant in the shop but decided there was no need.

"Really," replied Young, sounding confused. "But what is she doing in amongst all those articles the professor gave us?"

Jenna strained to read the details below the caption. "According to this, she is suspected of being part of that cult the professor said my uncle was investigating." Jenna thought for a moment, then continued. "Oh, my god, and I was standing just a few feet from her; she seemed perfectly normal, charming in fact!"

"Are you sure it's her?" Young tried to keep any scepticism he had out of his tone. "I mean, how long were you with her for? Long enough to recognise her in a line-up, or at least in a dodgy photocopy?"

Jenna studied the print once more.

Then she said, "I'm sure it's her." She turned to face Young. "But I need to see her again, just to make sure."

Young threw her a quick sideways glance. "Now, hold on just a minute. If it is her, and she's got something to do with this cult business, then I'm the one who needs to speak to her, not you. The last thing we want is her knowing that you are related to the man who's been investigating them."

"But if she is," Jenna protested, "then she might know where my uncle is, and if he's still alive."

Young nodded. "I realise that, but by the same token, if she is part of this cult, then we know how dangerous they are, and it wouldn't be safe for you to just barge in there and start demanding answers from her."

Jenna was frustrated by Young's retort, but she knew he was right.

Either way, this was a lead at least, and right now, the first one they had discovered since her uncle went missing, and Jenna was determined to make sure that she had the right woman, regardless.

Chapter Twenty

As they turned off the motorway for Huntley, Young turned to Jenna.

"Are you hungry?" he asked, glancing over at her once he was sure there was nothing ahead.

Jenna nodded. "Peckish more than hungry. I can't stop thinking about that woman in the book shop and wondering if she knows anything about my uncle's disappearance."

Young changed gear, then allowed his hand to slide off the gear stick and rest momentarily on Jenna's thigh.

She covered his hand with hers and gave it a gentle squeeze.

"Let's try and not think about her tonight," suggested Young. "Tomorrow, I promise you, I will interview her, and if she does know anything, I will ferret it out of her, even if it involves taking her in for a formal interview."

Jenna smiled at him, then leaned across and kissed him on the cheek.

She trusted him, and she knew that he would stand by his word. It was just hard for her to appreciate that he was constrained by procedure and protocol, whereas she just wanted to get to the bottom of her uncle's disappearance.

"I'm sure I can talk Audrey into giving us a quiet little booth away from the masses. She makes a wicked toasted cheese and ham," suggested Young.

Jenna frowned. "You know, I hate to say it, but I think that woman is a tad too inquisitive for my liking, and that place is just...weird!"

"How do you mean, weird?" asked Young quizzically.

Jenna took a deep breath. "Well, I wasn't going to say anything to you, mainly because I did not want you thinking I was going crazy, but yesterday morning I was assaulted by a kid outside my door."

Young immediately pulled the car over and parked on the soft verge beside the road.

"Are you being serious?" he asked, clearly shaken by her statement. "Tell me what happened!"

"It's gonna sound stupid, but I was leaving my room to meet you, and when I opened my door there was this little boy standing there. He's staying there with his terribly conservative parents. I was so shocked to see him that I dropped my keys, and when I bent down to retrieve them, he..."

"What?"

"He... reached out and fondled my boob. I was so shocked that at first I didn't react, but when I stood up, he ran back into his room."

Young looked perplexed. "Did you tell his parents?"

Jenna nodded. "Straight away, but that's what's so strange, they swore blind that he hadn't left their room all evening. The father even went so far as to make me feel as if I'd made the whole thing up. "

Young thought for a moment.

Then he said, "You know, if you want to make a formal complaint, it's not too late."

Jenna shook her head. "No, thanks, but it all seems so silly now, almost as if I dreamt it."

Chapter 20

"Well, I can have a quiet word with the father, just to assure him that you could take things further if you wanted. He's clearly in denial."

"No, let's not make a big thing about it. I shouldn't have said anything."

They sat in silence for a while.

Young felt that he should do more about the situation, but without Jenna's consent, he was not prepared to go behind her back and risk embarrassing her.

He had witnessed enough situations during his time in uniform where it was one person's word against another, and neither was willing to back down.

After a while, he said, "Tell you what, I've got some cheeses and pate at home, plus a couple of lovely bottles of red I picked up in France last year, how do you feel about coming back to my place rather than eating at your hotel?"

Jenna looked over at him. The thought of spending a cosy evening in with just the two of them suddenly sounded very appealing.

She leaned in for another kiss, but this time she made sure that their mouths met.

Young's flat was far larger than she had expected. But then, Jenna was used to the tiny, cramped spaces which passed for flats back in London. Some of her friends lived in flats virtually no bigger than her bedroom and paid a fortune for the privilege.

That was one reason why Jenna had never seriously looked for a place of her own.

The other was that with her uncle being away so much of the time, his place did kind of feel like hers, anyway.

She wondered for a moment what would happen if indeed her uncle had been killed. But then she shook the feeling away, deciding instead to concentrate on her evening with Young.

His choice of wine was indeed delicious, although rather

potent, and by the second glass, Jenna could feel her whole body relax.

Young laid a fine table, with cheese and crackers, pate, a dish of olives, and grapes and crunchy seasonal apples for dessert.

His living room had one of those gas fires which resembled a real coal fire, and with the lights dimmed and some gentle music in the background, Jenna felt a million miles away from her worries and concerns.

Once they had finished eating, they moved to the couch with their second bottle of wine. Rather than sitting, Jenna immediately lay back with her head against the armrest.

"You don't mind if I make myself at home, do you?" she asked, her voice starting to slur slightly from the wine.

"Not at all," smiled Young, taking his seat at the other end and turning in so that he could still face her. "Why don't you kick off your shoes and really get comfortable?"

Jenna did as he suggested without bothering to bend down and use her hands.

Once both her shoes had hit the floor, she manoeuvred herself around so that her feet were propped up on Young's lap.

He handed Jenna her glass, and they clinked before drinking.

"This is gorgeous stuff," Jenna commented as she reached over to place her glass back on the coffee table.

"Mmnn," Young agreed, "I wish I'd bought more now."

"Do you go to France often?" Jenna enquired dreamily.

Young nodded while still drinking. He put his glass next to Jenna's and began to gently massage her feet while he talked. "I used to try and get over there whenever I could. I love the whole way of life there."

Jenna slipped back against the sofa, the feel of Young's strong hands manipulating her bare soles sending a slight shiver throughout her body. "What's your favourite part?"

Young thought for a moment. "That's a hard one. I love Paris, of course, but sometimes I'd rather opt for the peace and serenity of the countryside. Paris, of course, has all the restaurants and art galleries and museums, not to mention the nightlife. But then at other times I would just rent a little cottage in some backwater village and spend my time going for long walks and then feeding myself in the local pub. It sort of depended on what kind of mood I was in when I booked up. Like I say, it's a hard one."

Jenna raised her head and gazed down her body.

She could feel Young growing aroused where her feet rested on his lap.

Without warning, she began to rub his growing hardness with the heel of her foot.

Young let out a gasp of surprise but did not attempt to move her foot.

"Not the only hard one, I see," joked Jenna, continuing her movement.

Eventually, Young lifted Jenna's feet off of him and slid along the couch towards her, so that they could lie together, side by side.

———

Mary Cranley opened her eyes and sat up in bed with a start.

Her bedroom was bathed in total darkness, save for a sliver of light creeping in through a gap in the curtains. She strained to hear the noise that had woken her, but there was no evidence of it now.

She was sure that whatever it was, it had emanated from downstairs.

Mary reached over instinctively to switch on the bedside lamp, but then she stopped herself.

She continued to listen for the sound to reoccur, her eyes growing accustomed to the dimness the longer she waited.

It had sounded like a window breaking, or perhaps a vase had fallen off a shelf.

Mary was by no means a timid woman. She prided herself on that fact. So, if it turned out there was something to investigate, she was more than prepared to carry out that investigation herself.

She waited a moment longer in the darkness, but there was no other sound to be heard.

Finally, assured by the fact that she would be unable to return to sleep without inspecting the house first, Mary threw back the covers and swung her legs over the bed. She slipped her feet into her slippers and retrieved her dressing gown from the chair by her bed, where she had left it the previous evening.

She crept over to her bedroom door and listened through the wood for any sound.

There was none!

There was no telephone in her bedroom, but Mary did keep one on each landing for the benefit of her lodgers. But even so, she felt no immediate threat, and the idea of phoning the police to report a possible intruder seemed to her a trifle impetuous at this stage.

After a moment, she carefully opened her door and peered out into the corridor.

The house appeared completely still, with no noise whatsoever to cause her alarm.

Mary considered returning to bed but then decided that as she was awake, she might as well complete her search of the house, even if just to satisfy her curiosity.

Switching on the landing light, Mary cautiously began moving through the rooms on her floor. Her house was on three levels including the attic, and her bedroom was on the second floor. There were two more bedrooms on this floor, plus a separate bathroom and toilet.

Mary checked each room without finding anything untoward.

Chapter 20

As she made her way down to the next level, she switched off the upper landing light and turned on the one for the second level. Again, everything appeared to be in order, so Mary continued her search of the rooms on this floor.

Having checked two of the bedrooms, she stopped once she was outside Jenna's uncle's room. Mary had always made a point of not entering her gentlemen's rooms in their absence without prior notice. But under the present circumstances, and considering what that charming police officer had said yesterday, she decided that there could be no objection to her breaking one of her own house rules.

She turned the handle and pushed open the door, reaching for the light switch on the wall as she entered.

Mary flicked the switch down and up several times before accepting that the bulb had blown. She wondered if that had been the noise she heard. They did make a rather loud popping sound when they blew.

But then she considered that in order for the bulb to blow like that, it had to be switched on in the first place.

Mary scanned the darkened room, but with the curtains fully closed, she could make out nothing other than meaningless shadows.

Just then, from the corner of her eye, she was sure that she had caught a movement over by the wardrobe.

She strained to see more clearly, but now everything appeared still.

Mary shook her head. "You're starting to lose it, girl," she reprimanded herself.

As she turned to leave the room, something massive struck her from behind and sent her flying forward until she crashed into the bannister post in the hallway.

Stunned by the shock, Mary stayed where she had landed, trying to make sense of what had just happened.

Her whole body ached from the sudden jolt of the attack.

As she started to come to her senses, Mary could feel, more than hear, something standing behind her. She rubbed her eyes and attempted to turn around on the floor, but the pain in her hips and shoulders made movement excruciatingly painful.

Then she heard the thing breathing!

It was a kind of low, guttural noise, which began to sound more like a growl the longer it continued.

Eventually, Mary found the strength and the courage to turn herself over, just enough to see what was standing behind her.

But when she saw the silhouette of the werewolf, her mind refused to acknowledge what she was looking at.

A scream caught in her throat.

Desperately, she tried to pull herself along, using the bannister struts for leverage, but her arms were so weak from the fall that progress was almost non-existent.

Her eyes filled with tears of fear and dread. Mary began to moan out loud but softly enough so that she could barely distinguish that it was her own voice making the noise.

With her futile efforts spent, Mary just managed to twist her body enough to prop herself up on one arm.

The creature looming over her was still very much in shadow, but she could just make out its hairy outer covering, pointed ears, and claw-like fingers.

Her mind now gone, Mary pulled up her knees and crouched forward into a foetal position, oblivious to the pain that spread through her frail body.

The werewolf's attack lasted less than ten seconds before Mary could feel the pain no more.

Chapter Twenty-One

JENNA AND YOUNG SAT OPPOSITE EACH OTHER IN THE tea shop. Being early, they had managed to snag the same table by the window that Jenna had used on her first visit.

Young had parked in front of the book shop to avoid any larger vehicle taking the spot and restricting their view across the road.

They had woken entwined in each other's arms. Their first time together had been an energetic as well as passionate experience for both of them. Jenna was pleased to discover that Young was a very considerate lover who appeared to care more for her needs than his own.

This was something she had not experienced in a long time.

Certainly not while she was with Roger, who seemed to think that him ejaculating inside her was all she ever dreamt of.

Having showered, they decided against breakfast, preferring instead to set off immediately to find the tea shop. Jenna was confident she could remember how to get there, but in the end, it had taken several trips down wrong turnings before they finally found it.

By the time they arrived, it was a little after ten o'clock. The sign on the book shop door stated that the shop should be opening soon, so they both opted to sit across the road and monitor the place before Young ventured inside.

By ten fifteen, Jenna noticed movement from across the road. She reached over and grabbed Young's wrist, indicating to the book shop with a nod of her head. Typically, the only other patrons of the tea shop, an elderly couple, had opted to sit at a table directly behind them, so they had to keep their voices down so as not to arouse any suspicion as to what they were doing.

They watched as the door to the shop opened, and Katerina appeared framed in the doorway.

Jenna squeezed Young's wrist harder. "That's her," she whispered, struggling to keep the excitement out of her voice.

Young gazed at the smudged photocopy Pudelko had given them and nodded.

There was no mistaking her striking form and appearance, even from this distance.

Young drained his cup. "Right then," he announced, "I'm going over there."

Jenna reached into her handbag. "I'll pay for our tea, then we can…"

"No!" Young cut her off. It was as if he had been expecting some opposition, despite the plan they had agreed on. "I need to go in alone, Jenna, this is an official investigation. There's a protocol I must follow."

His words were firm, but his eyes belied the fact that he was asking, more than telling her.

Jenna pouted. In truth, she knew that there was no way Young was going to agree to her accompanying him inside. All she really wanted was to stand in the background and listen to Katerina's answers to his questions.

However, it appeared she would have to wait for Young to relay them to her, after all.

Young rose from his chair and kissed her warmly on the mouth.

Jenna watched as he walked over to the shop. She shifted her chair to obtain a better view through the net curtains.

As Young entered the book shop, he was immediately struck by the delicate aroma of honey and herbs that hung in the air. He breathed in deeply, allowing the fused mixture to fill his nostrils. It was certainly a heady combination.

There was no sign of the woman, so Young continued to stroll further into the shop. As he did, he could feel his whole body growing weightless, as if he could float away at any time.

As ridiculous as it seemed, he saw his arm shoot out in front of him to grab hold of the iron railing of the spiral staircase to keep him weighted down.

His head began to swim. He rubbed his eyes between his thumb and forefinger and pulled himself closer to the railing for support.

"It does take some getting used to, doesn't it?"

He looked up and saw Katerina standing before him. Young was perplexed as to where she had appeared from, so he simply surmised that she must have crept down the winding staircase from above.

Young blinked several times as he took in the full embodiment of the woman's incredible beauty. That picture they had did not do her justice.

As Young's vision regained its focus, he could not help but stare at the woman's face.

He surveyed her like an antiquarian admiring a rare piece of china. Her perfectly chiselled cheekbones, her voluptuous lips, her long, sleek, flawless neck, eyes of a pure emerald green that were so hypnotic he just wanted to dive into them and drown, and to top it all, her flowing black hair, so thick and lustrous it took him all his willpower not to attempt to run his hands through it, right here and now.

All at once, Young realised that he was staring directly at her. It took all his willpower, but he managed to turn his eyes away, just for a moment. He could feel his face growing hot. This was no way for a police detective to act, he chided himself. Being intimidated by a suspect simply by her appearance.

"I...I'm sorry, I don't know what came over me," he apologised.

Katerina laughed. "No need to apologise, it's probably just the incense I'm burning, it can be a little potent if you're not used to it. But it is very good for the sinuses."

Young attempted a laugh, but another cloud of dizziness wafted over him, and he gripped the bannister until his knuckles turned white.

His head plopped forward until his chin rested on his chest.

For a moment, he concentrated on the woman's feet. She was wearing flip-flops, and her toenails were painted the same deep shade of red as her lips. As he slowly moved his eyes up her sublime figure, Young also noticed that her fingernails were painted in a similar hue.

By the time his vision reached her face again, there was a subtle, almost cruel smile playing at the corners of Katerina's mouth. She knew full well that he had been ogling her, and she seemed to revel in the attention.

The room around him slowly began to drift in and out of focus, and although he tried to focus on the woman's face, his vision appeared to zoom in and out like the viewfinder on a telescope.

In his more lucid moments, Young watched as the woman's tongue slid out between her red lips and traced a trail around them, moistening her lipstick.

As she slowly opened her mouth, Young felt sure he could see elongated white fangs peeking out.

He shook his head to clear the vision.

Chapter 21

By the time he looked back, Katerina had her mouth closed once more.

Young could feel himself being drawn towards her, as if invisible arms were pulling his forcibly. He felt powerless to resist. Part of him wanted to rest in those arms. To be held close to her bosom so that he could hear her heartbeat and become one with her.

The enticing seductiveness of her smile was momentarily replaced by a fleeting glance of anger and frustration.

Young could not understand why. He was lost to her and was happy to accept the consequences.

But then he heard a voice in the distance. A sweet, familiar voice which conveyed love and protection. He knew it, but he could not place it, such was the hold the woman before him had over him.

Young continued to stare at Katerina. The sudden change in her demeanour was unmistakable. He could feel her hold over him starting to diminish, but he wanted it back. He was desperate to be with her.

"Alan…Alan…?" He could hear the voice. It did not belong to Katerina.

As the mist began to clear, he looked to his side, and there was Jenna, trying her best to support him.

Young shook his head as if to clear away the haze that had invaded his brain.

He could feel the beginning of a thundering headache taking hold, and all of sudden, he knew that he needed to leave this shop and go far away.

Young leaned on Jenna as they made their way slowly to the front door of the shop.

In the background, he could hear the remnants of a conversation taking place between Jenna and Katerina. He managed to pick up on the occasional word or sentence, but his focus continued to drift in and out as they walked.

Once outside, the sudden rush of fresh air helped to clear the last of the misty haze from Young's head. The throbbing sensation from his oncoming headache took its place, and Young could feel his legs starting to lose their support beneath him.

Jenna helped him into his car.

As they drove away, Katerina turned and stormed back into the book shop.

She could feel her anger rising within.

She had realised the moment the man set foot in her shop that she had to have him, make him one of her own, but she had let the chance slip away.

When Jenna first came to Young's aid, Katerina did consider turning them both, but she knew she might have a struggle on her hands, especially in the daylight with people walking past outside who may have raised the alarm.

As she stood beside the cast-iron railings of the staircase, Katerina lashed out with her fist. The wrought iron post offered little resistance to her blow, and when she removed her fist, she saw the ball-size dent she had left in the frame.

———

When Jenna arrived back at Young's flat, he was still very groggy and virtually uncommunicative. With a great deal of effort on her part, Jenna managed to get him inside and onto the couch. She did consider calling a doctor, but as he was breathing normally and merely seemed exhausted, she decided to just let him sleep.

Jenna sat in the living room so she could keep an eye on Young.

Once she grew bored with watching television and reading the somewhat limited array of magazines he kept on the lower shelf of his coffee table, Jenna busied herself by tidying up the flat and washing up the dishes from the previous evening.

Chapter 21

As the hours passed laboriously by, Jenna's concern for Young grew more fervent.

On a couple of occasions, she did try to wake him, but each attempt failed and resulted in his merely turning over like a reluctant teenager refusing to get up for school.

As afternoon gave way to early evening, Jenna was starting to feel the pangs of hunger. She had existed on nothing all day save for tea and a couple of digestive biscuits. She considered making dinner for the pair of them, but as she had no way of knowing when Young would wake up, she decided not to bother.

Finally, she snuggled up next to him on the couch, and eventually she, too, fell asleep.

She was woken some time later by the frantic buzzing of her mobile, which she had placed on the coffee table in front of them.

Moving to a sitting position, Jenna looked at the screen and saw that it was Trisha calling.

She answered it immediately. "Hello, friend," she said, desperate to hear the voice of another human being.

"How are you?" Trisha enquired. "Are you still in the sticks?"

"Yes, I'm afraid so," sighed Jenna, initially keeping her voice low in case she woke Young, but then realising the futility of her action, she switched to a more normal tone.

"I take it things aren't going so well in your search for your uncle?" The genuine sympathy in her friend's voice made Jenna wish that she was there with her now. She could definitely do with a friendly hug right now.

"Oh, Trisha, I've got so much to tell you, it's hard to know where to start."

"Now you are going to make me feel guilty," replied Trisha, sounding forlorn.

"How do you mean?" asked Jenna, picking up on her friend's sudden change of tone.

Trisha took a deep breath. "I just called to touch base with you, I'm actually on my way out, but by the sound of your voice, you need to unload."

Trish was right, Jenna did indeed need to unload on a friend, and she knew that Trisha was the perfect candidate. But as desperate as she was, she was not prepared to ruin her friend's evening by bringing her down.

"Listen," said Jenna, trying to sound more cheerful. "You go out and have a fantastic time. I'll call you tomorrow and give you all the dirt."

There was a brief pause on the line.

Then Trish said, "Look, why don't I just cancel tonight? It's not exactly life and death. Then we can have a good long chinwag and you can bring me up to speed."

"No way, I won't hear of it," Jenna responded. "You go and enjoy your night. It'll keep 'til tomorrow, don't worry, I'm just being overdramatic."

Trisha could sense that her friend was covering up her true feelings and that in reality, she needed to unload, preferably in person.

They had known each other a long time, and Trisha, being the older of the two, had always treated Jenna like a little sister, having no siblings of her own.

She thought for a moment.

Then an idea struck her. "Hey, how about this, I'm due a couple of leave days from work, why don't I come down there tomorrow and you can show me the sights?"

Jenna laughed. "Oh, babe, that would be wonderful, but are you sure you want to drive all the way over here? It's not exactly the life and soul of party town."

"It'll be an adventure," Trisha assured her, "and besides, it'll give us a chance to catch up properly. What do you say?"

Jenna could not believe her luck. With everything else going on at the moment, a chance to meet up with her best friend was a tonic she could definitely do with right now.

Chapter 21

"Thank you, thank you so much, I can't wait to see you."

"Same here," Trisha assured her. "Now, listen, I've got to dash, or I'll be late. Text me the details of where you're staying, and I'll see you tomorrow around lunchtime, ok?"

Jenna thanked her friend again, and they said their goodbyes. Hearing Trisha's voice on the phone was like a breath of fresh air to Jenna, and she was genuinely excited at the prospect of seeing her the following day.

She looked over at Young, who was still sleeping peacefully.

"Well, it looks like I'll get to show you off tomorrow, as well," she said rhetorically, bending over to plant a kiss on his lips.

The thought of her friend's arrival inspired Jenna to change her mind about dinner.

She lifted herself off the couch and went into the kitchen to rummage through Young's fridge and freezer for inspiration.

There was an open bottle of chardonnay in the fridge door, so she poured herself a glass while she pondered what to prepare dinner.

She hoped that the smell of her cooking might be enough to rouse Young from his slumber.

Chapter Twenty-Two

Roger switched his wipers on to full power. The intensity of the rain spattering his windscreen had increased considerably during the last few minutes, and it was becoming increasingly difficult for him to see ahead.

According to the read-out on his car's satellite navigation system, he should be in Huntley within the hour, and once there, he would head straight for the local police station to make a formal complaint against their Detective Constable Young.

He had spoken to their company lawyer that afternoon, and apparently this upstart was breaking all kinds of rules by involving himself with a client during an ongoing investigation. At the very least, Roger would demand that the officer be disciplined, perhaps even dismissed from the force altogether.

Then Jenna would think twice about going out with an unemployed individual, compared to someone who would one day be running the entire company.

How dare she think that she could just cast him aside like some unwanted article of clothing. She had had her fun and rubbed his nose in it for shagging that little tart of a temp, so now they were even.

Chapter 22

What's more, if she wanted to keep her job, she knew on which side her bread was buttered.

Roger had watched his mother destroy people in the boardroom on many occasions, and once he was finished with this upstart copper, Jenna would see that he was a man not to be trifled with.

What she did not appreciate was that Roger had already decided that he was going to marry her. After all, she was a looker, well educated, decent enough education, and more than capable of knowing how to conduct herself in social situations.

In truth, he would be doing her a favour!

Where else would she find a man of Roger's qualities?

True, she was not as adventurous in bed as he would have liked. He always seemed to be the one having to instigate matters whenever he felt rampant. Obviously, the woman had a low sex drive. But not to worry; once they were married, Roger knew that finding women for a bit on the side would be no problem for a company director.

Yes, the future was certainly looking bright for our Roger.

But first, there was this little matter of the copper who could not keep it in his trousers to sort out!

Kevin's ears pricked up at the sound of the approaching vehicle. It was still a little way off, but the street ahead was deserted, and Kevin's heightened senses told him that other than a few night-creatures, there was no one else in the immediate vicinity.

He crouched down a little lower on the branch he had been squatting on for the past ten minutes or so, his powerful legs primed like coiled springs waiting to pounce.

His latest metamorphosis had been his least painful to date. It seemed that with each change, the process grew less arduous and more natural. He was beginning to feel as if his transformation phase was a far more natural state than his human guise.

Kevin had not feasted on human flesh since that night in the woods with those two girls. Katerina had not allowed him the freedom of stalking and killing his prey at will. She had informed him through his dreams that he must remain patient until the time was right.

Worse still, she had forbidden him to visit her as he had when she transformed him to quench his carnal lusts. Although she had promised him that they would enjoy further unions in the future.

But his needs were growing ever stronger with each passing day, and the nights were the worst of all. With him unable to satisfy his desires, Kevin had spent agonising hours in his bedroom, tossing and turning fitfully in an endless nightmare of lust and want.

Worse still, he was forced to listen to the endless moaning from his bitch of a mother as a result of him not being able to open the shop. In his present state, he was unable to contemplate the wearisome monotony of standing behind that counter, having to deal with the dregs of society who were not even fit to feed his most basic instinct.

Hour after hour he lay there, unable to quench his thirst for the warm fulfilling blood that coursed through the veins of so much human fodder. Forbidden to relieve himself of his newfound sexual aggression.

Unable to do anything but lie there, dormant. His hungers denied.

Until tonight!

For tonight, as Kevin lay beneath the damp, sweat-stained sheets in his bed, contemplating another agonising night of starvation, Katerina had come to him in a vision to praise him for his obedience and to reward him for his allegiance to her.

With the message received, Kevin rose from his bed in

Chapter 22

excited anticipation for the night ahead. As he looked in his wardrobe for suitable loose-fitting clothing he could discard easily, he heard the familiar patter of his mother's slippers on the landing outside his door.

This could only mean one thing!

Yet another barrage from her, bemoaning his lack of enterprise and general laziness.

As usual, she did not even bother to knock but instead just threw open the door, allowing it to smack into the dresser on the adjacent wall.

As Kevin turned, he could see the puzzled look on her face at the sight of his nakedness. His newly toned and sinewy torso was a vast change from his old flabby self.

But it was as her eyes rose to his face that Kevin noticed the look of sheer terror on his mother's face.

Before she had a chance to react, Kevin leapt forward and grabbed her roughly by the arm. With one tug, he sent her flying through the air towards his bed. With a scream of shock and surprise, her nightdress billowing around her hips, she landed face-down on his mattress with solid thump.

Before she had a chance to recover, Kevin was upon her. His massive frame pinned her down, preventing her from any chance of escape.

Unable to fathom what was happening to her, Kevin's mother remained in that prone position while he ripped open the flimsy material of her nightie and entered her roughly from behind.

The excruciating pain of the onslaught caused his mother to cry out in agony, so Kevin forced her face into his pillow to muffle her screams. Her futile struggles merely fed the flames of his lust, and with each blubbering whimper she released, Kevin increased the intensity of his thrusts.

He revelled in the stench of her sex!

But even more intoxicating than that was the other smell

which exuded from her. The same one he had caught a brief whiff of earlier when she first opened his door.

The unmistakable smell of fear!

It drove his pleasure to new heights.

Once he was spent, Kevin left his mother's prone body in situ and quickly dressed before heading out. With his sexual need satisfied, he was ready to concentrate on his other appetite: his craving for human flesh!

Kevin shifted impatiently as he watched the car approach. The driving rain did nothing to hamper his view of the vehicle, nor of the substantial occupant. His elongated tongue swept across his yellowed, pointed fangs as saliva drooled and dribbled down his fur-covered chin.

He could almost taste the succulent, meaty juices of the approaching human prey.

Roger squinted through his rain-splattered windscreen. This was supposed to be the main road leading into Huntley from the motorway, but it appeared to be more like a country lane. The road ahead was very narrow and extremely poorly lit, but he supposed that this was what one should expect, being out in the sticks.

The glare from his car's headlights illuminated the approaching woodland. This could not be right, surely this road must be a dead end?

Kevin shifted slightly along the branch, just far enough so that it could still withstand his weight without risking it snapping and giving away his position.

He readied himself to pounce.

Roger slowed down and pulled over to one side, keeping the engine on. This was obviously the wrong route, despite what his navigational system was telling him. He would just have to turn around and head back the way he came to see if he could find a decent road sign in this god-forsaken place, which might at least send him in the right direction.

Chapter 22

Kevin held his breath for a split second, then leapt off the branch. He sailed through the darkness for a few well-timed seconds before landing directly on the bonnet of Roger's car.

The impact caused the bonnet to buckle, and before Roger had a chance to react, Kevin had sprung forward and crashed through the windscreen, showering Roger with shards of tinted glass.

Roger threw his arms up to protect his face from the sudden onslaught. In his panic, his foot slipped off the brake and rammed down on the accelerator. The car shot forward and sped off out of control. Before he knew what was happening, the front tyres clipped the kerb and mounted the pavement before careering down a muddy verge and crashing headlong into a tree.

When Roger finally opened his eyes, he was not sure how long he had been unconscious for. He lifted his head from the steering wheel and immediately felt a fresh trickle of blood start a path down his face.

The steep angle of the verge was causing the seat belt to cut into his upper body, so Roger attempted manoeuvring his posture to release the catch.

As he turned, he heard the low growling coming from the back seat.

Unable to turn fully, Roger glanced up at the rear-view mirror in front of him and saw Kevin's burning red eyes staring back at him menacingly.

The werewolf's mighty jaws snapped around Roger's exposed neck before he had a chance to scream for help!

Young opened his eyes to find himself lying on his own settee. He could hear Jenna in the kitchen, busying herself to the soothing sounds of Bach drifting through the air.

As he propped himself up on one arm, the smell of something delicious hit his nostrils, and he breathed in deeply, savouring the aroma.

His recollection of how he managed to end up asleep in his own living room was, at best, hazy. But for now, he was more interested in seeing Jenna's welcoming smile, so he thrust himself off the couch and, in an attempt to rise to his feet, sent himself crashing to the floor.

Young hit the floor with a jarring thud, the sound of which brought Jenna running in from the kitchen.

"Alan!" she almost screamed his name as she ran over to him. "Oh, my god, you're awake!"

She began showering him with kisses whilst simultaneously helping him to his feet.

Jenna wrapped his arm around her shoulders to try and help support his weight as Young used the coffee table to take the strain.

He was still a little wobbly, but he managed to lift himself into a standing position, and once upright, Young threw his arms around Jenna and they supported each other in a warm embrace.

When they parted, Young asked, "How long have I been out?"

Jenna looked him straight in the eyes. "You really don't remember?"

Young could detect the note of concern in her voice.

He shook his head. "Not really. I seem to remember having tea with you in that shop this morning, and then... Did I pass out?"

Jenna placed a comforting hand at the side of his face. "You don't remember going into the bookshop and seeing that woman?"

Young thought for a moment. "Not really. I do sort of

remember a cloud of mist and feeling sleepy all of a sudden, but nothing about the woman. What happened?"

Jenna explained the events of that morning, right up until she managed to bring Young back up to his flat.

Young seemed more bemused than concerned at his lack of memory, and when Jenna suggested that she drive him to hospital to have him checked out, Young assured her that he felt fine.

"What is that gorgeous smell?" he asked, looking over Jenna's shoulder towards the kitchen.

"Only my world-famous shepherd's pie, just out of the oven."

Young breathed in deeply. "Mmnn, you certainly know the way to a man's heart, and no mistake," he said, smiling.

"You must be starved; you haven't eaten all day."

"You can say that again," Young agreed.

Jenna linked arms with him. "Well, come with me, officer, and we'll soon fix that."

Young polished off two large helpings, and together they finished a bottle and a half of wine.

Afterwards, they sat together on the sofa listening to music and allowing their food to digest.

To Jenna's surprise, Young could not stop yawning.

He apologised several times and assured her it was not a result of being bored in her company.

"I can't believe you're still sleepy!" Jenna exclaimed, ruffling his hair.

Young closed his eyes and leant gently against Jenna's breast. "After a meal like that, any man would be ready for his bed."

They stayed on the couch for a while longer before taking themselves to bed.

Within seconds of his head hitting the pillow, Young was fast asleep.

Jenna lay awake for a while, listening to his breathing and

praying that whatever charm or spell the woman in the book shop had used on him had left no permanent damage.

Furthermore, they still had not managed to ascertain what, if any, connection this Katerina woman had with the disappearance of her uncle.

Chapter Twenty-Three

Young spent a fitful night. When dreams came, they centred around a combination of what Professor Pudelko had told them, his experience with the woman in the bookshop, and his feelings for Jenna.

He was in a vast expanse of open land, probably somewhere in Huntley wood. All around him were naked men and women, some of whom he recognised, whilst others were totally alien to him.

Together they formed a circle surrounding him. As he scanned the crowd, Young could see the malevolent stare in each of their eyes, accompanied by something else.

Could it be hunger?

Suddenly, he realised that he, too, was naked and immediately felt self-conscious, like a first timer at a nudist colony. In his dream he tried to cover his modesty with his hands, but somehow, he was unable to move. That was when he realised he was being restrained by two huge men, each holding on tightly to one of his arms.

There was a massive bonfire off to one side, and Young could feel the warmth from it playing against his naked flesh.

The crowd moved in menacingly, and each set of eyes appeared to be trained upon him.

Just then, the woman from the bookshop appeared and cut a swath through the crowd as she approached him. When she reached him, the woman reached out and placed the palm of her hand on Young's chest. She kept it there for several moments as if trying to monitor his heartbeat.

It was then that Young noticed the group trailing behind her. There appeared to be six of them, each supporting one end of a large wooden frame on their shoulders. They stopped just behind the woman and together they lifted the apparatus until it was vertical. That was when Young noticed that Jenna was fastened to the wooden frame by ropes tied at her ankles and wrists.

She was calling to him. Begging him to free her and get her away from this awful place.

He tried to lunge forward, but the two men holding him did not yield.

He looked straight at Katerina and began to plead with her to let Jenna go. Even if she kept hold of him, his only concern was for his girlfriend's safety.

But the woman merely laughed in reply.

The crowd surrounding them began to move in closer.

As he looked up, Young could see their appearance beginning to undergo some form of metamorphosis. From the glow of the bonfire, he could just make out the appearance of thick, black hair starting to sprout from their skin, covering them from head to foot.

As they drew nearer, he could see their faces twist and contort as snouts grew where their noses and mouths had been. Some seemed to cry out as if the change caused them immense pain, but the noise they made was not human but guttural and animal-like.

Young looked on helplessly as the crowd transformed into

creatures that more resembled giant dogs than human beings. He knew what was happening, but he could not understand how he had allowed Jenna to be brought to this terrible place and how they had somehow managed to undress him and leave him so vulnerable without him at least putting up a fight.

In spite of his circumstances, Young could feel himself growing aroused as Katerina began to caress him with her bare hand.

He glanced over at Jenna, a weak apology on his lips as if he felt that he was somehow being unfaithful to her, although his adultery would be the least of her concerns at this time.

Katerina seemed to revel in the response she was receiving from her caresses.

Young was powerless to resist her touch.

As her hand slowly meandered a path towards his throbbing member, Young sucked in a deep breath as she curled her fingers around his shaft and began to stroke it gently, back and forth.

Young could feel his seed starting to rise.

He could not even look in Jenna's eyes, such was his feeling of overwhelming disloyalty.

He closed his eyes and threw back his head in resignation.

The sound of Katerina's scornful laughter permeated his eardrums, blocking out everything else.

He was hers now!

Young woke with a start. His body was drenched in perspiration.

For a few moments he just lay still, breathing deeply and trying to block out the nightmare which had pervaded his sleep.

Beside him, Jenna breathed quietly. The comforting sight of her naked breasts rising and falling made Young feel even more aware of his guilt from his dream.

He reached down between his legs and heaved a sigh of relief when he realised that he had not ejaculated. It reminded him of when he hit puberty and the guilt he would feel upon waking to find that his erotic dream had caused him to come, unwittingly, while he slept.

Now he thought about it, the guilt had often manifested itself as a result of the content of his dream, rather than the actual act of releasing his sperm. Some of his dreams had been downright bizarre, but over time he had learned how the human psyche worked, and eventually Young had stopped trying to figure out the reason behind them.

But this latest dream had been very real, and as much as he hated to admit it, he now remembered having an instant attraction to the woman in the bookshop the moment he met her. What was more, it was not just her face or her divine body but the fact that she seemed to emanate an aura which was tantalisingly sexual in nature.

Young wondered now what might have happened had Jenna not interceded when she did to take him out of there!

Young carefully threw back the covers and made his way to the bathroom.

He cupped some cold water from the tap and splashed his face several times.

Looking at his reflection in the mirror, he knew that he was going to have to take action to avoid any chance of his strange dream ever coming true.

The question was, what?

―――

Katerina opened her eyes and smiled.

The connection with the man had been a good one, and she had learnt much from him that was going to come in handy during the ceremony.

She swept back her covers and strode naked over to the bay window that looked out over the town. Protected from prying eyes by the flimsy net curtain, she gazed out over the main

Chapter 23

street, which was presently devoid of human beings due to the inhospitality of the hour.

Katerina closed her eyes and concentrated on making contact with her followers.

She knew that the time was near, and they would need to prepare.

———

Young sat in his kitchen, watching his coffee go cold.

As a police officer he had often felt frustrated at being unable to act on his suspicions because of the rule of law and the restrictions placed on him and his fellow officers by the police and criminal evidence act. But it did not make such situations any easier to bear.

He knew that if he went to his sergeant with some wild story about fearing that there were werewolves lurking around Huntley wood, he would be laughed out of his office and possibly the force after undergoing compulsory psychiatric tests to see if he was fit for duty.

Young knew that he was going to be alone on this one and that his avenues for help would be few and far between.

The easiest and possibly best solution would be to convince Jenna to go away with him, as far from Huntley as possible.

They could start a new life together, even if he had to leave the force. Not that Young had any idea what else he would do. He had only ever dreamed of being a copper since as far back as he could remember. But Jenna's safety was paramount.

On the other hand, he knew that she had not given up on finding her uncle alive, so he knew that any suggestion to abandon the search, even if ultimately it would be in her best interest, would go down like a lead balloon with her.

So, what next?

Young stayed at the kitchen table contemplating his next

move when an idea came to him that, if not an ideal solution, might at least give him some much-needed ammunition.

He checked his watch. It was still early, but he could not just sit there and do nothing.

Tiptoeing back into the bedroom so as not to wake Jenna, Young grabbed his mobile from the night table and walked over to the chair upon which he had draped his trousers the previous evening. He retrieved his wallet from one of the pockets and took it back with him to the kitchen, closing the bedroom door behind him.

He riffled through his wallet until he found the business card the professor had given him. Young heaved a sigh of relief when he saw that there was a mobile number on the card, as well as the university's main switchboard.

Young dialled the number and waited.

After several rings, the phone was answered by a very tired-sounding professor.

"Good morning, professor." Young spoke in hushed tones, conscious that his voice carried and there was only a plaster wall between him and Jenna. "I'm sorry to be calling you so early, but I have a question only you can answer."

"Please, go ahead." The professor sounded intrigued.

"Professor… According to your extensive research, how can someone kill a werewolf?"

Chapter Twenty-Four

TRISHA'S PHONE BUZZED INTO LIFE, SIGNALLING IT was time for her to wake.

Reaching over, she grabbed her mobile and from years of experience managed to negotiate depressing the snooze button without looking.

It seemed only seconds before the alarm went off again.

She opened her eyes and tried to focus on the unfamiliar surroundings.

After a moment, the details from the previous night came flooding back to her.

Trisha turned her head and glanced over at the shaved head on the pillow next to her. She strained for a moment, then she remembered the owner's name, Peter. Trisha was sure that he must have mentioned his last name at some point during the evening, but for now, it escaped her.

She reached over to check the time on her phone. It was already after eight, and she was supposed to be on the road in an hour on her way to see Jenna. The trouble was, she was on the other side of London from her flat, a decision she had made last night when it came to the 'your place or mine' part of the conversation.

Trisha decided that it would be easier for her to slip away from Peter's place than the prospect of having to kick him out, especially if he was one of those reluctant lovers who wanted to hang around for seconds.

In his case, he was not worth the effort. Trisha was not exactly impressed by his selfish lovemaking. He was doubtless used to going with women with far less experience than her. *Serves me right for going with a man twenty years younger,* she thought.

Trying not to wake him, Trisha slid out from under the sheets and crept around the bedroom retrieving her clothes and belongings. Once she had everything, she tiptoed to the door and went out onto the landing and then followed the corridor until she reached the bathroom.

Trisha dressed as quickly and quietly as she could. She checked herself in the mirror and used some toilet paper to remove her make-up that had smudged during the night.

She was about to leave when it dawned on her that her bladder would not last the entire journey home. Trisha peed as quietly as she could, feeling the instant relief as her bladder drained. Once she was finished, she wiped herself with some tissue and closed the lid, ready to flush.

Deciding that the noise of the flush was bound to wake Peter up, Trisha thought better of it. She carried her shoes back out onto the landing and left the flat, closing the front door behind her as quietly as possible.

A taxi home from Peter's place would cost a small fortune, so Trisha opted for the underground, even though it would mean changing trains twice.

When she finally emerged from the station around the corner from her flat, Trisha sent Jenna a text to apologise for the fact that she was going to be late but promised to be on the road within the hour.

———

Young had been on the phone for most of the morning, but each call was as important as the next, and he was glad that he had made them. Now at least he had the formation of a plan in his mind.

The question now was, what was he going to do with Jenna while he drove back into London? Some of the people he was going to meet with were not the sort he wanted to expose her to.

Young put the kettle on and made them both a strong coffee. He carried the cups into the bedroom and placed them safely on the bedside table before attempting to wake Jenna. He gazed down at her sleeping form for a moment and realised in a rush of exhilaration just how lucky he felt for having found her.

Leaning across the bed, Young placed a gentle kiss on Jenna's nose and then rubbed the tip of his own against hers. Slowly her eyes opened, and she smiled up at him.

They kissed good morning, and Young could not resist letting his mouth wander down the side of her neck. Jenna moaned and turned her body so that she could wrap one of her legs around his hips.

When they broke apart, Young reached over and brought Jenna's cup towards her.

Jenna propped herself up in bed. "Well, now," she said, "this is what I call room service."

Young grabbed his own cup and supported himself on his elbow as they both drank.

"Did you sleep well?" Young asked, wiping his mouth with the back of his hand.

Jenna nodded. "Like a baby. I didn't realise how tired I was until we crawled into bed. Mind you, you were off before I even had a goodnight kiss!"

Young frowned. "No way, as if I would let you go to sleep without a kiss." He tried to sound hurt, but they both knew he was faking it.

"Listen, Jenna," Young continued, this time with a genuine tone of seriousness in his voice. "There are a couple of things I need to do today." He stared into her eyes. "It's police work, so I can't take you with me, but at the same time I don't want to leave you here alone."

Jenna shook her head. "No problem. While you were out yesterday, I called my friend Trisha back in London, and she's coming to Huntley for a couple of days' holiday, so I gave her my hotel's address, and she's going to meet me there this afternoon."

Young relaxed visibly. He was going to suggest that he drop Jenna back at the Grange so at least she would not be alone while he was away. But this sounded even better.

"That's great." He smiled. "At least I don't have to be worried about leaving you at the mercy of Audrey and her strange clientele while I'm away."

Young did not want to go into detail about what he planned to do that day, so he hoped that, as he had mentioned it was police work, Jenna would not enquire further. Fortunately, she seemed quite excited at the prospect of seeing her friend, so Young managed to brush it off without concern.

They both showered and ate breakfast together in the kitchen.

While she was drinking her second cup of coffee, Jenna noticed the text from Trisha.

"Oh, that's a bummer," she said, looking back at Young across the table. "Trisha's running late, but according to this," she indicated to her phone, "she should already have left."

Young did not relish the prospect of leaving Jenna, but he

Chapter 24

knew that he had a long drive ahead of him, and he needed to make tracks as soon as possible. So once breakfast was over, he convinced Jenna that he had a meeting back at the station that he could not afford to be late for, so they bundled into his car and he drove her to the Grange.

He still felt guilty for leaving her alone at the hotel, but the thought of her friend's imminent arrival helped to ease his self-reproach.

Young drove straight for the motorway. Once he was on it, the way ahead seemed fairly clear, so Young put his foot down and stayed, for the most part, in the fast lane.

His first port of call was to be his old convent where he went to school. The church attached to the school was still presided over by the same priest who had given him his first holy communion and who knew all his teenage secrets from the confessional.

Father Spencer had been somewhat surprised to receive Young's call that morning, but the old priest still sounded as cheerful and as friendly as Young remembered from his time as an altar boy.

The old priest's part in Young's plan was vital, far more so than Young had divulged.

Speaking to Pudelko earlier on had left Young with something of a conundrum.

According to the academic, there were only two ways of killing a werewolf, according to his extensive research. The first was by burning them. The second was by spiking them through the heart with an object made from silver that had been blessed by a priest.

This was where, according to the professor, the old theory about shooting them with silver bullets had come from. But as Pudelko took great pains to reiterate, even silver bullets would not work unless the silver had been blessed first.

Pudelko left Young with one final thought. He claimed that

he had uncovered documents and drawings that showed villagers throughout history attempting to execute anyone accused of being a werewolf.

"The severing of one's head from their body had always been a sound way to slay demons of all types," the professor explained. "But the sad truth was that those who were innocent of the charge would die, just like any other human being. Whereas those who really were werewolves would regenerate three days after they had been killed."

It was a terrifying thought, but it made Young all the more fervent in his quest.

"Before you go," cut in the professor, "there is something which might be of interest to you. There is a legend that if you kill a werewolf, all those it has turned will also die as a result. I hope this is of some help to you."

Young was not sure of the significance of the statement, but he thanked the professor for all his help and ended the call.

It took just over two hours before Young saw the first turning for Surrey. The way so far had been exceptionally clear, but he knew that once he drew closer to the London exits the traffic would probably treble in volume.

Young continued to stick with the overtaking lane on the dual carriageways that meandered through the county until he finally reached the turning for Croydon.

As he drove down the leafy lanes, the familiarity of the location brought back fond memories from his childhood and the many hours he and his friends had trekked along them on their way to go fishing or hunting golf balls at the local club.

Young pulled into the car park for St Mark's and pulled up just outside the rectory door.

The middle-aged woman who answered his knock eyed him suspiciously when he announced that he was there to speak to Father Spencer.

Chapter 24

"The father is very busy; do you have an appointment?" she snapped.

To save any argument, Young took out his warrant card and held it out to her.

After studying the card for what Young considered longer than necessary, the woman made a loud "Humph" before standing back and allowing him to gain entrance.

She led him through the familiar dark wood panels until she reached the main door for the priest's private residence. She knocked loudly and waited for an answer before entering. Young felt as if she were purposely blocking his view as she announced him but then decided it was probably just a combination of the considerable size of her frame and the way she stood, square on.

The old priest rose from the chair behind his desk and moved around to the front. He gestured with his hand for Young to enter, which in turn seemed to act as a signal for the housekeeper to stand aside and let Young in.

Father Spencer extended his hand towards Young as he approached.

"Well, now, Alan Young as I live and breathe. How lovely to see you." They shook hands, and the priest clapped him affectionately on the shoulder with his free hand. "Please sit down." The priest indicated to the chair opposite his own.

Young thanked him and sat down. He glanced over his shoulder and saw that the woman was still standing in the doorway, eyeing him in her suspicious manner.

"Now, then," began the priest, "can I press you to tea or coffee, it's a little early for something stronger, or is it?" he said with a wink.

Young held up his hands. "No, thank you, father, I'm fine, really."

The priest turned to his housekeeper. "Thank you, Mrs Hobson, that will be all for now."

Without a word, the woman turned and left, shutting the

door behind her.

Once they were alone, Young allowed the old priest to reminisce about what he remembered of Young's time at the convent. Some of the stories he revealed had nothing to do with Young, but he allowed him to continue as he appeared to relish the chance to delve into the past.

After a while, Young decided that it was time to cut to the chase.

"Father, I don't mean to be rude, but have you got what I asked you for on the phone this morning?"

The old priest eyed him curiously before opening one of the drawers in his desk and taking out a clear plastic bag containing several silver crucifixes, each one housed in its own individual plastic bag.

The priest placed the large bag on the desk between them.

"Just as you asked," Father Spencer stated, "twenty silver crucifixes, all of which blessed by me this morning after we spoke."

Young leaned forward and took hold of the bag. He held it up in front of him while he scoured its contents. Each crucifix came with its own chain, and the crosses themselves were approximately the size of a fifty-pence coin and quite solid from what he remembered.

He turned the bag around slowly while he surveyed the contents.

Young hoped that there were enough.

There had to be!

He thanked the priest and placed the plastic bag inside his jacket pocket.

Once they were secure, he removed his wallet and took out his debit card.

He looked up at the priest. "You did say this morning that you had the facility to take cards, didn't you, father?"

"Oh, we're very well versed in modern technology these

days, you know." As he spoke, the priest pulled out an automatic card-reader from the other drawer in his desk and slid it across the table towards Young.

As Young punched in his PIN number, he could feel Father Spencer staring at him across the table. While the machine processed the transaction, Young glanced up and smiled back at the old priest. He could tell that the priest was curious to discover why Young needed so many crucifixes, but possibly out of respect for the fact that they had known each other for so many years, he did not ask.

Father Spencer escorted Young back to the front door himself.

Young could not help but notice the housekeeper loitering in the background as they entered the main hallway that led through the presbytery.

Young shook hands with the priest and thanked him once again for all his help. He felt guilty for the fact that his visit had been so short and also that he did not feel able to bring the priest into his confidence concerning the necessity for the crucifixes. But he consoled himself by the fact that Father Spencer had seemed genuinely pleased to see him, and he hoped that his visit had at least given the old boy a chance to catch up on old times.

Young knew that his next port of call was not going to be anywhere near as cheerful.

Trisha's navigational system informed her that Huntley was the next turning. She began to indicate and eased off the throttle as she checked over her left shoulder to ensure that it was safe to cross over into the left-hand lane.

Her tummy let out another low rumble. She knew in retrospect that she should have taken the time to eat something before she left home, even if it had only been a slice of toast. But she felt so guilty at running late that she skipped breakfast altogether, barely managing a cup of coffee after she showered before leaving her flat.

Not to worry, though. Even though they had not made firm plans to eat, Jenna knew roughly what time she was due to arrive, so hopefully, she would not have had lunch yet. That way they could catch up over something filling at the hotel, washed down with a well-deserved bottle of wine.

The road ahead was fairly clear. Being a Londoner, Trisha was not used to such open roads and abundant parking as the country offered. It was one of the things she hated about living in town, though not enough to ever consider moving. Trisha loved the nightlife the city offered, and although she did not go out as often now as she had in her twenties, she still knew how to have a good time, and it was very important to her to have all that on her doorstep.

According to the voice on her navigator, the Grange was less than a mile away.

Trisha relaxed and eased back in her seat. She was starting to look forward to the prospect of spending a couple of days away with her friend, and now that she had left the motorway, her break could really start.

Up ahead, Trisha could see a Mercedes parked on the main road with its hazard lights flashing. Not an uncommon sight in London, but out here, it almost stood out like the proverbial sore thumb.

As Trisha approached the vehicle, a woman appeared from behind it and started waving her arms in the air, frantically trying to signal for Trisha to stop.

In London, Trisha would not have thought twice about stopping, such was the climate of street crime. But somehow, in the present circumstance, she was far more willing to give the woman the benefit of the doubt.

Chapter 24

As Trisha slowed down, she pressed the button to lower her window.

When she stopped, the woman walked over to her and leaned in.

She looked to Trisha as if she had just stepped out of a salon. Her hair and make-up were done to perfection.

"Thank you so much for stopping, you really are a dear." The woman spoke with a clear-cut accent that exuded wealth and privilege.

"That's ok," replied Trisha openly. "I take it you're having car trouble?"

The woman sighed. "Can you believe it, that dope of a husband of mine did not bother to fill up the car, and now it's out of petrol. I only came out to book a nail appointment, and now I'm stranded without my purse or my mobile or anything." She gave Trisha a beseeching smile. "I wonder," she continued, "there's a hotel just around the corner where they know me, do you think you could possibly give me a lift there? I would really appreciate it."

"Would that be the Grange?" asked Trisha, smiling.

The woman's eyes lit up. "Why, yes, you clever old thing, that's the very place."

"Hop in," said Trisha, releasing the door lock for the passenger side and lifting her handbag off the seat before throwing it in the back to join her suitcase.

The woman opened the door and slid in beside her. "This is really wonderful of you; I cannot thank you enough. You must let me buy you a drink when we reach the hotel, are you planning on staying there?" The woman glanced over at Trisha's suitcase on the back seat.

"I am, as a matter of fact," replied Trisha. "By the way, my name is Trisha." She extended her hand.

The woman took Trisha's hand and wrapped her well-manicured fingers gently around it. "I'm June, June Le Vant."

Chapter Twenty-Five

Young made his way from Surrey through to southeast London. As he had expected, the traffic through this part of town was far heavier than it had been so far, and it was not just the sheer volume of traffic that caused so many delays but equally the result of bad driving, poor parking, road rage arguments and double-decker buses blocking the way ahead in groups of three and four, which all helped to exacerbate the overall condition.

Young was tempted on more than one occasion to turn on his siren and blue lights to try and cut a swath through the traffic, but from past experience he knew that some drivers in the vicinity would make a point of purposely blocking his progress. It was a sad example of modern times that so many individuals, especially in certain parts of town, considered the police as the enemy.

Young's final destination was in what was considered by most serving officers as one of the least salubrious areas in London. The transfer rate alone from the local stations was far higher here than anywhere else in the country.

Young himself had been seconded to one of those stations

when they were short-staffed, and he remembered how there were certain estates where officers refused to go unless they were in groups.

As he turned off the main high street, Young noticed the usual groups of young boys hanging around on the corners. These were the future villains, having already been groomed by the thugs and hoodlums they looked up to. They were there specifically to act as lookouts should rival gang members decide to venture into their territory.

In the distance, Young could see the four high-rise tower blocks that made up the Crafton estate, the mere sight of which caused a cold shiver to run down his spine. As he drove along the road, Young could see curtains twitching from the houses that lined the street. An unknown vehicle was a rare sight around here, and Young was in no doubt that some of the more streetwise occupants could recognise a police vehicle, even when it belonged to a plain-clothes detective.

When young reached the second of the four blocks, he parked his car as far out in the open as possible in the hope that even the most brazen thief might think twice before attempting to break in when everyone could see them.

As he approached the block, Young noticed a Harley Davidson parked in front of the lift lobby. It gleamed in the sunlight and appeared to be in pristine condition. Young could not image what possessed the owner to leave such a glorious machine out here in full view of some of southeast London's worst villains.

He made his way to the lift lobby, where he was met by a group of six or seven young male teenagers. Some were sitting astride bicycles, while others either stood leaning against the lift doors or sat slumped on the floor with their backs against the cold concrete pillars which helped support the block.

They all stopped talking when Young came into sight. From the way he was dressed, Young presumed that they either took him to be a copper or a salesman; although no salesman with any sense would venture onto the Crafton estate, no matter how desperate he was for his commission.

Young nodded to some of the boys as he made his way towards the nearest lift.

He hit the button, but not surprisingly it did not illuminate.

"Lift's broken," one of the boys called out, looking at Young sideways.

Young sighed and thanked the youth before he turned and headed for the stairwell.

It was a long climb to the ninth floor, but Young was at least grateful that at the end of each staircase he could glance out and see that his car was not being molested.

When he finally reached his floor, Young stopped and took in several deep breaths. He was by no means unfit and certainly was not carrying any extra weight, but nonetheless the climb had taken it out of him.

When he was ready, Young pushed open the stairwell door and turned right. In the distance he could see two men blocking the corridor leading to the flat he was visiting.

Young tried to appear nonchalant as he approached them. Each had an open can of lager clutched in his hand, and they both eyed Young as he grew nearer, making a point of not moving aside for him. He waited until he was as close to them as he could be without bumping into them before he spoke.

Young cleared his throat. "I'm here to see Duggan," he announced. "He's expecting me."

The two men exchanged glances with one another, then one of them reached over and knocked three times on the front door behind them.

Young waited patiently.

After a moment, the door opened, and the two men moved apart to allow Young access. He offered them a cursory 'thank you' as he passed. The man who had opened the door was quite possibly the largest human being Young had ever set eyes on. In Young's estimation, he was close to seven feet and was as broad as he was tall.

The man stared directly at Young, and instinctively, Young could feel his knees starting to buckle.

Somehow, managing to maintain his dignity, Young looked back at the monster before him and repeated what he had just said to the two men outside.

The big man seemed to consider Young's explanation for what seemed to him an agonizing moment before he moved to one side and signalled Young to enter.

Young slid past his massive frame, noticing that his eye level only just came up to the man's chest. There was only one open door at the far end of the corridor, so Young made his way towards it slowly, just in case fresh orders were barked at him en route.

When he arrived at the door, the angle of the wall obscured his view, so not wishing to enter without permission, he knocked on the wooden frame.

"Yes!" came the gruff response from inside.

Young recognised the voice immediately, so he ventured in until he had a full view of the man inside. "Hello, Duggan, thanks for seeing me at such short notice."

The man stood up and offered his hand. "Well, well, well, Sergeant Young, or is it Inspector Young by now?"

Young took his hand. "No, still only constable, I'm afraid."

The man tutted. "You must be greasing the wrong palms, my old son, what you need is to sign up to one of those masonic lodges, then you'll make the right contacts. Please, take a seat."

Young slumped down on the couch opposite the one Duggan was using.

"Drink?" asked Duggan.

Young nodded. "I could use some water, it's quite dry out there."

The man chuckled. "Water, yeah right…Butch!" he called out.

Seconds later the big man entered the room, eyeing Young suspiciously.

"A couple of Bushmills," Duggan ordered, "oh, and put a drop of water in his for me and bring the box back with you."

The big man left without saying a word.

Duggan noticed Young's concern etched into his face.

"Don't you worry about Butch, 'e's as good as gold. I looked after his old mum for him when in clink; now she's dead, 'e won't leave my side."

"He certainly looks as if he could handle himself," Young observed. "I'll bet he could stop a riot just by shouting at them."

"Ah, well now, not exactly," continued Duggan. "Yer see, 'e had 'is tongue ripped out during a prison riot, so 'e can't actually speak."

"Oh." Young nodded his understanding.

"But don't be fooled by that!" Duggan wagged his finger. "'e may not be able to speak, but 'e's only bin out a couple of months and 'e already 'as this manner under control."

"I'll bet."

Just then, Butch re-entered the room carrying a tray with two tumblers of whiskey and a black cardboard box on it. He placed the two glasses on the coffee table between the two men and handed the box to Duggan.

Duggan took the box and set it down on the table. "There you go," he said, "see what you think of that!"

Hesitantly, Young leaned over and picked up the box. It was far heavier than he had anticipated. He turned it over in his hands a couple of times before ripping open one of the side flaps and putting his hand inside to pull out the contents.

The handgun was wrapped in plastic, which Young removed and shoved back inside the box. He hefted the object in the palm of his hand to grow accustomed to the weight. During his time at Hendon, he had spent some time on the police gun range, but his training had only been with rifles. Therefore, the object in his hand felt completely alien to him.

"What'd 'yer think?" asked Duggan proudly. "Not bad for such short notice."

Young looked up. "Thanks, this'll be just fine. I owe you one."

Duggan held up his hands in objection. "No, like I said on the phone, I still owe you from before, you played a decent 'and fer me, unlike the rest of your lot, an' I never forget a favour." He reached over and picked up the two glasses, handing one to Young. "To debts paid and slates cleaned," he announced before clinking his glass against Young's and draining its contents in one go.

Young took a tentative sip of his drink. It was supposed to be watered down but still almost tasted neat to him. Not wishing to cause offence, he took a decent swig and pulled a face as the liquid burned its way down his throat.

Duggan laughed. "Good stuff, eh?"

Young nodded, turning his attention back to the revolver.

"Now, then," continued Duggan, "are you sure you don't want any ammo? I've got some 'ere I can give yer."

Young shook his head. "You said over the phone that you knew someone who could make me bullets to order."

"Yep, that's right, me mate can make you customised ammunition out of any metal you want."

"That's just what I need, can you take me to him?"

Duggan sighed. "Ok, suit yerself." He turned to his bodyguard. "Butch, take my friend 'ere down to slippery Pete's place, 'e'll be expectin' you."

Butch nodded his understanding and turned to leave the room.

Duggan rose to his feet, and Young did the same. As they walked to the front door, Duggan slapped his hand on the detective's shoulder in a gesture of warmth and companionship. "Now, then," he began, waiting just inside the door. "You know the score, this thing can't be traced back to me, but all the same, you won't be tempted to tell anyone where yer got it."

"No," Young assured him. "You'll have to trust me on this, but I promise no one will ever know."

Duggan furrowed his brow and squinted at Young. "Why can't you tell me what it's fer? Are yer goin' to knock off a bank or someink?"

Young smiled wryly. "Take my word for it," he sighed, "you wouldn't believe me if I told you."

Butch was waiting for Young at the end of the corridor by the lift.

As he approached, Young saw that the door was open. He realised that he should have known better than to believe the teenagers downstairs.

They rode down together. Young kept his eyes concentrated on the floor, though he suspected that Butch kept his on him. He had the gun tucked away in his jacket pocket and instinctively kept patting it as if to make sure that it was still secure.

Once they reached the ground floor, there was no sign of the youths outside the lift.

Young followed Butch outside and saw him head towards the Harley Davidson he had seen on his way in. Now he knew why it remained untouched!

When Young turned to walk towards his vehicle, he saw the teenagers from outside the lift gathered around it. Some were actually sitting on the bonnet, and a couple were peering in through the windows, suspiciously looking as if they were checking out if there was anything inside worth stealing.

As Young drew closer, the boys all looked over to him, but none of them moved.

Young reached inside his jacket for his warrant card, as it seemed to him to be his only chance of making them scatter.

Chapter 25

Even on this estate, youngsters did not want the hassle of having to spend time locked up for a minor offence.

From behind, Young suddenly heard the roar of an engine.

To his surprise, the boys all stood up and moved silently away from his car without looking back. Young turned to see Butch on his Harley, waiting for him to get behind the wheel.

Once he started his engine, Young watched Butch pull out onto the street in front of the block and head on down towards the main road. He hoped that the biker would appreciate that Young would not be able to swerve in and out of the traffic and that he would need to stay back for Young to follow him.

As it was, he need not have worried. Butch pulled over every time he noticed Young falling back. They stayed on the main road until they had reached Dulwich, and then Butch turned onto a side road and followed the back-doubles until they reached their destination.

The back-street garage had a yellow facia, which showed more rust than paint. The sign outside was for Pete's Motors, and from here it looked, at least to Young, to be closed.

Butch parked outside and dismounted. He went to the closed door, which was built into the roller shutter, and banged on it several times. Eventually, the door was opened by a skinny man in his mid-forties, wearing blue overalls covered in dried oil.

Once the man, who Young presumed was Pete from the sign, saw Butch, he nodded. That was the signal for the big biker to climb back on his bike and roar off into the distance.

Young parked up and climbed out of his car. He walked over to where the man in overalls was standing, and when he was close enough so that no one else could overhear him, he said, "Duggan sent me."

The man ushered him in without formality and slammed and locked the shutter door behind him. Pete headed for an office situated at the far end of the garage. The floor of the shop was littered with various shells from different cars, with metal shelving on each side of the walls bursting with exhausts, tyres and a host of accessories, most of which looked used.

Pete shut the door of the office behind them. He slumped down in an old worn swivel chair behind a desk overflowing with paperwork, most of which was stained with oil.

"So, what you got for me?" Pete asked in a matter-a-fact way.

Young hesitated for a moment, then he pulled out the gun Duggan had given him and placed it in front of Pete.

"I need you to make me some ammunition for this!" he stated, trying not to let his voice quiver. This entire circumstance was so far removed from Young's usual behaviour that, not for the first time that day, he was starting to question his actions.

Pete picked up the gun and frowned. "So, what's the problem? Didn't Duggan have any to spare?"

Young took a deep breath. "It's not that. Duggan told me you could make bullets to order out of any metal, is that true?"

Pete nodded. "You give me the metal, I make the ammo, plain and simple."

Young removed the plastic bag of silver crucifixes from his pocket and placed them on the table.

Pete put down the gun and inspected the holy ornaments.

He looked up at Young. "Are you fuckin' serious?" he snapped. "Silver fuckin' bullets, what are you, the Lone Ranger?"

Young tried to keep his cool, but he could feel the tension rising within him. "Can you do it for me, or not?"

Pete thought for a moment. "Yeah, I can do it, keep yer 'air on," he replied, removing one of the crucifixes from its container and hefting it in his hand.

"Can you do it now?" asked Young urgently.

"It'll take about an hour, that ok for you, kemosabe?" Pete laughed scornfully.

Young waited while Pete disappeared into his workshop to undertake the task.

He decided to check in with Jenna.

She answered on the second ring. "Alan?" she sounded a little terse.

"Hiya, just thought I'd check in, how's your reunion going?"

"It's not," Jenna replied.

"How do you mean?"

"Trisha still hasn't arrived, and she should have been here ages ago."

"Perhaps she's had some car trouble," Young said helpfully. "Have you tried calling her?"

"Several times, and each time her phone goes straight to voicemail. Alan, I'm really getting worried about her, this isn't like her at all."

Young felt helpless. As much as he did not want to cause Jenna any undue concern, he did not like the thought of her being all alone at the hotel without him or her friend for company.

"Alan?" Jenna asked tentatively. "You don't think she's had an accident, do you?"

"No, listen, I'm sure she's fine, perhaps she forgot her mobile and didn't realise it until she broke down. There's a million reasons why she might be late."

"Name them!" Jenna demanded, trying to introduce some levity into the conversation. She was glad to hear Young's voice, and she realised she should have called him earlier instead of just sitting in her room, growing more anxious by the minute.

"You know what I mean!" Young scolded her. "Listen, I should be on my way back soon, and I'm sure she will be there by the time I arrive. Then I can have the pleasure of taking the two of you to dinner, how's that?"

There was a brief pause before Jenna answered. "Ok, what time will you be here?"

Young remembered that he had not told Jenna where he was going today, and the chances were that she presumed he was still in town.

"I've just got a couple of things to clear up and speak to my sergeant...when he gets back from his conference, then I'll be on my way. Just call me if you hear anything."

He felt a sharp pang of guilt at having to lie to her, but he convinced himself that she would panic even more if she knew he was so far away.

"Ok, I'll see you later, bye."

"Bye, darling." Young could not help but detect the tone of Jenna's voice.

She sounded scared, even if she did not want to admit it to him.

As much as he wanted to remain rational, there was something deeply coincidental about Jenna's friend's lateness, which did not sit easy with him.

Chapter Twenty-Six

YOUNG GREW INCREASINGLY IMPATIENT WAITING FOR Pete to return. From behind the back door of the office, he could hear the rasping sound of metal being shaved, and it reminded him of his time spent in metal work at secondary school.

He had always hated that sound, but at least this time it was muffled by the closed door between them.

Although he had tried to keep it from Jenna, he was really concerned by the fact that her friend had not turned up yet. The entire situation was starting to become a little too real for his liking. First, with the disappearance of Jenna's uncle; then with everything Professor Pudelko had told them; next, his strange encounter with the woman in the book shop; and now, the unexplained tardiness of Jenna's friend.

He needed to be with Jenna. In hindsight, he should never have left her alone in Huntley, but then, what alternative did he have. He certainly did not want to expose her to the kind of villains he needed help from today.

What's more, with Trisha's pending arrival already arranged, it would have been rude, not to mention a tad possessive, to insist that Jenna accompany him and tell her friend they would have to rearrange their get-together.

Young stood up abruptly, almost knocking his chair over, and began to pace the floor. Being so far away from Jenna made him feel completely powerless. He needed to get back to her as soon as possible.

What was taking this bloke so long?

Young considered venturing into Pete's private workshop to enquire how much longer he was likely to be. But then he stopped himself. He knew that Pete had no reason to keep him waiting any longer than was necessary. After all, he was not being paid by the hour.

Young just hoped that the mechanic knew what he was doing. After all his efforts from today, at the very least he wanted to be able to return to Jenna with a viable option to protect her if it became necessary.

―――

Jenna finished the chapter she had been reading and discarded her book on the table. She stood up and wandered back into her room to fetch a jumper. The late afternoon sun was already on its downward slide towards the horizon, and she could feel that the wind was picking up.

This was not like Trisha!

The longer she waited, the more Jenna grew convinced that something had happened to her friend. When Young first dropped her off that morning, Jenna had half expected a barrage of questions from Audrey, demanding to know where she had been and why she did not take the trouble to inform her that she planned on staying away for a while.

Walking towards the reception, Jenna had begun to formulate some off-the-cuff answers to placate the inquisitive hotelier.

But to her surprise, for once, Audrey was not standing guard, and one of the young waitresses gave Jenna her key.

Jenna spent the rest of the day in her room waiting for Trisha's arrival.

Now, she was not only concerned, she was also hungry and in desperate need of a drink.

She decided that she would go downstairs and retrieve the papers the professor had given them from her car and read over them again in the bar while she waited for Trisha to arrive.

Before she left her room, Jenna tried her friend once more, but again her call went straight to voicemail. As she had already left her several that afternoon, Jenna did not bother to leave another.

When she entered the lobby, the reception desk was unmanned, so Jenna skipped passed it and made her way out to the car park.

As she made her way across the gravel floor to her car, something suddenly caught her eye. Frowning to herself, Jenna altered her direction and began walking towards the side of the hotel, where the overspill car park was situated.

For a moment, she thought that the fading light was merely playing a trick on her. But the closer she came the more convinced she was that Trisha's car was parked at the far end of the lot.

She knew what type of car her friend drove, as she had seen it on several occasions when she had visited her at home, but right now Jenna wished that she had paid more attention to the vehicle's number plate or other distinguishing features.

Once she had reached the car, Jenna stared at it for a moment. She was sure that the colour was the same, although to be fair, she had mainly seen it in darkness when she and Trisha had gone back to her place after work for dinner.

Jenna walked around the vehicle twice. There were no distinguishing markings that she remembered, but there was an ugly dent across the driver's door, and now she thought about it, she was sure that Trisha had mentioned an incident a couple of months ago where a cyclist had rammed into the side of her car while she was waiting at a junction.

Why on earth would Trisha be at the hotel without contacting her? It just did not make any sense. Jenna was sorely tempted to try the door handles, just in case the car was unlocked. Perhaps then she might find something in the glove box that proved that this car belonged to her friend.

Jenna looked around her. There was no one else in sight, but even so, her natural in-built caution convinced her that she was not being rational, and if she did try the doors she would suddenly find herself being shouted at by the genuine owner who was watching her suspicious behaviour from their hotel window right this minute.

Before walking away, Jenna studied the number plate. Again, nothing jumped out at her. She decided to memorise it and check at reception, just in case they knew who the owner was.

Having retrieved her papers from her own car, Jenna walked back into the hotel.

There was still no one on reception, so reluctantly she rang the bell, half-expecting Audrey to appear with a barrage of questions. But to her surprise, it was another of the waitresses who had served them at dinner.

The girl smiled warmly. "How may I help?" she asked cheerily.

"I'm sorry to be a nuisance, but would you happen to know who the owner of that purple Golf in the car park is?" Jenna could tell from the girl's puzzled look that she was going to have to elucidate a little more before she received an answer. "It's just that I have been expecting a friend to arrive all day, and I'd swear that car is hers."

The girl seemed to relax at Jenna's explanation.

"I'm sorry, but I don't, we don't make a note of customer's

registrations as we have a lot of drop-ins who just come for dinner or a drink. I'm really sorry."

"That's no problem," replied Jenna, a little deflated. "It's probably not her car anyway."

The receptionist moved over to the computer on the desk and began hitting keys.

"What's your friend's name? I can check if she has booked in already."

Jenna held up her hand. "That's ok, she hasn't booked a room yet, I told her not to worry because Audrey told me you had plenty to spare," Jenna lied.

The girl looked up and smiled. "That's true," she confirmed, "your friend will be spoilt for choice at the moment."

Jenna nodded. "Thanks for your help. I think I'll just wait for her in the bar."

When Pete finally emerged from his workshop, Young was almost at his wit's end and was unable to hide his expression from the mechanic.

"You can't rush a professional." He grinned in response, showing a set of teeth with several gaps in them.

Pete dumped the plastic bag on his desk. Young moved in closer for a better look. The bullets within certainly looked real to him, though he had to admit he was no expert on the subject.

"Well, open it!" Pete said roughly. "They won't bite!"

Young reached for the bag and pulled out a handful of bullets. He rubbed a few of them between his fingers. They were perfectly smooth to the touch, and he had to admit, they did appear to have been well crafted.

Young looked up at Pete, who was busy lighting a cigar. "Will they work?" he asked sceptically. He could see the anger flash across the mechanic's face. Young held his hand up. "I mean, they look perfect and all, but they will fire, won't they? These aren't for fun!"

Without speaking, Pete reached over and grabbed a handful of bullets from the bag. Picking up the handgun, he released the chamber from the handle and proceeded to slot the bullets into the holder. Each one slipped in effortlessly.

Once the chamber was full, Pete shoved it back inside the handle and pulled back on the firing catch across the top of the barrel.

He handed the gun to Young, handle first. "You wanna try it out? Be my guest," he growled, obviously still furious that Young had questioned his craftmanship.

Young hefted the loaded weapon in his hand. He was not at all comfortable holding the firearm, but this was what he had come all the way to London for, so he had no reason to complain.

Young looked back at Pete sheepishly. "I'm sure it's fine, I didn't mean to question your craft, I'm just not used to handling such things as this."

Pete seemed to accept Young's apology, and he slumped back in his wing chair to concentrate on his cigar.

Young aimed the gun at the floor and felt the trigger.

"Hold on." Pete leaned over and tentatively took the weapon from Young. "You see this catch at the side?" he asked, pointing to a ribbed lever, barely perceptible from where Young was standing. "Well, this is your safety catch. I advise you to keep it on unless you are about to fire the weapon."

Pete slipped the catch forward, and Young heard it take hold.

He handed the gun back to Young.

Young thanked him and asked him what he owed.

Pete thought for a moment while chewing on his cigar.

Finally, he said, "Nah, that's ok, Duggan said 'e'll see me right."

Young stuffed the remainder of the bullets into his side

jacket pocket and tucked the firearm into the one on the other side. As he left the garage, he almost expected to be met by a group of armed officers from London, who would demand that he dropped his weapon and lie down on the floor.

That would certainly leave him with a lot of explaining.

Young wondered if what he was experiencing was the same feeling those on the other side of the law had under similar situations.

As he pulled away from the kerb, Young could feel himself relax. The tension from the whole experience thus far was still there, but now that he was on his way back home, Young at least felt as if the worst was over.

Chapter Twenty-Seven

Jenna sat in the bar sipping her wine, aimlessly spinning her mobile around in front of her on the table. Her concern for Trisha was palpable. In all the years she had known her, her friend had never once let her down. It was completely out of character for her to be this late without at least contacting Jenna with the reason why.

Therefore, as far as she was concerned, Trisha must be in trouble. Jenna's worst fear was that she had met with an accident on the motorway. But she had checked the news earlier in her room and looked up the BBC website for an update, and there was no information concerning a pile-up or a serious accident of any kind.

Also, there was that car in the hotel car park. Jenna could not be a hundred percent sure, but she was convinced that it belonged to Trisha, which also made no sense because if she was already at the hotel, surely she would have contacted Jenna by now.

Jenna wished that Young were here with her now. Being stuck on her own for the majority of the day was not helping her paranoia that something weird was going on in Huntley.

Chapter 27

They were no closer to finding any details concerning the disappearance of her uncle. That strange woman who ran the bookshop definitely needed investigating, only not by Young, or at least not on his own after yesterday. Those weird theories Pudelko had filled their minds with had certainly done nothing to alleviate Jenna's fears with regard to her uncle, and now this business with Trisha not showing up as arranged.

It was all becoming too much for her; she needed answers.

From the corner of the room Jenna saw Audrey appear. The woman gazed around the bar until she spotted Jenna, then she made a beeline for her.

Jenna sighed. This was the last thing she needed. More senseless questions from the interfering busybody who clearly had too much time on her hands, not to mention an unfathomable interest in Jenna's comings and goings.

Jenna drained her glass. She needed fortification if she was about to be interrogated.

Audrey's smile grew wider as she crossed the floor towards Jenna's table.

There was no way Jenna could pretend not to have seen her, so she attempted the warmest smile she could muster when Audrey finally reached her side.

"Well, hello, stranger," Audrey began. "I was beginning to think that young Alan had kidnapped you."

Jenna tried not to betray her sheer annoyance at the woman's presence to show through her fake smile.

"Is he not here?" Audrey asked, turning to check the bar area.

"No, I'm afraid he's still at work, but I am expecting him later."

"Lovely," beamed Audrey, "I've just been speaking to young Ellen on the desk. She said you were making enquiries about your friend, and, well, I just escorted her up to her room not more than five minutes ago, we must have just missed each other."

Jenna's eyes lit up. For the first time that day she felt a positive energy surge through her. "Trisha?" she asked excitedly. "Are you sure?"

Audrey nodded. "Yes, dear, when she arrived, she told me she was your friend, so I didn't bother with the formality of booking her in, I took her straight up as she said you had been expecting her. We knocked on your door, but there was no answer."

Jenna shot up, almost knocking over her chair in her haste. "I must have been out in the car park," she replied, "I needed to get these papers from my car." Jenna collected up her paperwork and crammed it into the cardboard folder, the order and sequence of the sheets no longer a priority.

"Right, well, I've put your friend in room 412. I've just left her in there to unpack; why don't you pop along up and surprise her, I'm sure she can't wait to see you."

Such was her relief, Jenna had to stop herself from hugging the landlady. Instead she gave her a gentle pat on the arm and thanked her again.

Although Audrey had put Trisha on the top floor, Jenna was too excited to wait for the lift. She bounded up the stairs two at a time, unaware that she was holding her breath until she reached Trisha's floor. Then she finally let the air out of her mouth before having to take in huge gulps as she walked along the corridor to room 412.

Right this moment, Jenna did not care why her friend was so late or why she had not contacted her earlier to explain her delay. The fact that she was here now was all that mattered, and Jenna could not wait to see her.

By the time she reached the door, Jenna's breathing was back under control. She knocked several times in succession and waited.

Chapter 27

After a moment, when there was no answer, Jenna wondered if by chance Trisha had made her way down in the lift while Jenna was rushing up to meet her. That would be just about typical after the kind of day she had been having.

Just as she was about to turn back and head towards the lift, Jenna heard a voice inside the room call for her to enter.

Jenna grabbed the handle and twisted it. She nudged the door open and walked into the room, expecting to see her friend waiting with open arms.

When she entered, the room appeared empty.

The main light was off, and the room was illuminated by a small table lamp on the far end of the bed.

Jenna squinted in the dim light. "Trisha, where are you?" she called out, surveying the room. It was a good deal bigger than hers, but that was not the issue.

Where was her friend?

"I'm over here," a voice called from the shadows.

Jenna strained to see more clearly, and then she noticed her friend was standing outside on the balcony, which seemed to stretch the entire width of the room.

The net curtains billowed in the breeze from the open door, so Jenna could barely make out her friend's silhouette in the poor light.

"There you are!" Jenna exclaimed, relieved. "Where on earth have you been?"

Jenna rushed around the king-size bed, dropping her file of papers on it as she made straight for the veranda.

Jenna reached out for her friend as she crossed the threshold, her arms outstretched to the willowy figure who stood with her back to her, gazing out at the darkened woodland beyond the hotel perimeter.

But then she realised that something was wrong!

Trisha was small and petite, just like Jenna, but from this close the woman with her back to her appeared taller.

Jenna stopped short in the doorway. "Trisha?" she called, tentatively.

It was then that June Le Vant finally turned around to face her.

"Hello, you. I've been waiting!"

———

Young had been mostly fortunate with the weight of traffic on his return journey back to Huntley. At times he had noticed his speedometer needle leaning towards a hundred miles per hour, instead of the seventy the law demanded.

The last thing he needed was to be stopped by the motorway police, especially with an unlicensed firearm in his possession. He reasoned that if such a situation did occur, a flash of his warrant card should hopefully be all that was needed.

But he knew from conversations with colleagues that there was still an awful lot of overzealous uniformed officers who would insist that he go through the motions, regardless of the fact that he was one of them.

He decided it was best to err on the side of caution.

Reluctantly, he slowed down to a more reasonable speed but kept in the fast lane to ensure he still made it back to Huntley in the quickest possible time.

Young knew that all he had achieved that day was necessary, but by the same token he was wracked with guilt at having to leave Jenna all alone.

Mind you, if her friend had played her part, that would not have been the case.

Young wondered if Jenna had heard from her yet.

He glanced at his mobile sitting in the handsfree holder. He had not missed any calls from Jenna.

He decided to give her a ring just to make sure everything

was alright and assure her he would be back with her within the hour.

Young hit the speed-dial for Jenna's phone.

He listened over the speaker.

Jenna's phone rang twice before the call was cut off.

Young tried again. This time the number would not go through.

He attempted to make the call twice more, but each time, the number he was trying to reach came up as unavailable.

Now he no longer cared about being stopped.

Young switched on his blue light and hit the siren, shoving his foot down hard on the accelerator.

Jenna gasped when she saw the figure of June Le Vant looming over her. The tall, elegant woman that she had seen on only a couple of occasions appeared now to be far less refined, with an almost animalistic quality about her.

The two women stayed where they were for a moment, surveying each other.

Jenna could not comprehend what the woman was doing there in her friend's room.

Audrey had definitely told her room number 412. So, unless she had misheard her, or the landlady herself had accidently given her the wrong room, she was definitely in the right place, just with the wrong person.

"I'm very sorry," Jenna offered, "it appears I have the wrong room. I was looking for my friend."

June laughed and slowly let her tongue sweep across her teeth as if in anticipation of a sumptuous meal about to be laid before her. "Oh, you have the correct room, make no mistake about that, young lady," June drawled, taking her first step towards Jenna.

Jenna automatically backed off, almost tripping against the veranda step as she moved backwards.

There was something decidedly sinister about this woman, and she was sure that it was not just her imagination playing with her.

Without warning, June Le Vant moved forward with an ease that caught Jenna completely unaware. Before she had a chance to move back, June was standing directly in front of her with her hands on her shoulders.

The woman's grip felt almost vise-like to Jenna. Whether intentional or not, Jenna knew that she could not free herself without a major struggle ensuing.

From this proximity, Jenna could not help but notice the woman's features. They appeared more animal-like than human. Her nose and mouth were elongated and more resembled a muzzle and a snout, than a normal person's visage. Her ears had taken on a pointy extreme and stuck up through the woman's thickly tousled hair.

But it was her eyes which caused Jenna the most distress. They had formed themselves into blood-red orbs with tiny black dots for pupils, and there was a malicious rage burning behind them, which was aimed directly at her.

June pulled Jenna reluctantly toward her. The fetid breath that emanated from the creature's jaws struck Jenna full on in the face, and she felt as if she were about to gag from the stench.

Jenna steeled herself and tried to break free for the creature's grasp. But it was to no avail. June threw back her mighty head and laughed maniacally with a guttural roar.

"What's the matter?" she growled. "No big brave Officer Young to protect you now. Well, don't you worry, I will be waiting for him when he returns. He has always been mine, and you tried to take him from me."

Chapter 27

Jenna had no words of response. She could feel her entire body quivering in fright.

Keeping her gaze fixed directly on June, Jenna reached into her pocket and slipped out her mobile. If possible, she wanted to try and dial Young so that at least he could hear what was going on and would know just who — or what — to go after if he arrived there too late.

But as she managed to free her phone from her jeans, it buzzed into life.

Before Jenna had a chance to respond, June grabbed the phone in one of her claw-like paws and stared at the screen.

"Well, well, speak of the devil," she growled. Holding the phone up, she closed her hand around it and squeezed.

Jenna heard the sound of metal, glass and plastic shatter, as June crunched the phone down to a mass of twisted remnants before dropping the useless remnants to the floor.

With only one hand on her shoulder keeping her in place, Jenna wrenched herself free and turned for the bedroom door.

In a blinding flash, June suddenly appeared in front of her, blocking her way.

"Now, just where do you think you're going?" she snarled, baring her huge pointed fangs.

June held her arms out to her side as if to stop Jenna from snaking around her.

Jenna watched transfixed as the woman's fingers seemed to grow longer, her fingernails curling into elongated, razor-sharp claws.

Jenna automatically took a step backwards. Although she knew that her only chance of escape was back behind the creature, her first instinct was to just move away from it and try and put some distance between them.

For a second she considered making a dash for the veranda and leaping over the balcony. But as they were on the fourth floor, Jenna reasoned that her chances of survival would be minimal at best.

What was more, she knew that if she managed to scream for help, even if she was heard by some of the other guests, June would be upon her before any help could be summoned.

As if reading her mind, June began to advance. "Now, don't go thinking about screaming for help, you know that won't do you any good," she warned. "Because then I will have to kill you straight away, and I was hoping for enough time to play with you until I get bored."

Jenna knew her situation was hopeless.

With no way of escape, she stared back at the creature that had once been June Le Vant. "Oh, for the love of god, just kill me and be done with it, you bitch!"

The creature shook its shaggy head as it closed in on its hapless victim. "No, no, no, that won't do at all," it chided, and the voice coming from deep within its throat no longer held any resemblance to June's sultry tone. "First, I'm going to torture you until you are begging me to kill you. Then, and only then, if I am feeling generous, I will put you out of your misery. So, you'd better behave and speak nicely to me, or else your demise will be far worse than anything you could ever imagine!"

Jenna had almost reached the veranda step.

She knew that she was fast running out of options.

Before she had a chance to try and think of something, the creature leapt forward and grabbed her by the front of her blouse. Its claws ripped through the fabric and scraped against her bare flesh, causing Jenna to wince.

With one move, the creature picked Jenna up and threw her to the floor beside the bed. The landing caused the wind to be knocked out of her, but before Jenna could regain her breath, the creature jumped on her, straddling her meagre frame and trapping her beneath its mighty physique.

Chapter 27

Jenna looked up into the malicious, burning red eyes of the beast and waited for her torment to commence.

From out of nowhere, another shape leapt through the dim light and smacked into the creature, knocking it sideways off Jenna.

Jenna scrambled backwards, shoving at the carpeted floor with her feet until her back reached the corner of the bed and the wall beside it. She crammed herself into as tight a ball as she could, while the two werewolves rolled and tussled with each other before her.

The two creatures tore and clawed at each other in a frenzied battle.

Jenna's mind could not comprehend what was happening. Why this other beast had suddenly appeared and attacked one of its own was incomprehensible.

Jenna wondered if they were fighting over her, with the winner enjoying the spoils.

The thought made her feel sick, but due to some horrendous fascination akin to rubberneckers who could not help but slow down to watch the suffering of road traffic victims, she was unable to tear her eyes away from the onslaught before her.

The two creatures continued their battle, and neither seemed to Jenna to be an obvious victor. They hefted each other off the ground in turn and smashed their opponent down on the floor and against the walls, but neither beast looked to be any worse off for being on the receiving end.

Jenna did notice that the second werewolf, which had saved her momentarily from June's clutches, did appear to be much smaller than its opponent. But that did not seem to prevent it from holding its own against a much bigger adversary.

The bloody combat continued for what seemed to Jenna to be ages. Each time she felt as if it might be worth her climbing onto the bed and making her way to the door, they seemed to bring the battle closer to where she was. Even though the second werewolf had, at least temporarily, saved her from June, Jenna was in no doubt that it had only done it so that it could feast on her itself.

It was like watching two hungry animals fighting over the spoils.

Finally, the smaller of the two sank its fangs in June's neck and kept hold while it shook its head back and forth like a mongoose wrestling with a snake.

June let out a cry of anguish as blood spurted out of the gaping wound in her neck, spraying the room in an arc of crimson.

Jenna could feel herself being splattered. She held her hands over her face, but she could already taste the coppery tang of June's blood on her tongue. She turned towards the bed and wiped her tongue on the duvet, keeping her head turned away as the pitiful creature cried out its last.

Eventually, Jenna heard a massive thump as the lifeless werewolf slumped to the floor.

Jenna turned back, overcome by a ghoulish compulsion to watch as the dead creature transformed back into her nemesis. The transformation took seconds, until June's naked form lay a few feet in front of her, her head lolling dangerously to one side as a result of the other werewolf's bite.

For a moment, Jenna felt a modicum of pity for the woman. Jenna had no idea how she had been transformed into such a hideous beast, but she was sure that June Le Vant never asked for it, and once she had been changed, perhaps she could not fight the compulsion to feed on human flesh and blood.

Just then, Jenna remembered the victor!

She turned her head slowly and saw the other werewolf standing to one side. Its huge chest was rising and falling from the exertion of the fight. It was looking down at its conquest. But as Jenna watched, it slowly turned its head to survey its prize.

Chapter 27

Jenna felt her body stiffen. She knew that her time had come. It was the only reasonable explanation for why the creature had intervened and killed one of its own.

The beast strode over to where Jenna lay huddled next to the bed.

Its salivating jaws dripped as it prepared for the feast to follow.

Jenna looked into the beast's eyes. Just like June's, they glowed red with rage, and yet, as the beast drew nearer, there was something odd about them that Jenna could not place.

The werewolf was now standing directly over Jenna. It dropped to all fours, its face only inches away from her own.

"Jenna. Jenna." The words came out in a guttural low growl, but there was something about them, just like with the eyes, that Jenna recognised.

The creature moved one of its mighty paws forward, and Jenna flinched. But instead of slashing her with its elongated claws, it merely rested its paw on Jenna's hand.

"Jenna," it spoke again, desperately trying to form words with its tongue lolling over its massive jaws. "It's me, Trisha."

Jenna stared back in disbelief.

Could this thing before her actually be her friend?

A rush of emotions flooded her senses.

"Trisha, is that really you?"

The beast nodded its head.

"But how? Why?" Jenna could feel her throat starting to clog as a huge lump formed there. Her eyes brimmed over with tears as she mourned the loss of her friend. For surely there was no way back from what she had become.

Trisha pointed to June's dead body. "She turned me. She thought she had killed me, but instead she made me one of them."

Before Jenna's eyes, her friend began to transform back into her old self.

Jenna reached forward and threw her arms around her and hugged her tightly.

Trisha responded likewise. Her arms, still part beast, were powerful and strong and almost crushed the breath from Jenna's lungs as she squeezed.

When they released, Jenna saw her old friend kneeling before her with virtually every trace of the werewolf gone.

Jenna grabbed Trisha's hand. "Come on, we need to get out of here, I'll take you to Alan's place, and we'll call him and tell him what's happened. Everything is going to be fine. All we need to do…"

"No!" Trisha cut Jenna off in mid-sentence. "You don't understand, I'm one of them now!"

Jenna stared at her friend incredulously. "But you just saved my life; if you were one of them, why would you do that?"

Fresh tears were now streaming down Trisha's cheeks, as well. "Because I have only just been changed, so the human part of me is still there. But I can feel it moving further and further away. Even now, I'm fighting the urge to attack you. You can't stay with me; you won't be safe."

Jenna could not believe what she was hearing, but she knew that she had no choice.

Right now, Trisha was human. But seconds ago, she had been a raging animal tearing out the flesh of another beast in a frenzied attack.

But then, her reason for doing so was to save her friend, so that must count for something.

Jenna wiped away her tears. "This can't be it — I won't accept it!" she demanded. "You just saved me from a horrific death, so there is still good in you. Part of you is still Trisha, my best friend."

Trisha grabbed Jenna's wrists tightly. Jenna yelped at the sudden pain, and Trisha immediately loosened her grip. "Listen to me, Jenna, please understand I cannot stay like this for long,

Chapter 27

the draw is too much for me to withstand. You need to get away from here, as far as you can. They are coming for you, and there are too many of them for me to fight them all off. Now, please, just go, run!"

Trisha's words took hold. Jenna leaned in, and the two women hugged each other once more, this time for the last time.

"Well, now isn't this simply lovely?"

The two women let go and looked back at the bedroom door where the voice had come from.

Katerina stood there, flanked by several werewolves of all sizes, staring down at the two women with salivating jaws.

Jenna instinctively shuffled back into Trisha's comforting frame.

Katerina threw her head back and laughed scornfully. "She can't save you now, she's with me whether she likes it or not. She knows she has no choice!"

Jenna could feel Trisha's body beginning to shake and convulse.

She moved away and turned back as her friend began to transform once more into a werewolf. Jenna stared into her friend's eyes and watched as the humanness began to dissolve, only to be replaced by the animalistic stare she had seen earlier.

Jenna knew her last chance for survival had gone!

Her friend was powerless to defend her now!

Trisha rose to her feet, her full transformation now complete.

"Bring her!" Katerina demanded, indicating with a nod of her head towards Jenna's cowering form.

The beast bent down and grabbed Jenna under the arms and lifted her off the floor with ease. Then it turned with Jenna's limp body in its arms and carried her over to the veranda, placing her on one of the chairs on the balcony.

The beast turned back to face Katerina and her troops.

"You dare to defy me? I am your mistress, now bring her to

me!" Katerina's voice had changed since her last order and now she too had a guttural depth to her tone.

Trisha shook her head defiantly, and closed the veranda doors behind her, locking Jenna out.

Jenna stood up and glanced over the balcony once more. She knew her only chance was to jump. That was doubtless what Trisha's human side — what was left of it — had meant for her to do. But the drop was far too high, and even if she did survive, Jenna doubted she would make it without breaking something. Then she would just be a sitting target.

Jenna turned back to the room. Trisha's werewolf was still blocking the doors with her huge frame, but Jenna could still see Katerina through the glass, her face contorting into a mask of hideous rage and malevolence.

Katerina took a couple of steps into the room. Trisha tensed in anticipation of attack.

The other werewolves began to flood in around their mistress, awaiting her command.

There was silence for a moment, and no one moved.

Katerina took in a deep breath. She appeared calm and completely in control and not the slightest bit concerned anymore by Trisha's defiance.

Finally, she spoke. "Kill her!" she demanded. "And bring the other one!"

In unison, the werewolves began to advance on Trisha.

Trisha stood her ground, still barring the doorway that led to Jenna.

In panic, Jenna took another look over the balcony, but it was still not a feasible option in her mind.

She turned back to see that the werewolves were almost upon her friend.

Trisha was poised like a wrestler about to link up with its opponent.

Jenna knew that strong as she was, Trisha would not be able

to handle all the advancing beasts by herself. Trisha had risked her life to save her; now it was Jenna's turn to try and repay the favour.

She burst through the veranda doors. "No, wait, there's no need for this, I'll come quietly, please just don't hurt my friend."

The other werewolves stopped in their tracks.

Trisha turned on the spot and growled menacingly at Jenna. For a split second, Jenna was convinced that her friend was about to attack her. She pulled back slightly. She mouthed the words, 'It'll be ok,' without speaking and attempted a smile.

Trisha turned her attention back to the beasts surrounding her.

From the other end of the room, Katerina reiterated, "Kill her, and bring the other one!"

The werewolves moved in to attack as one.

Chapter Twenty-Eight

YOUNG SCREECHED TO A HALT INSIDE THE HOTEL CAR park, his tyres kicking up a cloud of dust and gravel. Even with his siren and lights flashing, the journey had taken far longer than he would have liked.

He scanned the car park as he ran towards the foyer. There was no sign of Jenna's car, but he presumed that in the dim glow of the car park lighting, he could not be certain if it was parked there without searching the entire area, and he did not have time for that.

Young arrived at the reception desk, breathless. There was no one on duty, so he slammed his palm against the bell on the counter several times, trying to attract someone's attention.

When no one responded, Young ran through into the bar and restaurant areas. He scanned the tables for any sign of Jenna, but she was nowhere to be seen.

He noticed some of the other diners looking at him, but he ignored their stares and turned back to the reception area.

Young knew that Jenna had a view of the woods from her room, but that could cover a plethora of options, so he needed to know exactly which room to aim for.

Chapter 28

Since his earlier attempt to contact her, Young had re-tried several times, and each time his call refused to go through. He had considered calling the hotel, but after Jenna had shared her suspicions with him about Audrey and some of her guests, he decided it was better to just try and make his own way there as soon as possible.

Young was just about to hit the bell again when a young waitress appeared from the door behind reception.

She smiled when she saw Young. "Good evening, sir, may I help you?"

Young fumbled in his jacket pocket for his warrant card. When he found it, he opened it and held it up for the young lady to see.

She studied it for a few seconds, then turned back to him. "Is there some trouble?" she asked hesitantly.

"Where's Audrey, the proprietor?" he asked, more sharply than he had intended.

"I'm afraid she is out for the evening. One of the assistant managers is on duty if you would like me to get her?"

"No time." Young walked around the reception to stand beside the young girl. He could tell she was not comfortable with his presence on her side of the desk, but she managed to maintain her professional stance.

The computer booking system was open. Young tried tapping in Jenna's details, but nothing showed up on the screen.

"Is there anything I can do?" the girl asked tentatively.

Young moved back, allowing her access to the screen. "Yes, please, I'm looking for the room of a Miss Jenna Wilkinson, she's a guest of yours."

The girl hesitated for a moment, then moved forward and began typing in Jenna's details using a different page on the screen.

"Is this her?" she asked, stepping back to allow Young an unrestricted view.

Young scanned the booking, noting Jenna's room number at the hotel.

"Thanks," he said, running back around the reception and heading for the staircase to the upper floors.

The carpeted stairs were slippery under Young's leather soles, and in his haste, he almost lost his footing a couple of times.

Finally, he made it to Jenna's floor and strode purposefully down the corridor towards her room. It was now that he realised that he should have asked for a spare key. But circumstances being what they were, he decided if Jenna did not answer his knock, he had no option but to break the door down.

Counting down the numbers, he arrived outside Jenna's room.

Bracing himself, Young pounded on the door with his fist. As he feared, his call went unanswered.

Young tried the handle. It turned with ease, and the door opened.

Quickly checking over his shoulder to make sure no one was following him, Young entered the room.

"Jenna," he called out. The room was silent.

Reaching for the switch, Young flicked it down, but the room remained in darkness. He hit it several times back and forth, but to no avail. The light filtering in from the corridor barely illuminated the space where he was standing.

Young took a deep breath. He felt for the gun in his pocket, and reassured by its presence, he ventured in further.

The room was still. The open balcony door let in a cool breeze, which fluttered the long net curtains in front of it. There was only this room and the separate bathroom for him to investigate, and he already suspected that Jenna was not going to be in there.

As he took a tentative step towards the other room, Young suddenly caught a glimpse of something moving from his right-hand side. He stopped in his tracks and turned toward the balcony. It was then that he noticed a figure sitting in one of the chairs outside.

"Jenna," he called, relieved, "is that you?"

As he drew closer, he realised that whoever was outside could not possibly be Jenna after all. For one thing, their overall stature was far too big and bulky to be hers.

Young stood still and surveyed the shadowy figure masked by the flowing curtains.

"Who are you?" he demanded, using the tone he had cultivated during his training at Hendon.

The figure stayed put.

There was nothing for it. Young moved forward and drew aside the curtains and stared down at the smiling face of Kevin Roop.

The two men stared at each other for a moment before Young spoke.

"I said, who the hell are you? And where's Miss Wilkinson?"

Kevin continued to smile like a man with all the time in the world to play with. His huge frame barely squeezed into the iron chair the hotel provided as part of their veranda furniture ensemble.

Young could feel his frustration rising.

Whoever this was, he was in Jenna's room, so doubtless he knew something of her whereabouts, and if he thought for one second that Young was in the mood to be messed with, he had another thing coming.

"I'm only going to ask you once more: where is Miss Wilkinson?"

"Or else what?" The reply was in a deep, husky voice, which unnerved Young, although he managed to cover it.

Young cleared his throat. "Or else, I'm taking you down the station for questioning. You're trespassing in a private room, so you'd better start answering my questions, now!"

Kevin laughed scornfully. "So, you're going to slap the bracelets on me and drag me down the station, is that the plan? Now that I would really like to see."

With that, Kevin rose to his full height, which, even though he was one step down from the level Young was on, still meant that he towered over the officer's frame.

Without realising it, Young took a step back.

Using that as his cue, Kevin climbed into the room from outside. His massive shoulders almost blocked the entire doorway.

Even with all his training, Young knew that he would not be able to take Kevin into custody on his own, and what's more, he knew that his suspect knew it, too.

A guttural laugh began to emanate from deep within Kevin's throat.

In the dim light, Young could just make out the man's sneering smile as he watched Young helplessly trying to figure out what to do next.

Kevin tensed his muscles, clenching and relaxing his fists as if in anticipation of battle.

As Young looked on, he was sure that the man before him was growing right before his eyes.

"You want to know where your little girlfriend is, don't you?" Kevin's voice seemed to grow deeper with each syllable. "Well, the mistress has her in the woods, and boy, does she have some wicked plans for her."

For a moment, Young ignored Kevin's strange metamorphosis and concentrated on his words. "What do you mean, plans? What does she intend to do with her?"

"Oh, Mistress Katerina has been waiting a long time to find a victim like your little missy, and I intend to be there to revel in the sacrifice, just as soon as I've finished with you!"

Katerina! The name hit home immediately. The woman in

Chapter 28

the bookshop who had hypnotised him. Was that who he meant?

Young watched as Kevin tilted back his head and turned his neck from one side to the other in slow motion. Each time he moved, Young could hear what sounded like joints cracking and popping.

He strained to see what was happening to the man without having to move in any closer. Kevin's clothes began to rip as his body grew. When he dropped his head to stare back at Young, his face had contorted into a grisly, grotesque visage that more resembled an animal than a man.

Young quickly realised that everything Pudelko had told them was true.

There were indeed werewolves in the world, and one of them was right before him now — and would soon be ready to rip him to shreds if he did not react fast.

Young felt for his handgun. He removed it carefully from his pocket and held it out in front of him.

Kevin's transformation was almost complete. His shredded outer clothing lay sprawled around his feet, and even in the dim light, Young could tell that his naked body was coated in thick black hair-like fur.

The gun in his hand shook as Young tried desperately to take control of himself, as well as the situation.

The werewolf noticed the trembling hands of his opponent and laughed heartily.

This time, the sound of his mirth seemed to come from a far deeper source than before. His voice carried a menace and a loathing which only served to stiffen Young's resolve.

"Why don't you shoot me, copper!" The werewolf moved forward. "Come on, you can't miss from there, take your best shot!"

The werewolf held out its mighty arms to its sides, as if allowing Young the best possible target from this distance.

Young moved back until the back of his legs hit the side of the bed, and he almost lost his balance.

In desperation, he pulled the trigger.

Nothing happened!

The werewolf let out another almighty laugh. "What's the matter, forget to load it? Well, don't feel bad, bullets don't hurt us, anyway."

There was nowhere left for Young to go. He was blocked by the bed behind him.

He squeezed the trigger twice more, but still nothing engaged.

The werewolf continued to close in. They were so close now that Young could actually feel the creature's fetid breath against his skin.

With a guttural laugh, the werewolf launched itself into the air.

As Young fell back on the bed, his finger touched the safety catch, and he flicked it back and squeezed the trigger almost simultaneously.

The noise of the shot that rang out almost deafened Young.

The werewolf slammed against him, pinning him down on the mattress.

Young could feel the beast's massive fangs rubbing against the flesh of his neck.

He closed his eyes in anticipation of the bite he was about to receive.

But it never came!

Young lay there for a full minute with the weight of the dead werewolf on top of him.

Once he had realised that his shot had found its mark, Young heaved at the massive form, which even now threatened to crush him to death.

Unable to move it, Young managed to roll it enough to crawl

out from under it. He took himself to the bathroom and immediately vomited into the toilet.

After splashing his face with cold water, Young re-entered the bedroom to find the dead body of Kevin Roop draped across the bed.

He stood there for a moment, breathing hard. He walked over to the bed and retrieved his weapon, which he had dropped in his haste to make it to the bathroom.

Young slipped the safety back in place and slipped the gun back into his pocket as he left the room.

There was no one outside in the corridor, which surprised him, considering the sound of his gunshot had not even been muffled behind a closed door. But he did not have time to ponder the reason why.

Young decided to use the fire exit to leave the hotel.

Something told him he did not want to be seen leaving by the staff or guests.

Chapter Twenty-Nine

JENNA FELT HERSELF BEING SLAPPED AWAKE ROUGHLY. When she finally opened her eyes, it was to discover that she was lying on some sort of wooden platform, surrounded by a crowd of eager, malevolent faces peering down at her.

When she tried to move, she realised that her hands and feet were being held down by two men standing on either side of her. They had her stretched out into a bizarre sort of human star. From her position, she could tell that she was high up off the ground on some form of platform.

Jenna struggled against her captives, but she soon realised that such an effort was futile. The more she fought, the tighter they held onto her.

Once she stopped fighting, Jenna gazed around at the faces peering in at her. To her surprise, she seemed to recognise a couple of them. Audrey, her landlady, was there, as well as the father of the young boy who had fondled her outside her hotel room.

There were a couple of other recognisable faces from the hotel. The large woman she had seen at breakfast on her first day, one of the bartenders, and even one of the cleaners she had noticed a couple of times pushing her trolley along the corridor.

It was only now that she noticed that all those gathered were completely naked. Then, to her horror, she realised that she was, too.

Jenna opened her mouth to scream, but a huge hand clamped over it before the sound could leave her throat. The grip was so tight that Jenna was only able to breathe through her nose, so she attempted to relax once more in the hope that the assailant would loosen their grip when they realised that she was no longer struggling.

But the hand stayed fast, so she just concentrated on inhaling and exhaling using just her nose.

The cool night air caused Jenna to shiver involuntarily, and for a moment she was afraid her captors might take the movement as another sign of her trying to break free. But their hold on her was already so tight that they merely stayed in position.

Without warning, the two men holding her down suddenly wrenched her up into a standing position. The hand across her mouth fell away, and Jenna was allowed to stand by herself, with her jailors holding her steady by her wrists and elbows.

As Jenna scanned the crowd, which almost filled the field they were in, she could not help noticing that all the men had erections proudly on display. Some of them were stroking themselves, whilst others were being assisted by the women in the crowd. Men were standing behind women, their hands draped over their shoulders, fondling their naked breasts, while the females in return grinded their naked buttocks back against their partners' raging hard-ons.

Jenna closed her eyes in disgust at the orgy taking place before her.

When she opened them again, she saw the naked figure of Katerina standing before her.

The bookshop owner moved a step closer, and Jenna instinctively tried to move back but was held in place by those restraining her.

Katerina reached out and traced a line down Jenna's naked torso with her index finger.

"Get off me!" Jenna demanded as she squirmed at the woman's touch.

Katerina smiled and turned back to the crowd. As if a silent command passed between them, they all dispersed and set about collecting branches and discarded logs, which they built into a pointy hill in front of the podium on which Jenna was being held.

Some of the crowd appeared with petrol cans and doused the wood pile before finally setting light to it.

As the fire caught and the flames licked hungrily against the wooden structure, Jenna could feel the heat generated by the flames waft against her bare skin. It was a small comfort from the night chill.

Once the fire was blazing, Katerina returned her attention to Jenna. She walked around behind her and gently began to stroke Jenna's hair from behind.

Jenna's instinctive reaction was to try and move out of reach, but she realised that would be impossible due to the two men holding her. Instead, she decided to just remain calm and pretend as if she was not disgusted by the woman's touch.

"That's better," purred Katerina, leaning in closer so that her mouth was right beside Jenna's ear. "There's really no point in you trying to fight, so you might as well just relax and enjoy it."

Jenna felt a sudden heaviness in the pit of her stomach as if she had just swallowed a lump of concrete. "What exactly do you have in mind for me?" she asked timidly.

Katerina moved back around so that she could look in her prisoner's eyes.

"Something wonderful," she assured her. "Something which no one else can share." She gently moved Jenna's hair away from her eyes. "You're going to be a mummy to a very special child, and I, for one, am a little jealous of you."

It took a moment for her words to register with Jenna.

She looked past Katerina at the pack of eager, hungry-looking men in the crowd, then at the two holding her. "Oh, I get it, this is some sort of gang-rape initiation, you twisted bitch!"

Katerina laughed as she reached out and started to stroke Jenna's hair once more.

Suddenly she grabbed it tightly and pulled Jenna's head back.

"Ow!" Jenna squealed, taken by surprise.

"No, my pretty one, the father of your child is not of this world. He is the one who walks in darkness, and you should be honoured that I have chosen you to be his vessel."

With her head still being held back, Jenna glanced downwards to try and see Katerina's face. "Well, if it's all the same to you, I'd rather not be anyone's vessel."

Katerina released her grip on Jenna's hair and laughed wildly. "Well, you might just change your mind when you see the master — very few people alive have ever laid eyes upon him, and those that have usually don't live to tell about it!"

"Master!" screamed Jenna. "What master? What the hell are you talking about?"

Jenna began thrashing about, but once again those holding her tightened their grip until she cried out in pain.

Once the cuffuffle was over, Katerina stood directly in front of Jenna, shaking her head. "You need to relax," she advised, "otherwise the experience will be a very intense and painful one."

Jenna felt the weight in her stomach grow heavier. Any way she looked at it, she was destined to be raped by whatever mental case Katerina and her pack had chosen to be their leader.

There was no way out. She was trapped!

Where the hell was Alan?

How could he have left her at the mercy of these monsters?

Jenna looked Katerina directly in the yes. "So, he's going to rape me, this master of yours. When it comes down to it, that is what this is all about?"

Katerina shook her head. "No, you mustn't think of it in those terms. When the master has mated with you, in six weeks' time you will give birth to a gorgeous little girl, and in time, she will take over from me and lead the army for the master. Regrettably, you will probably die during the birth, but that is a small price to pay for the immense honour being bestowed upon you."

Jenna's mind raced to take everything in. "Six weeks! Are you nuts? No one gestates for only six weeks!"

"I can assure you that is all the time it takes. Alas, your feeble body is too delicate to survive being host to the master's spawn, which is why you will most likely die after I remove the baby from you."

Jenna turned her head away. She could feel the bile rising in her throat and had to fight to keep from throwing up.

"There, there, you must understand what an incredible privilege is being bestowed upon you." Katerina's voice was soft and kind, like a mother calming her child after a nightmare. "Our civilisation goes back thousands of years before your Christianity first came about. The master is the last remaining warrior of our race, but through his seed we have the chance to start a new race for him to guide and teach, and the birth of your child will mark the beginning of this new becoming."

"Not if I kill myself before it's born!" Jenna almost spat the words out.

Katerina's eyes narrowed, casting a shadow of pure evil over them, which caused Jenna to flinch when she saw it.

"There'll be no chance of that!" Katerina assured her. "You'll be very well looked after until the birth."

It sounded to Jenna more of a threat than a statement.

Chapter 29

"Why did you kill my uncle?" With nothing to lose, Jenna felt she had a right to demand some answers.

Katerina frowned. "We have to dispose of many of your race in an effort to keep our existence a secret. Whoever gets in our way must be taken care of."

"And what about my friend, Trisha, back at the hotel. You'd already made her one of you, so why did you have to kill her, as well?"

Katerina stood back, looking flustered. "We do not have to justify ourselves to the likes of your kind." She turned and surveyed her followers gathered in the field, some of whom had already begun their transformation. It was too early; she had not given the command. But Katerina could well understand their impatience. They, too, had waited a long time for what was about to happen.

Standing on the edge of the platform, Katerina raised her arms above her head.

All those gathered surged forward, their eyes wide in anticipation.

"The time is coming," Katerina informed them. "Prepare to meet the master."

The crowd all turned in unison towards the full moon, which beamed down at them form the far end of the field.

Katerina watched as each of them went through their metamorphosis.

She waited until the vast majority were werewolves before she turned back towards Jenna.

The two men holding her were now also both more werewolf than man, and Jenna screamed and cried as she tried desperately to free herself from their vise-like grasp.

But it was all in vain.

Katerina looked on and smiled at Jenna's hopeless struggle. "Make her ready," she demanded, smiling as the two werewolves complied with her order.

Chapter Thirty

Young raced through town with his blue lights on and siren blaring. From what Kevin had told him, Jenna was being held captive for a ceremony somewhere in the woods that surrounded the town, and the only area he could think of that would afford enough privacy for something like that typically lay at the far end of Huntley.

He had considered calling the station for reinforcements, but on reflection he decided that the explanation of what he was expecting to find would either result in him being laughed at by the desk sergeant or being ignored for trying to be funny.

After his encounter with Kevin back at the hotel, Young was in no doubt what was waiting for him when he arrived at the woods. His one saving grace was that he had proven that the silver bullets worked. He only hoped now that he had enough to protect Jenna and would be able save her from whatever horror they had planned for her.

At the edge of town, Young took the woodland turning that led up to the largest expanse of open ground he knew of. He had only visited it once since coming to Huntley, and that had been as part of a search for a missing schoolgirl, which turned out to be a waste of everybody's time when she was finally found hiding under the bed at her boyfriend's house.

Young switched off his blue lights and siren, not wishing to announce his arrival just in case it caused Jenna's kidnappers to panic and harm her in some way. He also surmised that it might be advantageous if he were able to creep up on her captives unobserved, giving him an opportunity to complete an assessment of the situation before moving in.

The road leading up to the woods was a little rocky and strewn with potholes, which made the going rough. Fortunately, there was no other traffic using it, so Young took full advantage and picked whichever side of the road looked the least hazardous to drive on.

With less than a quarter of a mile to go, Young killed his headlights. Once he had driven up the steep incline, he decided to ditch his car altogether, just in case the sound of his approaching engine was enough to warn those gathered of his approach.

Leaving his vehicle and continuing on foot made Young feel extremely vulnerable. He could feel his heart racing as he moved forward, and he prayed for Jenna's sake that he had not made an error in judgement by not calling for reinforcements.

Through the trees ahead of him, Young could see what appeared to be a fire on the horizon. He was suddenly overtaken by the irrational fear that there were people lurking in the dense foliage that surrounded him, ready to pounce at any given second.

Young carefully retrieved his weapon from his pocket and removed the safety catch.

With his gun firmly in his grasp, Young felt his courage begin to return. Even so, as he moved forward, he swung the gun back and forth in front of him, ready to shoot at the first thing that moved in his line of fire.

Trying desperately not to step on any loose branches that

might give his position away, Young edged his way through the trees towards the clearing beyond.

When he emerged from the cluster of bushes, the sight that met his eyes sent a shiver of dread through his entire body.

For a start, Young had not anticipated that there would be so many of them. The entire central area of the field was literally crammed with werewolves, far more than he could ever hope to take out with his gun. Young watched them in forced fascination like someone witnessing a tragedy unfold who cannot turn their head away.

The werewolves frolicked and cavorted with each other in a macabre orgy, their revelling illuminated by the firelight, the highest flames of which leapt some thirty feet into the air and cast eerie shadows over the ensemble.

But worse than that was the sight of Jenna on the podium, being held fast by two burly werewolves who seemed to be in the process of tying her to a giant wooden cross with her back to the crowd. For a second it reminded Young of Fay Wray in the original King Kong.

Through the glow of the fire, Young could just make out the woman who seemed to be commanding the two beasts. It was the one from the bookshop, Katerina, the woman who had hypnotised him.

Young could feel a lump forming in his throat. He swallowed, but it was hard and with difficulty as if something inside him was pushing the air back up his windpipe.

Once the woman was satisfied that Jenna could not escape, Young watched as Katerina walked to the end of the podium and stood facing the crowd. The glow from the firelight showed her in all her naked glory, and Young felt a pang of guilt at how attractive he found her, even at this moment.

Katerina held her arms above her head, and the crowd immediately stopped their orgy to pay attention to her. From this distance, Young could just about hear as the woman recited some form of ritualistic incantation. The crowd seemed to be growing more fervent as she spoke.

Young shifted his position to avoid feeling cramped, careful not to draw any attention to his movement. He shifted his gun from one hand to the other as he wiped the perspiration from his hands on his trousers to ensure he would have a tight grip on his weapon.

In an instant, the werewolves listening to Katerina all fell to the ground, crouching on all fours, as the huge bonfire began to spit and shoot sparks high into the air like a Roman candle. With each mini-eruption, those gathered bowed their heads as if in solemn prayer, but Young knew that there could be nothing holy or pious about these ceremonial proceedings.

Suddenly, there was an almighty bang, and a large, brightly coloured ball of fire shot out from the flames and landed right in front of the podium. As it made contact with the ground, the ball exploded, and there in its place stood a gigantic werewolf, far larger than any of those in the field before it.

Young looked on in horror as the latest arrival gazed up at the podium. It was so tall that its head could see over the parapet, and Katerina immediately dropped down into a curtsey before her master.

The monster turned slowly to survey those assembled in the field.

Each werewolf now lay as close to the ground as its frame would allow, in respectful subservience.

After a moment, the beast turned back to face the podium. The two werewolves Young had watched fasten Jenna to the cross stood aside, both with their heads bowed.

The huge werewolf slowly climbed the makeshift steps to where Katerina waited. Even from this distance, Young could not help but notice the enormous protrusion of the beast's organ in the firelight.

When it reached the top, Katerina turned sideways as if to present Jenna to her master.

Young instinctively crouched and began to move closer to the stage. The attention of all those gathered around the fire appeared totally focussed on what was taking place on the podium, so none of them seemed to notice him moving through the darkness.

As Young approached the podium from the side, the full horror of what was about to take place dawned on him.

The grotesque beast stood poised with its huge arms out by its sides as if in some macabre mockery of saying grace before dining. Katerina meanwhile moved closer to it and, reaching out, took its gigantic erection in her hand and began stroking it up and down before taking the thick end in her mouth and sucking on it deeply.

It was so large that she could barely manage to force the head of it between her willing lips.

The beast lifted its head back and roared into the night. The sound seemed to fill the entire field, reverberating off the trees surrounding it.

Once Katerina was satisfied that she had completed her duty, she stood up and walked over to where Jenna was tied. Jenna, for her part, was unable to turn around completely due to her restraints, but Young could see that she was tugging and thrashing against them in a vain effort to free herself.

There was no doubt in Young's mind what was about to take place.

Young raised his gun and took aim as the beast approached the helpless Jenna.

But, as he was about to fire, he stopped himself. From this distance it was too risky. He knew that his aim was not sufficiently proficient to eradicate the risk of hitting Jenna. He considered letting off a warning shot but quickly reconsidered. Such an action would waste a precious bullet, and considering he already knew that he did not have enough to take out all those present, the thought of intentionally missing his target seemed ludicrous.

The monstrous beast took up position behind Jenna.

From this distance, Jenna was able to look back over her shoulder just enough to see what was about to impale her. She screamed out in terror, her mind racing to try and rationalise her situation. But it was to no avail. She could feel the hot breath of the creature on her naked flesh, and she knew she was only seconds away from unimaginable agony.

Then, from out of nowhere, a shot rang out!

For a split second, time appeared to stand still. No one moved or even dared to breathe.

Katerina, uncharacteristically flustered by the sudden halt to the ceremony, scanned the surrounding area and saw Young emerging from the trees, his gun held out in front of him.

Katerina pointed to him and screamed to the crowd, "Grab him, bring him here to the master. Now!"

As if shaken out of a trance, the werewolves turned as one and began to advance on the lone figure facing them.

Young glanced back up at the podium, but he was still too far away to risk a shot in that direction.

He turned his attention back to the advancing army.

The werewolves crept towards him, unafraid of anything he might have in his arsenal.

As they drew closer, Young could feel his reserve starting to leave him once more, but another cry of despair from Jenna managed to stiffen his resolve.

The lead werewolves were no more than ten feet away, and from this distance, Young could see their glowing eyes and salivating jaws as they jostled one another in a bid to be the first one to reach their prey.

Young held his weapon out in front of him and aimed it directly into the crowd.

"Stop, armed police!" he called, trying desperately to maintain a believable level of authority in his voice.

But the pack did not acknowledge his command and continued with their advance.

Young fired a shot. Then another, and another, then he continued until the chamber was empty and the hammer merely clicked in response to him squeezing the trigger.

The howling of those before him filled the night, and they watched in astonishment as several of their number slumped to the ground, dead.

Young used their moment of confusion and disbelief to reload his gun. He fumbled with some of the bullets while keeping his eyes fixed firmly on those before him, afraid to turn his attention away even for a moment.

The werewolves turned their attention form their fallen colleagues back to Katerina, as if seeking direction.

Young's actions had, for the moment at least, stopped the head werewolf's assault on Jenna, and it had turned its attention towards him. Doubtless realising that Young's ammunition was more than just lead, it grabbed hold of the two werewolves who had secured Jenna to the wooden cross and pulled them in front of it as if to form a human shield.

Katerina was beside herself. "Take him!" she screamed, frantically pointing to Young.

Obediently, the mob turned their attention back to Young, but none of them moved forward. Instead they growled menacingly in his direction, as if threatening an attack should he dare to try using his weapon against them.

Young was sure that they knew, even in their bestial state, that if they rushed him, he would at best take out another seven of them before the others would have the chance to grab him and tear him apart.

But still, none of them seemed willing to offer themselves in sacrifice.

Chapter 30

Young glanced back up at the podium. He could see Katerina standing at the edge, her hands planted defiantly on her hips, waiting for her orders to be carried out. With the two werewolves protecting their master, Young was unable to see Jenna behind them, but he comforted himself with the knowledge that for the moment she was unharmed and alive.

He turned his attention back to the beasts before him.

They still had not advanced, but Young felt sure that it was only a matter of seconds before they did.

His position was hopeless. Even if he had had enough ammunition to despatch them all, he would never be given the chance to reload in time. As it was, he could barely take out a quarter of them with what he had left.

For a second he considered the possibility of shooting Jenna and then himself, just to save them both from what was surely a fate worse than death.

But he knew in his heart that regardless of the circumstances, he could not harm Jenna, and there was no way he was going to take his own life without fighting for her with his last breath.

From the corner of his eye, Young noticed one of the pack making its way towards him. Young took aim and fired, sending the creature staggering to the ground. He turned back just in time to catch another advancing from his other side. He shot that one, too.

The other werewolves shuffled on the spot, looking from one to another as if for some sort of plan or idea as to how best to deal with the situation. Some of those from the back began to push forward, causing those in the front line to move closer to Young.

He let off two more shots, taking out some of the frontrunners.

Those directly before him now began to heave backwards,

afraid that they might be next if they were jostled into the firing line.

This gave Young an idea.

He remembered Professor Pudelko telling them that if they killed the lead werewolf, then all those it had created would die also. Young could tell from the way the head werewolf cowered behind his followers that he was afraid of Young's weapon, so it stood to reason that it knew it could be killed with one of his silver bullets.

Young slowly began to move towards the stage, swinging his gun from left to right in front of him to warn off the mob. None of them backed off, but Young could tell that they were wary enough to ensure that they did not advance on him, either.

He needed to be close enough to the podium to ensure that he could take a shot at the head werewolf without risking his bullet hitting Jenna. It was the only plan he could think of that had any hope of success.

As Young moved closer to the stage, his eyes still fixed on the crowd, he could hear Katerina screaming orders at them to kill him before he reached their master.

Young knew he had only three shots left in the chamber, and now he was convinced that whatever else happened, he was not going to be allowed a chance to reload again, so he had to make his final shots count.

If he failed, he had no doubt that he would die by being torn to shreds by the baying mob before him.

As he neared the podium, Young glanced over just to check on the exact location of the head werewolf. It still cowered behind its followers but was close enough that Young felt confident he could make his shot count.

Turning back to the crowd, Young took aim at one of the lead werewolves. Seeing the barrel pointed in its direction, it scuttled backwards, causing those nearest to it to act in a similar vein.

Young took his time and waited until the crowd were stumbling over each other in a bid not to be in Young's direct line of fire.

At that moment, Young turned and aimed his weapon towards the podium. He let off two shots in rapid succession, and the two werewolves guarding their master fell to the floor.

With one shot left, Young looked into the eyes of the head werewolf and carefully took aim. He fancied at that moment he could see fear in the beast's eyes.

At that moment, Katerina ran in front of Young's target and grabbed Jenna by the hair, pulling her head back. She looked down at Young. "Now, put your gun down or I'll break her neck!" she demanded.

For a moment, Young was perplexed. If he shot the werewolf, surely Katerina would die along with all the others. But if she was quick enough, she could easily snap Jenna's neck in a heartbeat before she died.

Young paused, his gun still out in front of him aimed directly at the large werewolf.

From this distance, he was confident he would find his target.

He could feel the crowd to his left moving in closer. Somehow, they, too, seemed to know that his options were severely limited.

Young held his ground.

He glanced quickly at Katerina, then back to the beast beside her. She seemed far calmer and more in control than her master.

It was a risk. But Young was out of options.

He held his breath and levelled his barrel at the beast's chest.

As he squeezed the trigger, the lead werewolf reached over and grabbed hold of Katerina by the arm, yanking her in front of it.

It was too late. Young's last bullet left the chamber and hit Katerina directly in the chest.

For a moment, no one moved.

As Young watched, Katerina turned to her master. Her mouth was open, but no words came out. Her expression conveyed a look of surprise and incomprehension that it had used her to save itself, after all that she had done.

The lead werewolf released his hold on his subordinate, and she slumped to the ground.

Within seconds, Young noticed the mob falling back and clutching at their throats, as one by one they, too, slumped to the floor, writhing around in agony.

Realising they were no longer a threat, Young turned his attention back to the stage.

The head werewolf stood alone with his back to Jenna.

The beast stared down at Young as its enormous chest rose and fell. Young could see the great clouds of air streaming from its jaws as it began to survey the carnage taking place before it.

With trembling hands, Young reloaded a couple of bullets into the gun's chamber.

The sound of him slotting it back home brought the beast out of its reverie.

Young raised his weapon as the beast leaped from the stage and landed in the burning pyre from which it had risen.

Young let off the two shots, but with the flames rising and spitting as before, he had no way of knowing if his bullets hit their target.

In the same instant, Young watched as the werewolves writhing in their death throes began to self-combust. One by one they burst into flames, and those that were still able howled in agony as the flames consumed them.

Young turned back to the podium and saw that Katerina, too, had started to burn. Her dead body lay crumpled at the edge of the podium, and it was already impossible to tell how beautiful she had been only minutes before.

Young bounded up the wooden stairs and went straight to

Jenna. He noticed that her head was slumped forward on her chest, and he immediately feared the worst, that Katerina had managed to carry out her threat before her master had used her to save itself.

Young gently lifted Jenna's head and was overwhelmed to see that she was alive.

Her eyes were streaming tears, and he kissed her, desperately, before untying her and carrying her from the podium and across the field down to his waiting car.

Epilogue

YOUNG FILLED BOTH FLUTES WITH CHAMPAGNE AND carried them over to where Jenna lay on the bottom bunk. He kissed her gently on the lips, then handed her one of the glasses. They clinked and drank as the train thundered through the darkened countryside.

It had been a month since that night in Huntley, and Jenna was still suffering from nightmares. Although, mercifully, they were becoming more sporadic over time.

Having rescued Jenna from the woods that night, Young had driven them back to his place, where they had stayed up until the dawn drinking coffee and holding each other.

Once daylight had come, Young had managed to cobble together something for Jenna to wear from his own wardrobe before he drove to his office. As much as he hated the thought of leaving her alone, he knew that the station would be the safest place for now.

His plan was to venture back up to the woods alone and see the result of the carnage they had fled from. However, when he arrived at the station, he was informed that someone had already reported the fire in the woods, and once the fire brigade had arrived, they'd called in the police as there appeared to be dead bodies — or what was left of them — strewn amongst the ashes. Young was told a forensics team was already up there.

Coincidentally, there had also been a fire at the Grange, which had gutted several rooms on two floors. Fortunately, someone had raised the alarm in time and managed to evacuate everyone, other than those in the rooms in which the fires had started. Their remains, like those up at the woods, were more skeletal than flesh, so the pathologist would have to concentrate on DNA and teeth for positive identifications.

Due to the volume of bodies involved, an outside team of detectives had been called in who had more experience in this area. From what Young could glean, his team were not at all impressed with the Assistant Chief Constable's decision, but there it was, so they had to just keep quiet and get on with it.

Taking this news into account, Jenna and Young decided to keep quiet about their involvement. Young knew that the whole investigation was going to blow up because it was by far the biggest in the county's history, and by that morning the press and television crews were already starting to arrive. If the pair of them started talking about werewolves, they would either end up being detained under the Mental Health Act or just laughed out of the station, and Young could kiss his career goodbye in the process.

Young realised that eventually his bullets would be found amongst the debris. But he was not overly concerned. He knew that they would be untraceable, so there was no way of them being linked to him.

In his official capacity, Young went back to the Grange to see if any of Jenna's belongings were salvageable from her room. But alas, Kevin's self-combustion had taken out the entire room, furniture and all. So he picked her up and took her into town to buy some essentials.

That night, Young decided it would be best for Jenna to go

back to London while he set about sorting things out in Huntley.

She was reluctant to leave him and made no bones about it, but Young assured her it would only be temporary until he could officially book time off.

As Jenna's keys were all lost, she had to arrange for a breakdown service to tow her car back for her. Fortunately, one of her neighbours held a spare front door key for her uncle, so Jenna was at least able to gain access to her flat without calling a locksmith.

Whilst back in London, Jenna arranged to meet with Professor Pudelko once more. Out of respect for her uncle's work, she told him all about Katerina and the werewolves, and he eagerly made notes on every aspect of her ordeal.

Pudelko even asked if there was any way Jenna and Young might consider making a presentation in front of a few select members of the Royal Society, but Jenna declined in no uncertain terms. She could see the look of disappointment in the professor's eyes, but at least she had given him some new information about the werewolves' ceremony and the fact that they self-combusted when killed, or even if the one who turned them was killed.

Plus, there were the details concerning the giant werewolf Katerina had summoned from the fire and the fact that it had wanted to mate with her to continue its race.

So, all in all, Jenna did not feel too guilty about refusing the professor's request. She had given him more first-hand information than he could ever have hoped for without actually being there himself.

Over coffee they talked about Jenna's uncle, and Pudelko reiterated how guilty he felt for his death and how much he was going to miss his old friend. Jenna assured him that her uncle would have been completely aware of the risks involved and that knowing him, it would have only served to spur him on.

Epilogue

When they parted company, Jenna saw a tear in the corner of the old man's eye. Instead of merely shaking hands, she hugged him and thanked him for being such a good friend to her uncle.

Young put in for an immediate transfer and was offered a post in Cornwall. When he asked Jenna if she would move in with him, she jumped at the idea. Being practically minded, she informed Young that initially she intended to rent out her uncle's flat, just on the off-chance things did not work out and she had to return to London.

For his part, Young understood and did not try and talk her out of it.

The two of them spent a week in Cornwall looking at places to rent and eventually found one they both liked reasonably close to Young's new station.

The week before their move, they decided on an impromptu weekend break in Scotland, as both of them confessed to always wanting to visit Edinburgh.

They decided that taking the train would be more romantic than driving or flying, so they opted for the overnight journey.

"Mmmm, this stuff is good," said Jenna, licking some spilt champagne from her fingers.

"Only the best for milady." Young smiled.

He picked up the bottle and refilled their glasses. As he poured, he noticed Jenna had a faraway look in her eyes.

"Penny for them?" he asked, concerned.

Jenna looked back at him. "I'm sorry," she apologised, "I was just thinking about my uncle and Trisha, that's all."

When Trisha's remains had been identified, the police could find no evidence of any living relatives. Jenna was convinced that her friend had once told her about some distant cousins, but she knew that both her parents were deceased and that she had no siblings.

In the end, Jenna, with Young's help, had taken on the responsibility of arranging her funeral. It had been a small affair, and Jenna had made a silent promise to her friend that whenever she was in London, she would always put fresh flowers on her gravestone.

Young put down the bottle and placed both their glasses on the table beside it before wrapping his arms around Jenna and holding her.

When they parted, Jenna's cheeks were lined with tears. Young rubbed them away with his thumbs and then kissed the end of her nose.

Jenna smiled up at him and reached for the cord of his silk dressing gown. She pulled at it and watched as the fabric parted, revealing Young's growing erection.

"Is that for me?" she asked coyly, lying back on the bunk and throwing aside the sheet to reveal her nakedness.

Norma Roop kicked off her bedsheet and rolled onto her side, holding her stomach. The excruciating cramps that had wracked her body for the last four weeks were worse than ever tonight. The tablets her doctor had prescribed were less than useless, and she had already taken three times the stated dose that day without relief.

Swinging her legs over the edge of the bed, she just managed to make it to the bathroom in time to lift the lid on the toilet before another hot jet of vomit spewed forth. This was at least the fifth time today.

She retched twice, then washed her mouth out before dragging herself back to bed.

As she lay in the darkness, she felt the thundering kicks in her abdomen start up once again. If she did not know any better, she would have sworn that she was pregnant. But as the only unprotected sexual intercourse she'd had recently was when her son Kevin had raped her a month ago, it seemed highly unlikely.

Epilogue

She had not bothered to mention the attack to anyone. At the time, it had been because she needed him to work in the shop to keep a roof over their heads. Norma had decided that when her son came crawling back begging with an apology, she would give him a good hiding like she had when he was little.

That would sort him out!

She regretted now that she had ever stopped whacking him when she thought he had grown too old for it to matter. Perhaps if she had continued with the beatings, he might have learned to show her more respect.

But as it was, soon after the assault the police showed up at her door to inform her that Kevin had been killed in a fire at a local hotel.

God knows what he had been doing there!

Robbing the place, more than likely.

Still, Norma was in for a nice little touch from the victim's support lot, so she was not going to complain. The silly little bugger was a no-good sod, just like his father and his older brother, so good riddance to bad rubbish. Once she received her insurance cheque, she could decide if it was worth paying someone to run the shop or just sell up and move away.

Either way, her future looked bright.

She doubled over as another spasm gripped her insides. Oh, god, this pain was becoming unbearable. She could definitely feel something moving about inside her.

The question was, what?

If her stupid son had made her pregnant, there was no way that she would be able to feel the baby kicking at this early stage.

Then why did she feel as if she was only a couple of weeks away from giving birth?

Who had ever heard of a pregnancy that lasted only six weeks?

Surely, that was impossible!

The End.

Dear reader,

We hope you enjoyed reading *Silver Bullet*. Please take a moment to leave a review, even if it's a short one. Your opinion is important to us.

Discover more books by Mark L'estrange at https://www.nextchapter.pub/authors/mark-lestrange

Want to know when one of our books is free or discounted for Kindle? Join the newsletter at http://eepurl.com/bqqB3H

Best regards,

Mark L'estrange and the Next Chapter Team

You might also like:
Ghost Song by Mark L'estrange

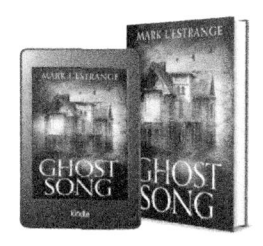

Click here to read the first chapter for free

Printed in Great Britain
by Amazon